"Should we go in, Chief?"

Just as the Chief was about to answer, heavy footsteps thudded from inside the house. The door squealed again and Heany appeared. His face was screwed up tightly and his mouth was just a slit.

"You guys better get in here and see this," he said.

Quickly, Braden and the Chief went into the house, following Heany up the steep line of stairs that lay on the right. They went all the way up to the top floor, turned down a short hallway, and approached a room in the front of the house. Braden remembered it as Nick's old bedroom. The two of them had played up there for many countless hours when they were kids. Through the doorway Braden saw police officers walking around as the room lit up with white flashes from a digital camera.

The stench grew more powerful; Braden had to breathe through his mouth to stop from gagging. They followed Heany's huge body into the room. He pointed at the floor in front of the only window. Stan Winslow lay on his back; his eyes were unfocused and staring up at the ceiling in one of those blank, unfocused stares only a dead man had. His arms and legs were bent at the joints, rigor mortis, and he had a gun hanging off the index finger of his right hand. There was a bloody bullet hole in his right temple and no exit wound that Braden could see. A clear case of suicide. Next to Stan's contorted body was a small black box. It had a flashing light and a switch on top.

"The remote detonator," Heany said as he knelt down over it. "It's been activated."

Champagne Books Presents

Firefighter 2070:
Flashover Point

By

G.C. Rosenquist

Champagne Books
www.champagnebooks.com
Copyright 2012 by Gregg Rosenquist
ISBN 9781927454527
May 2012
Cover Art by Amanda Kelsey
Produced in Canada

Champagne Books
#35069-4604 37 ST SW
Calgary, AB T3E 7C7
Canada

Dedication

To my son, Josh.

One

The massive yellow engine swooped down out of the gray sky, pelted by the cold needles of an early October rainstorm. Its red and white lights flashed through the gloom; its siren blared and honked, bouncing off the metal and glass surfaces of the surrounding skyscrapers like a racquetball. The dark figures of curious people appeared in windows, watching the spectacle below.

Braden Rathman, clad in his protective bunker gear, tightly gripped the ceiling strap in the crew cab behind Joni, the vehicle's driver. Sam Maxwell, truly a massive person, also in his bunker gear, sat in the seat next to her, checking the monitor that displayed exactly what the cameras mounted on Braden's helmet saw.

"You're coming through like a star, Probie!" Sam shouted over the siren, looked back at Braden, winked, and flashed a challenging smile.

Probie. It's what the veterans called a rookie because they were on probation. Braden didn't like the phrase because it sounded as if he was an ex-con fresh out of Joliet. He swallowed hard and took a deep breath. Nervous sweat gathered underneath his gear. He likened it to the stage fright an actor feels just before he goes on stage opening night. He couldn't wait until this was all over.

Through the crew cab porthole he saw dark rectangular, opaque windows rising up as if on a giant conveyor belt. Then the engine slowed, zeroing in on a window spewing black smoke into the air. Joni, watching her own monitor, which was connected to a camera on the outside of the apparatus, saw that they were close enough and stopped the Engine with a slight jerk. She hit a large black button on the dashboard and the wall in front of Braden hissed and fell forward in a slowly controlled descent, suddenly becoming a seven-foot bridge between the vehicle and the open window. Show time.

Braden felt a slap on his back. He turned his head around quickly. The Chief stood there, his ancient, weathered face staring at him from under the shadow of his white helmet. "Good luck, Probie!" he shouted.

"Thanks, Chief," Braden said and turned back towards the open, smoking window.

He was the last of three to face the two-story obstacle course that lay on the third and fourth floor of the station house. He had to go in, find "Victor, the Victim," and carry him to the safety of the engine crew cab in fewer than eight minutes (seven minutes, thirty-five seconds to be exact). The other two probies, Stan Winslow and Roger Kelly, both had had intense military training in the Army. They had scored seven minutes, thirty-eight seconds and seven minutes, thirty-five seconds respectively. And it didn't ease Braden's mind that Roger was the Chief's son.

The week before, they each had been allowed to tour and rehearse the obstacle course to format a plan of attack, but even so, both Stan and Roger sustained injuries. Braden noted where they received their injuries and was prepared. But there was always the unknown: a loose stairway railing could send him rolling down the steps; his helmet and jacket lights could fail, leaving him blind, or a rat could come out of nowhere, tripping him up.

The Chief's voice came through the speaker in his ear mic, "Remember, the clock starts as soon as you enter the building, Kid."

Braden nodded, took another deep breath, and threw down his blast shield. He let the ceiling strap go, his heart thumping relentlessly, then he ran across the bridge into the living darkness. *Enter, stage left.*

His feet, heavy with the weight of fireproof boots, hit the floor hard, but he was young and strong and the extra weight was nothing to him, especially with the adrenaline running through his body like an electrical charge. The air smelled of sulfur and gasoline.

Thick smoke, coming from generators in the walls, roiled like the tendrils of a hurricane. Visibility was almost non-existent, even with the lights on his helmet and coat activated. He turned on his self-contained breathing apparatus (SCBA). The SCBA mask kept all of the smoke out of his lungs, re-circulated clean oxygen, and, if there *were* fire in here, the heat also. He could see only a few feet above the worn, oak floor. They hadn't rehearsed the course with the smoke generators going. It was completely disorientating. He couldn't go any further without some help.

"Sam!" he shouted into his ear mic. "Sam!"

"Watcha want, Probie?"

"I need a GPS schematic of the course routed to my blast shield."

"You got it."

Braden knew that Sam was giving orders verbally to the engine's main computer and he knew the Chief was watching everything that was happening on his own monitor. Suddenly, the transparent alloy of the blast shield flashed and, like a video game appearing on a monitor, the schematic of the obstacle course, both floors, filled the right half of the blast shield. The other half was clear so that he could still see reality in real time. The schematic was bright and sharp as Braden's firefighter icon flashed with his current position; it showed that he faced west. It was a straight shot to the downward stairway at the other end of the room, but he remembered that there was a hole in the floor somewhere between him and the stairs. He'd have to keep an eye out for that.

"Thanks, Sam," he said and hurried forward, following the animated map. He ran into something immediately, stumbling forward. His gloved hands fell upon what felt like long pieces of wood and debris. He pushed himself backwards then stepped forward so that he could see what he'd run in to. The thick black smoke flowed outward and around the object, resembling storm clouds swirling around the crest of a mountain. He waved at the smoke, hoping to disrupt it enough to see through it. This didn't work; the smoke was too heavy and dark. It seemed to coagulate like blood in a wound. He had an idea: his chest speakers. If he could find the right frequency of an object, he could shred it to pieces. He'd seen it done before. He reached over with his right glove and turned the big button that was embedded in his left glove, up by the forearm. The speakers on the chest of his jacket vibrated, emanating a low hum. He turned the button a little more, the sound went lower, louder, and the smoke began to peel away like a curtain opening, slowly revealing what lay in his way.

It was a pile of trash and old debris about six feet high. It was made up of broken pieces of wood, sharp clumps of cement, spools of old electrical wire, old damaged bunker gear, twisted three inch hoses, and empty milk cartons.

"What the hell?" Braden muttered. This hadn't been there during rehearsal and it sure as hell wasn't there when Stan and Roger ran the course. He tried to go around the debris but it went many yards to the left and right; trying to find a way around it would cost him too much time.

"What's the problem, Kid?" the Chief asked.

"Look on the monitor," Braden said stiffly. "It's some kind of debris pile."

"I see it," the Chief said. "Where did it come from?"

Braden didn't answer. It would have wasted too much time. Angrily, he turned the button on his glove again and the speakers on his chest blasted a rolling, deafening hum, causing the debris in its wave path to shake as if in an earthquake, but nothing was being pushed away. He turned it again, this time the debris pile lifted into the air and separated like a ball of popcorn exploding. Jagged pieces of wood spun away into the smoke, the large chunks of cement rolled away over the spools of electrical wire; Braden could hear them clumping along the floor like horses stampeding. The spools of wire, free of the weight of the cement, shot off with the damaged bunker gear; the curled up hoses rose up, writhed like a gang of snakes, and slithered away into the darkness. He didn't see where the empty milk cartons went.

The path was clear for Braden now. He wasted no time. He left the speakers on just in case and it kept splitting the thick smoke in front of him like Moses parting the Red Sea. It closed up behind him, but he didn't care about that. The speakers would clear the smoke away again when he returned. He should've thought of using the sound dousers earlier. It was a safety feature designed to douse small fires in a firefighter's immediate vicinity, not clear open paths through smoke, but he was in the zone now and thinking outside the box.

Braden ran until he came to the hole in the floor. Smoke was coming up through it but the speakers easily blew it aside. He knew there was a supporting beam overhead. He looked up just to make sure. Yes, it was still there. They hadn't manipulated that, thankfully.

He reached down, under his jacket, and unhooked the thirty-foot, Kevlar/titanium lifeline from his breech belt. Then he threw it over the beam and let the two loose ends fall down through the hole in the floor. Satisfied, Braden jumped over the hole in the floor and headed for the downward stairway. That was where Roger got hurt. The smoke had been so bad that Roger hadn't been able to see the stairs and he had tripped, rolling down all the way to the bottom. He'd sprained his ankle and added thirty seconds to his time. But Braden's speakers made short work of the smoke rising through the stairwell.

He could hear Sam and the Chief talking to each other in his ear mic. Sam was concerned about Braden's heart rate; the detectors inside the jacket indicated that Braden's heart was going so fast it was on the verge of a seizure. The Chief told him to watch it closely. Sam counted off the time, "three minutes, twelve seconds."

Almost half the time is gone, Braden thought, trying not to panic. *I'm too slow! Too damn slow!*

The smoke wasn't as bad downstairs and Braden's lights fell upon the hanging wall of electrical cables. "Victor, the Victim" was in the closed off room just beyond them all the way on the other side of the room; the locked door needed to be kicked in. That was where Stan had hurt himself. He'd bruised his right shoulder running through the door. Braden was prepared for that, too.

"Sam!" He shouted. "Deactivate the GPS. I don't need it any longer!"

"You got it, man," Sam said. The animated image on Braden's blast shield disappeared.

He had to be careful. For each cable he touched, he'd lose ten seconds. They were attached to some kind of mechanical rig that shook them back and forth, and they went all the way to the floor so he couldn't crawl under them. He focused the sound douser on them but all that did was make them shudder even more violently. He had to find the right frequency; it was probably too low. He turned the button back a little, the low hum rose, and the writhing cables snapped up to the ceiling like octopus legs, each sounding like a gunshot as they hit. As long as he had the speakers pointing at the cables, they would stay pinned to the ceiling.

He ran through and heard the cables slap heavily on the floor as they came back down. Realizing he had to speed things up, he didn't stop as he approached the locked door. Instead, he pressed the button on his left glove that activated the compressor in the lining in the lower back of his jacket. He heard the compressor buzz as it filled all the individual bladders inside the jacket with helium. With his shoulders protected from impact and his momentum carrying him faster and faster, the door opened easily when he hit it. Almost too easy. Braden nearly tripped over Victor as he ran in but he managed to jump over him, right himself, and stop. He leaned forward, put his hands on his knees, trying to catch his breath. He looked up and saw an opaque window. He considered extricating Victor through that, but there was a piece of plywood cut and painted to look like fire sitting on the floor in front of it. That meant the escape route was blocked off.

"Four minutes, five seconds," Sam said in his ear mic.

Braden went back to Victor and knelt down next to him. Victor was designed to look as real as possible, to lend believability to the probie. Victor wore a three-piece suit, as the scenario was that it was an office building Braden was running through. The head, arms, torso, legs, and feet were filled with sand, a hundred and eighty pounds of it. Braden had been spending extra time in the station's exercise room on the fifth floor working out in preparation for this.

Like he'd practiced, he pulled a small, portable air pack from his jacket pocket and strapped it to Victor's face. Then he took Victor by the wrist and leg and lifted him up onto his right shoulder so that Victor lay face down against his back. Braden attempted to stand up but it seemed like Victor weighed twice what they'd told him he weighed. He tried again, straining with all his strength, and managed to get to his feet. Once his center of balance was sure, he ran out the door quickly, again facing the hazard of those flailing electrical cables.

He approached them confidently, expecting them to part as they did before, but they were only shuddering again. He stopped and waited, pointing the speakers at them, yet only the cables on his left actually rose out of his way. Then it struck him. Victor's legs were blocking the right side speaker. Braden could feel Victor's body vibrating because of it. He reached over, switching all power to the left speaker. Immediately, Victor stopped vibrating and Braden saw a clear path through the electrical cables.

"Four minutes, forty-five seconds," Sam said.

Braden ran as fast as he could, Victor weighing heavily on him despite his helium-inflated jacket. When he got to the lifeline he'd dropped through the floor earlier, he put Victor down and wrapped the line around Victor's chest, under his armpits. After securing the knot, he took up the loose end of the line and ran to the stairs at the far end of the room. The weight of Victor's body pulled the line taut, slowing Braden down. He pulled and pulled until he made the stairway. He turned around and saw that Victor's feet were hanging down, just below the hole in the ceiling. There was something strange about his ankles; they seemed disproportionately large. Quickly, he tied the line off on the railing, took his laser pen from his pocket, and scaled the stairs three at a time.

When he made the top, the smoke was thick again but the speakers were working perfectly. Without stopping, Braden leapt over the hole, stopped, turned, and grabbed Victor's left hand. He pulled Victor towards him, cut the line above him with the laser, caught Victor, and threw him over his shoulder again. The damned dummy seemed even heavier now, the muscles in Braden's legs were cramping, burning with every step. So he ran harder.

Then everything fell out from under him.

Two

Braden didn't realize he was falling until he hit the floor. He slid along the floor, losing Victor in the process. The dummy disappeared in the smoke. Braden's boots lost their grip on the floor somehow; he'd slipped on something smooth. Had someone coated the floor here with Vaseline? He got to his feet quickly, looking on the floor for the culprit, finding it a few seconds later. A plastic milk carton, crushed in the middle, the dirty shadow of his boot print on it. Well, at least he knew where one of the milk cartons had disappeared.

Again, Sam was informing the Chief about Braden's heart rate, but what could be done now? It was too late to stop the test. He was almost through it.

"Five minutes, thirty seconds," Sam said.

Braden cursed, he was letting precious ticks waste away. He turned back to find Victor, staying low on his knees, reaching out with his gloves. Once he found him, Braden scooped him up easily and began running again. This time his legs weren't burning or cramping. Adrenaline must have kicked in again. There was a wall that all marathon runners break through during their race; Braden had reached it.

The smoke was thinning and the soft glow of white light was illuminating the floor. *The window.* Braden pushed himself harder. Everything he'd ever done in his life had led to this moment. The course of the rest of his life would be set by how well he did here.

"Come on, Rathman!" the Chief yelled. "Hump that package outta there!"

Braden ran faster. Victor's weight wasn't an issue any longer. He'd gotten his second wind; he could be carrying the core of a neutron star on his back and it wouldn't faze him any. The white light was getting brighter. Suddenly the window appeared and he jumped through it, took the bridge in one step, and fell into the engine's crew cab face first, heaving painfully with Victor on top of him. *Exit stage right.*

Victor's dead weight suddenly disappeared as a pair of big hands grabbed him by the left shoulder and spun him around so that he lay on his back. Sam was kneeling over him, the Chief was standing at his feet, looking down at him with large, disbelieving, white eyes. They didn't seem as tired as they usually did.

"Wow, kid!" Sam said, a long, wide smile cut into his face. "That was really sumthin'!"

"It-it was?" Braden asked between gasps for air.

"You bet! Never seen anything like it. You scored a six minute, two second time. Bested the Chief's record by half a minute."

Braden hadn't known anything about the Chief's record. He looked up at the Chief and didn't see anger or disappointment in his big white eyes. It was more like pride and excitement.

"Congratulations, Probie," The Chief said. "You've made it. You're officially a cadet."

~ * ~

The Hot Zone was a bar located on the first floor of Chicago Engine Station 85. Every fire station in the city had one and the locals always heavily frequented them. The profits from the bar went directly to the station house, thereby offsetting some of the tax load the citizens had to pay in their particular district. There was a gift shop at the front of the bar that sold T-shirts with the distinctive Station 85 crest, firefighter costumes (including a fake helmet and axe), fire truck toys (both battery and non-battery operated), books about firefighters, CD's with songs that had firefighting themes, buttons, ties, anything, in fact, that had to do with firefighting and all with the relative station number in which the bar was located.

This being a Friday night, the Hot Zone was wall-to-wall people. Money and drink floated high, fast, and loose. A local band was performing their brand of Chicago blues on a stage in the back.

They were called Jake and the place rocked at the foundations.

The main bar was located in the middle of the room and was shaped like a giant "O". The bartenders came in from outside through a door in the back of the building, went down a flight of steps, tread a long hallway, and then went up another flight of stairs where they came out inside the rails. Sometimes firefighters were allowed to tend bar, but mostly they came, drank, played pool, darts, or virtual-reality boxing, and wagged tongue until the place closed down at 2:00 a.m.

When Sam, the Chief, and the rest of the station personnel came through the doors, leading Braden to a large table reserved especially for them behind the bar, many people cheered, applauded, and patted them on the back. This wasn't because they'd done something special that particular day, but because *they* were special. They were heroes in the neighborhood; they did many acts of charity for local food banks; they went to schools and educated the kids about fire; many of those kids dreamed of being firefighters.

After all the accolades, they reached their table: a big number "85" was inlaid in the wood and varnished over in a transparent layer that was, to Braden's eye, at least an inch thick. They put Braden at the head of the table, next to the Chief. Three waitresses, all wearing blue Station 85 T-shirts, took their drink orders. The crew told Braden that his money was no good that night, which was fine with him because he didn't have any money to spend. It smelled like fried food and Braden was hungry.

The waitresses weren't gone more than sixty seconds when they came back with their beers. Braden shouted an order for a double burger, well done, to a red-headed waitress. She punched the order in on a small wristband computer, which sent the order to a monitor in the kitchen where a cook saw it and filled it. Making sure everyone else at the table had what they wanted, the red-headed waitress turned to go to another table, but Sam couldn't let her get away without a slap on the rear.

She narrowed her eyes at him and then pointed to her hair. "This hair color ain't no lie, Sam. Beware," she said, and winked at him.

Sam lifted a beer to her. "I am duly warned, my lady," he said and tugged heavily at his beer. Everyone whooped and howled as she walked away. She had one of those walks that was inherently sexy: the way her hair flowed behind her, the way her hips swayed. Even for Braden, who was deeply in love with his wife, it was a pleasure to watch.

"All right, you ash holes!" the Chief shouted, raising his glass of beer. "Before we lose all sense of control and decorum tonight, let's give a toast, please forgive the pun, to our new cadet, Braden Rathman!"

They all lifted their glasses, gave out a guttural "Ugh!" and drank down; even Debbie, one of the EMTs, and Joni, the Engine driver, emptied their glasses. Sam waved the waitresses back over for refueling. Then they heard an electronic ringing noise below all the revelry. Debbie stood up and pulled her cell phone from her back pocket. She looked at the screen and frowned. "It's my husband," she said. "I'll be back, guys. Don't drink without me."

She went towards the entrance to the bar. Her walk, in contrast to the waitress' walk, was slow and jerky, almost as if there was an entire building weighing on her shoulders. She pushed the door open and went outside.

"Is there something wrong with Debbie?" Braden asked the Chief.

The Chief frowned. "Yeah, Kid. She's been married only three years and already her husband is playing *'Who's Messed The Sheets'* and it ain't with her."

"But Debbie's so attractive and so sweet—"

"That's the problem, Kid," the Chief interrupted. "A guy who lands a babe like Debbie figures he can line them up like bowling pins and knock them down whenever he wants, then he uses her sweetness against her so he can blame her later on."

"Why does she put up with it?"

"Well, again, she's only been married a short time; she loves the jerk. As long as it doesn't affect her work, I'm staying out of it and I suggest you do the same."

"Copy that, Chief," Braden said as Debbie came back inside. Her face was flushed and her eyes were red. She wiped her tears quickly with her fingers before she reached the table. Once she sat down with them again, she laughed and joked as if nothing had happened.

Braden could never understand men like that. Why cause all that pain for someone else? If that's what they wanted to do, then why did they have to get married? He was more than happy with his wife, Amy, and couldn't envision a scenario where he would ever cheat on her.

Braden had three beers under his belt by the time his parents came in and found their table. Sam and Paul Rose, the Foam Truck leader, got up and offered them their seats.

"Is your lovely wife here yet, Son?" his mother, Zoey, asked.

Braden shook his head, "Not yet. Amy said she had some errands to run and then she'd swing over here for a drink."

"She must be so proud of you, Son," his father, Gene, said.

"Oh, and we're so very proud of you," his mother said.

"I know, Mom. Thanks."

His mom and dad were the best. Good, honest, and ethical. Gene worked as an architect for an important agency downtown. He had clients all over the country. His mom worked as a phlebotomist for a doctor in Evanston. They'd brought him up, an only child, in a big house in Wrigleyville and, in an effort to downsize after Braden and Amy were married, they'd moved into their own apartment, a modest downtown condo with a great view of Lake Michigan. They were reasonably young, in their late forties, and quite active in their lives. They were so proud of him it almost embarrassed Braden at times, but he understood it. A parent always wanted more for their child than they had.

Just then, Amy's parents, Dennis and Barbara, came in. Braden and the Chief, after brief introductions, gave them their seats. The loud music and ambient noise made it difficult for anyone to have a meaningful conversation but the effort was made. Braden got along with Amy's parents wonderfully.

They were wondering where Amy was; all Braden could do was shrug. Amy had been acting strange lately, secretive, which concerned Braden. He'd been meaning to ask them if they knew anything but decided to leave it and wait until Amy arrived. She said she would be here and he believed her.

Sam, already comfortably buzzed, had that redheaded waitress under his massive right arm and had a full glass of beer in his left hand. She'd fallen enough under his charms to tell him her name, Maureen, which pleased Sam to no end; now he wouldn't let her go. Braden could tell there was something developing between the two of them. The waitress, trying to get away to serve other people, finally gave Sam a peck on the cheek and he let her go do her job. He pulled up a chair and sat with the parents.

"You shoulda seen him today" he said incredulously, pointing at Braden. "He did stuff I never seen done before. He used the sound dousers to blow the smoke away and then..." the story he told them vaguely resembled what had really happened; by the end of it Braden felt as if he should have been wearing a red cape with an "S" on it. Sam wrapped up the story by telling them that they got it all on holocube and it would make a fortune on the Internet. "He's a real clock." Sam said, taking a big gulp from his glass.

"Clock?" Gene asked.

"Yeah," Sam nodded. "He's a real clock, as in cuckoo."

Everyone laughed.

Sam's recounting of the obstacle course reminded Braden about the pile of debris, so he asked the Chief about it.

"Yeah, I saw it on your helm cam," he answered. "I have no idea where it came from. Why worry about it? It didn't seem to slow you down."

"Well, Stan and your son, Roger, didn't have to face it," Braden said. "It just seems unfair, that's all. What if I hadn't beat them out?"

"Tell you what," the Chief said. "I'll look into it tomorrow and if I find anything, I'll let you know."

"Thanks, Chief," Braden said. As if on cue, Stan and Roger came in. They went right up to Braden, Roger still limped on his sprained ankle. They held their hands out to him.

"We saw what you did today on the holocube," Roger said. "Unbelievable. We came to congratulate you. No hard feelings?"

Braden smiled and shook his hand. "Never had hard feelings, Rog." He reached out for Stan's hand but Stan couldn't lift it because of his shoulder injury.

"I'm left-handed anyway," Stan said, and held his left hand out. Braden quickly changed hands and shook it.

"Great. Can I buy you a drink?" Roger said. "Wait, are you even old enough to drink?"

"I'm twenty-two."

"He's legal! He's legal!" Sam shouted. Everyone "Ughed!" and drank some more. Everyone except Stan. He trailed off and stood alone at the bar. This made Braden suspicious. Could Stan be the one who had ried to sabotage his test? Braden watched as Stan ordered a glass of ginger ale and sat there alone at the bar, not even taking up conversation with the bartenders.

It was past 9:00 when Braden became really worried about Amy. Her parents and his had stayed as long as they could, until the thundering drums from the band frayed their nerves. The four of them had left at 8:30 to get dinner at a much quieter establishment.

Braden tried calling Amy on her cell but all he got was her voice mail. He'd give her until 10:00, after that he'd hit the streets to find her. In the meantime, something about "Victor, the Victim" had been bothering him all night. He told everyone that he was gonna hit the "lube and tube" and be right back. Sam was trying to talk Danny and Debbie, the ambulance team, into connecting him to a beer IV as Braden left.

And the night was still in diapers.

Braden made his way through the swirling mass of people and reached the elevators reserved for the firemen of Station 85. There was a big digital sign on the wall that flashed "For Station 85 Employees Only." He grinned proudly. He was now an official Station 85 employee. Life was good.

He stuck his hand into the metallic DNA swiper in the wall next to the elevator; it blew air on his hand. The detectors under his hand swept up the microscopic skin flakes the air blew off his hand, chemically treated them, then matched the results with his known DNA structure. The elevator door opened with a chime. He took the elevator all the way up to the dome, the seventh floor, where the apparatus, the kitchen, the showers, and the bunkrooms were. The cement floor was still wet from the washing of the apparatus; he could hear drips echoing from the six drains placed in the floor. It smelled like rubber and sweat up there; he loved it. Some of that sweat was his. The outer walls of the roof were six layers of brick and mortar, solid enough to support the weight of the giant white dome above. For Braden, every time he stepped out of that elevator onto the roof it was like walking into one of those ancient gothic churches in Europe. There was a solemn reverence, a sanctity about the dome and the station that came from the importance of what they did here. He thought that apt because firefighting was his religion and *this* was his church.

Braden went towards the line of utility lockers stacked against the outside kitchen wall, his feet clicking and echoing into the empty air of the dome, past the bunker gear assignment cubicles where the superconductors inside their jackets were being recharged. When he reached the utility lockers he stopped and opened the large one that held Victor. Victor was hung from a strap at the base of his skull, similar to a drag rescue device on the back of a firefighter's jacket. If Braden hadn't known any better, he would've sworn that it was a real person hanging there, dead and cold. He remembered how thick Victor's ankles seemed earlier. He knelt down and rolled up the left pant leg. Hanging from a Velcro strap and wrapped around the ankle was a thirty-pound weight. It was the same with the other ankle. Victor had weighed an extra sixty pounds for his test.

Braden was sure of his suspicions now and he couldn't swallow. The proof was in front of him. Someone was trying to sabotage him. But why and who? Stan immediately came to mind. He couldn't have acted more guilty downstairs. Braden would have to show this to the Chief and then come up with a way to prove that Stan was behind the wall of debris and the weights on Victor's ankles.

Then he thought about it. Nothing that was done had been illegal. Even if Stan confessed, nothing could be done to him.

Braden stood up, closed the locker, and went back downstairs. When the elevator door opened a wall of noise washed over him; he put his hands over his ears. The band was in the middle of a killer version of "Born Under A Bad Sign" and people were singing along to it.

He pushed his way back to the table. Sam lay on the table while the entire Foam Tender crew was trying to throw olives into his mouth. Much laughter ensued when an olive miraculously got lodged in one of his nostrils. They laughed even harder when he closed the open nostril with his finger and blew the olive out of his nose. People scrambled to stay away from it. And for some unknown reason, Sam had his shirt off, displaying a solidly chiseled upper body.

"Hey, hero!" he called and motioned for Braden to come stand by him. The words that came out of his mouth were blurred and garbled. "Be...be careful of Thom," he said, looking around, as if to make sure Thom wasn't within earshot.

"Why?" Braden asked, leaning over so that he could hear better.

"Why, what?" Sam asked.

"Why should I be careful of Thom?"

Sam sprayed a wet laugh into the air. "Oh, yeah," he said, then whispered, "Yellow knees."

"Yellow knees? What does that mean?"

"Yellow knees, man," Sam said. "He's got yellow knees."

Before Braden could quiz Sam any further, the waitress came around and Sam asked what kind of beer was in the pitcher. Braden checked his watch. Five minutes before 10:00. He couldn't wait any longer. He pulled out his cell phone; just as he hit redial Amy appeared through the entrance. She saw him and waved. Immensely relieved, he put his phone away and embraced her.

"Hi, honey," she said and kissed him. "I'm sorry I'm late. My errands took a little longer than I thought they would."

"It's all right," Braden said. "I'm just glad you're here."

"I wouldn't miss this for anything."

Braden smiled. "Why didn't you answer your phone?" he asked.

She hesitated. "I couldn't," she said and looked down.

"Why not?"

"I was at the doctor." Braden saw tears in her eyes.

"Oh, my God," Braden said. "Are you all right?"

"I'm fine, honey."

"Then why were you at the doctor?"

"Because we're going to be parents."

"What?"

"I'm pregnant."

Braden looked her right in the eyes to make sure she wasn't lying. She wasn't. And those weren't tears of sadness; they were tears of joy.

Somehow, through all the noise, Sam had heard Amy. He

shouted, "Amy's on the nest! Amy's on the nest!"

Another "Ugh!" was shouted, more beer was downed, and more beer was ordered.

Braden kissed Amy on the lips, then on the cheeks, then the chin, the nose, the forehead, the ears, the eyes, and finally back on the lips again.

"I'm gonna be a dad?" he asked in disbelief.

Amy nodded through a smile.

"Why didn't you tell me about any of this before?"

Her smile disappeared. "I didn't want it to affect how you performed on the test."

"I love you so much, Amy," he said and hugged her again.

"I love you too, Brad. I mean, Daddy."

The Chief came up and slapped Braden on the back. "Well, it's been one hell of a year for you, hasn't it, Probie?" he said.

"Yes, sir," Braden said and kissed Amy on the lips, then on the cheeks, then on the chin, the nose...

Three

The man watched Braden leave the Hot Zone with his wife. She was beautiful and he didn't deserve her. He didn't deserve most of what he got. Rathman was nothing but a young punk who got lucky. The thing about luck is that it runs out, it dries up like a puddle in the desert. The man would make sure of that.

The man followed them as they crossed the street together and went east towards the air-car docks at the end of the block. The man looked up. He saw the four octagon shapes of the docking towers, nothing more than brightly lit skeletal monstrosities against the black night. He saw the blinking navigation lights of air-cars docking and leaving the parking balconies in a slow, orderly dance. He saw how air-cars were stacked like cans of soup on a grocery shelf, twenty-five stories high. He saw people going in and out of the external elevators. It was still reasonably early, there were many people walking on the dimly lit sidewalks and there were many ground cars on the streets. That was helpful to him. He stayed well back in the shadows, hiding among the crowds on the sidewalk. Braden and his precious wife had no idea they were being followed. They walked close together, their arms entwined around each other's waists; they laughed and kissed each other playfully.

Enraged, the man hurried his pace, once bumping shoulders with a heavily dressed elderly woman. Her husband saved her from falling to the ground. She called the man a very derogatory name. The man grinned and pushed on, keeping his eyes on his targets.

The man remembered how it had taken him all night to gather up all that garbage, throw it in the trunk of his air-car, and sneak it through the leading window of the obstacle course on the fourth floor of the station house. It had taken him five trunk loads and he'd done it alone. He thought he'd made the pile high and wide enough. He was wrong. Rathman went through it as if it was a hologram. And then there was Victor, The Victim. Finding the time and place to sabotage that was like playing a game of chess with live pieces. But he'd done it and it should've worked. It should have been much too heavy for Rathman to shoulder all the way back to the Engine. But he found a way around that, too.

The man would have to be smarter the next time.

The breeze was picking up and the man smelled onion rings in it, probably coming from the Hot Zone. He kept his head low but his eyes up as he walked. His hands were in the deep pockets of his long, black coat; he made it look as if he were chilled even though the night was quite mild. But that bastard and his wife never even looked back…not once. Their attention remained on each other, damn the outside world.

Finally, they came to the entrance to the docking towers. There was a man in a heated booth wearing a cheesy, light blue uniform and cap that was supposed to make him look important. He was the guard of the west-side entrance; there were guards in a booth like his on the north, south, and east sides also. They were off-duty policemen trying to make an extra hundred bucks a night to make up for what they lost in a card game last Saturday, or to pay for the floozy they'd visit that night before going home to their wives.

The man watched as Rathman pulled a card out of his coat pocket and gave it to the guard. The guard swiped it under a laser, gave the card back to him. They waved at the guard as they went through the security arch. The man waited a few seconds for them to reach the elevator then he went up to the guard and gave him his card. The guard swiped it, gave it back to the man, and waved him through. The guard had a holocube of the Bear/Packer game going. The Bears were losing twenty-four to ten. They were having another rough season.

He went under the security arch without setting off the weapons alarm and headed for the elevator. Rathman and his wife were already going up. They were still cuddling and kissing each other. It made the man want to retch. They stopped at the eighteenth floor and got out. The man took a different elevator and stepped in. The doors kissed; he pressed button eighteen. The elevator jerked. His body became heavy, but that was temporary as the acceleration slowed the higher up the elevator went.

The elevator stopped on the eighteenth floor and the doors slid apart. The man casually stepped out, saw that Rathman and his wife were getting into their air-car on a west side balcony. It was an old blue Camaro. He didn't know the year but it was sharp. The man found a shadow under a crossbeam next to the elevator and hid in it. He watched as Rathman sat in the driver's seat, brought the door down, leaned over and gave his wife a long, passionate kiss.

He could feel the anger in him building. The unfairness of it all made his temples throb. Rathman activated the air-car, it responded by rising slowly into the air, away from the balcony, its navigation lights blinking in front, in back, and underneath. Then the Camaro turned and darted east, quickly becoming nothing more than a swiftly moving set of blinking lights.

A strange taste developed in the man's mouth. He spit it out onto the cement floor. It splashed dark and heavy. It was blood and he grimaced. He was so angry that he'd bit his lip. The cut throbbed painfully in his bottom lip as he turned and went to his air-car, an old rusty gold, '59 Spec, two-seater.

The man pressed the unlock button on his remote. The air-car chirped. He pressed the open button, the driver's side door inched up, sounding as if someone was torturing a dog. He quickly sat down on the cracked vinyl of the driver's seat and closed the door. It smelled like burnt plastic inside, the fading memory of the garbage he'd filled his car up with the night before. He hated this air-car but it was all he could afford. For now.

As he activated the superconductors and hovered away from the parking balcony, the man licked at the blood on his lip, but instead of spitting it out, he swallowed it. He liked the taste of blood.

Four

It was around 3:00 in the morning when Braden finally became fed up with his tossing and turning in bed. He got up to get some fresh air on the balcony outside their bedroom.

He and Amy hadn't stayed at the Hot Zone long after she told him the good news. The rest of the station crew understood, so he'd gone home, made love to his wife, and enjoyed his life. The Chief was right; it had been a great year for him. He was excited and deliriously happy. While Amy slept, presumably exhausted from their lovemaking, his mind wouldn't shut down.

It was a comfortable, breezy, October night. The city spread out in front of him like a big, black, jagged shadow. Some of the skyscrapers were still sprinkled with tiny dots of yellow light. It was sad that some people were chained to their cubicles, even at this hour. He saw the station house a few miles to the east; its great white dome lit externally and internally so that it glowed ethereally, like a lighthouse in the sea. Far in the distance he could see many lit domes of other stations and he knew that anyone who lived in the city could see the same thing. The city did that on purpose. Psychologically, to see those shining domes gave a feeling of safety and security to the citizens, the more domes there were, the better the city felt about itself. Braden knew that a city was a living organism treading a thin line between chaos and order. There was a balance that had to be maintained and a fire station dome was a comforting reminder of that order.

Braden had yearned to be a firefighter since he was nine years old. He remembered playing in his front yard with his neighbor friend, Nick, when they heard the sirens coming from somewhere up in the clouds. They looked up and saw, coming down out of the sky, a brilliant, yellow machine, large as a house, lights flashing all over it, even underneath. Behind it was a smaller vehicle, shiny with red paint, also flashing with lights. Their sirens got louder as they swooped down like eagles over their usually quiet Wrigleyville street, stopping in front of Nick's house across the street. He and Nick had been so engrossed in playing "Sky Cop", the big hit television show at the time, that they hadn't seen the column of brown smoke coming from Nick's roof. They hadn't even smelled the burning of wood and rubber since the breeze that day was eastward, towards Lake Michigan. The big yellow machine sprayed the houses next to Nick's house with water from a pair of large cannons ontop; the firefighters moved like a well-rehearsed dance troupe, each knowing their respective task. It was all so exciting. They were pushing Nick's father out of the house on a floating gurney, and into that smaller red vehicle before the fire in the house was even put out. In less than twenty minutes, they had saved Nick's father and his house. They were superheroes.

Braden remembered Nick crying, and how one of the firemen came over and gave him a strawberry-flavored sucker. The fireman stayed with him until Nick's mom came barreling down the street in her used '51 Ford Landspeeder. Braden remembered the man's big white eyes and his rugged, strong face covered in soot and scars. The passport on his coat said his name was Captain Neil Kelly. He would become Chief of Chicago Engine Station 85 a few years later.

From then on, it was nothing but firefighting for Braden. His parents got him one of those sleek, metallic, pedal cars that Christmas. It was shaped like an old fire truck from the twentieth century and was red and shiny just like the real thing. It had flames on the sides and a small, working bell on the front. There was a decal on the hood that said "Flame Thrower." He rode that thing on the sidewalk in front of his house until the plastic wheels fell off.

Fast forward eleven years. At twenty, Braden had completed two years at the University of Chicago, Circle Campus, studying to become an architect, but his heart just wasn't in it. Firefighting was his passion. As was Amy, whom he'd been dating since high school.

She didn't like the time they'd spent apart while he went to school so he quit college, got a job as a manager of the paint department at a local Maynerds, and moved into an apartment with Amy. They were married a year later.

As things sometimes went in life, Braden became close with Amy's father, Dennis, and joined their bowling team on Saturday nights at Lake's Bowl. By sheer luck, Chief Kelly and his team were bowling on the alley next to theirs. Dennis knew the Chief because he'd done some construction work for the station a few years before. He introduced Braden to Chief Kelly, and Braden remembered him. He relayed the story about Nick's house and the strawberry sucker. The Chief said he remembered it well. He added that Nick's father falling asleep with a cigarette still lit in his hand had caused the fire. An ash fell onto a stack of newspapers; the rest was public knowledge.

Braden subtly made known to the Chief his own interest in becoming a firefighter but nothing really came of it. Then, a few days later, Braden was at work when Elliot, a co-worker, came up to him.

"There's a firefighter here to see you, Braden," Elliot said.

"A firefighter? Is the store burning down?"

Elliot laughed. "No, man. There's a real firefighter here asking to see you. He's up at the front counter."

Braden meant to ask Elliot how he knew the man was a firefighter but Elliot had disappeared into Hardware before he could ask. Braden checked his watch; he was due for a break anyway so he quickly finished pricing a stack of paint cans and went up front. Sure enough, there was a firefighter standing at the counter making small talk with Jennifer, the Returns clerk. He was completely decked out in his bunker gear and was so cool that Braden imagined himself standing there in the man's shoes. It was a Frank Sinatra coolness that came from confidence and the fact that the man was doing what he was meant to be doing in life. The firefighter wore a white helmet; Braden recognized him immediately.

"Chief Kelly," he said and shook the man's hand enthusiastically. "This is a surprise. What are you doing here?"

"We were in the area doing a fire inspection and I remembered that you told me this is where you worked," the old man answered. "I was wondering if you'd like to come in for an interview."

Braden's heart skipped; he wasn't sure he heard the Chief correctly.

"An interview?" he asked.

"Sure, at the station, Wednesday, 9:00 a.m."

"I-I'll be there, Chief!"

"Glad to hear it," the Chief said and shook Braden's hand. "We have a single opening in the Engine crew. I think you'd be good for it. Bring in copies of your birth certificate, social security card, high school diploma, and your driver's license."

Braden was tongue-tied but managed to get out, "Thanks, Chief," anyway.

So that night, his blood pressure still racing, he sat Amy down on the couch in the living room and took her hand.

"What would you think about me becoming a firefighter?" he asked her.

She looked at him with those deep blue eyes and took a deep breath. He knew she was imagining him trapped under a pile of flaming debris or being blown up in a warehouse or the countless other terribly dangerous scenarios that went along with firefighting. He knew she wasn't going for the idea.

"I-I don't know, honey," she said, looking down at their hands locked together. "I can't lose you."

"You won't, baby... I promise."

She looked back up at him and he saw that she didn't believe him. He had to lay his feelings out slowly, calmly.

"I can't work at Maynerds for the rest of my life. There are middle-aged people who've been working there since they got out of high school, babe. You should see how unhappy they are. They look back at their lives and see nothing but time wasted. A whole lifetime wasted. I don't want to look back at my life when I turn fifty and see that all I've made of my life is that I'm a department supervisor who's in debt and can't afford to send any of my kids to college."

"But it's safe, Brad," she said. "And if I get a job as a chef, we'll make our bills and have enough left over to send our kids to college."

Braden nodded but wasn't going to give up. "Look, babe, how

many people get a chance to do what they were meant to be doing in their life? This is my chance and I may never get another one. I have to take it."

Amy looked at him and smiled. "Sounds like you've already made your mind up, Brad."

"I would love it if you were behind me in this decision."

"Of course I'm behind you," she said, bringing his hand up, kissing it. "But if you die in a fire I'll kill you." She said this with deep sincerity and Braden didn't know she was joking until she burst out laughing.

They talked more about the dangers of the job, the pay, the benefits. Amy's concern now was that being a firefighter would monopolize his time and she'd never see him. He explained to her the *On* one day and *Off* the next concept; it seemed to ease her mind.

That Wednesday came and Braden arrived for the first time at Station 85. He was a few minutes early but a big, bald man named Sam met him at the entrance to the Hot Zone and escorted him up. He seemed nice enough but he talked fast, as though he'd drank a gallon of Boltz Cola and was wired. They went up the elevator, stopping at each floor for a mini-tour. He met Stacey the dispatcher, and Old Lady Perry, the bookkeeper, Dr. Payne and his nurses, but the exercise room impressed him the most. Braden planned on spending a lot of time in there working on his abs.

Finally, Sam led him up to the seventh floor where the apparatus hovered quietly and the great white dome hung like an overcast sky above. The station crest was painted on the wall to the right, it was at least twenty feet tall: two axes crossed, a flame underneath them with the words *Chicago Engine Station 85* inside the flame. Above the crossed axe heads it said *Fire & Rescue* and below the flame it said *Strength & Honor*. He felt at home immediately. Sam showed him the bunk room, the game room, the conference room, and the assignment areas where the gear of the firefighters hung and charged. Not many people got to see this intimate part of an Engine station. It was like being welcomed into a secret, sacred organization and Braden was shaking in his excitement.

"Hey, Braden," a man's rumbling voice blared throughout the dome. Braden turned and saw the Chief standing in the doorway of his office. "Why don't you come on in, we'll get things started."

"Yes, sir," Braden said. Sam followed him into the Chief's office and closed the door behind them.

The Chief motioned at a pair of simple chairs that stood in front of a large, organized, and polished desk. He sat down on a big black leather hover chair. Braden sat down and Sam stood next to the Chief. The Chief asked for the personal information he'd requested, Braden handed over a green folder. Sam took it and began looking through it like a spy looking for secret weapons plans.

"All that information is going into an electronic file kept by the state of Illinois. It can be accessed by me and every other Fire Chief in the city," the Chief began. "This file will be continuously updated. It will show your entire training and firefighter education history; it will show your rank and just about everything that has to do with you as a firefighter, good or bad."

Braden had never heard of such a thing; it unnerved him. What if he made a mistake, like he crashed the Engine or was late to work? That would follow him for the rest of his life.

"We're not Big Brother," the Chief said, obviously seeing Braden's concern. "By state law and Chicago Firefighter Union Local 7 restraints, in order for a firefighter to be certified the state needs complete records of the firefighters it hires. That way, if a lawsuit should be filed by a taxpayer, the state, city, and station are protected. It sounds worse than it is but it's the same in every state."

"I understand, sir," Braden said.

"Good. Now, this is just a preliminary interview, Braden," the Chief said. "A kind of 'get to know you' session dealing mainly with personal information."

Braden nodded, and noticed that his palms were clammy. He suddenly realized he was nervous. *Keep it together.* he told himself. *Just relax and everything will be fine.*

"First question," the Chief said, leaning forward in his big, important-looking leather chair. He set his eyes on Braden, screwed down his big chin. "Why do you want to be a firefighter?"

The interview lasted an hour. As far as Braden could tell, things went perfectly. The Chief and Sam were friendly and joked with him. They made him feel at ease; he appreciated that. They'd been in the same position he was and understood what he was going through. The Chief ended the interview by giving him a sheet of electronic paper and a stylus. On it was an application for employment from the city of Chicago.

"Fill it out completely, even if it doesn't apply to you," the Chief ordered.

Braden nodded and once he filled it in he followed the directions at the bottom and looked with his right eye at the big red dot in the bottom corner. The dot took an electronic snapshot of the vessels in his eye, a signature much more accurate and easier to read than his fingerprint, and then he hit the *SEND* icon next to the red dot with the stylus. The image of the application shimmered then disappeared, leaving a blank sheet. The Chief reached over and took it.

"Thanks, Kid," he said. "That information has now been routed to every station computer in the city and to the main computer downstate. You're official. Once all that information has been processed we'll get in touch with you concerning an orientation meeting here in the station's conference room."

"Thank you, Chief, for this opportunity," Braden said.

"No problem, Kid," the Chief said. "I must tell you, though, in the spirit of honesty and fair play, that there are two other applicants for the position, and one of them is my son."

This was terrible news. Braden's heart broke. What chance did he have against the Chief's son? He was familiar with the role nepotism played in modern Chicago politics, and he knew that being a firefighter was a city job. Braden didn't know anyone who could pull the strings capable of playing his song. He got up, shook the Chief's hand, and was led out of the office by Sam. Sam escorted Braden back down the elevator and into the Hot Zone. At the entrance, Sam shook his hand, wished him luck.

Braden knew luck didn't have anything to do with it.

A month later he received an invitation in his email. It was for that orientation the Chief had spoken of at the interview. It was scheduled for the coming Saturday morning and would last approximately three hours. Lunch would be served. Braden knew the other two candidates would be there and sure enough, when he walked into the conference room, Stan and Roger were already sitting at the table. Sam introduced them, they shook hands, and talked as they ate doughnuts and drank coffee. Braden learned that both Stan and Roger had been trained to jump out of air transports in the military. It didn't come any more intense than that. His hope of ever winning the job was completely dashed.

The Chief walked in and everyone got down to business.

"Good morning and welcome, everyone," the Chief said as Sam closed the door. Braden could hear the firefighters outside doing a routine drill. "As you can hear outside," the Chief began, "my firefighters are doing their morning hose and ladder drills. Drills strengthen the backbone of the station. If that backbone broke during a rescue or fire, the station would be crippled, useless. Lives and property would be lost. So if you don't like to do drills, firefighting isn't for you. If you are scared of heights or claustrophobic, firefighting isn't for you. If you don't like the sight of blood or the smell of decaying guts, firefighting isn't for you. If you are scared of fire, firefighting isn't for you. I ask you to leave now so that I don't waste your precious time or mine."

Braden, Stan, and Roger remained in their seats, their eyes on the Chief.

"Good. Now that that's out of the way, the first thing I want to say to you is that eighty per cent of the calls we receive are rescue calls, things like auto collisions, overdoses, cats in trees."

Everyone laughed.

"The second thing I want to tell you is that the first five minutes of a fire station's response determines the ultimate success or failure of a fire or rescue operation. The sooner we get to a job, the better able we are to save lives and property. We expect blinding speed from you and complete competence. Will that be a problem for any of you probies?"

They all shook their heads.

"So if you should be the one lucky enough to become a firefighter for the great city of Chicago, you will have to go through a rigorous three month EMT/paramedic class. You will have to learn CPR. You will have to complete a six month Firefighter I class. You will have to pass a statewide test concerning WMD response and hazardous materials. You will have to pass the State of Illinois' Fire Marshall test—and re-certify it every six months. You will have to learn the behavior of a fire. You will have to attend a forty-hour

Operations class. You will have to learn how to tie every knot man has ever invented. If this is too much for you, firefighting is not for you. Leave now."

No one moved.

The Chief smiled and leaned forward, his large hands splayed on the table.

"Okay," he said. "The number one rule in firefighting is *never let the fire get behind you.* Always back out of the room when putting out a fire. And be patient. I was at a job early in my career, a house fire, working with a group of seasoned firefighters from another station. It was my job to stand at the threshold of the front door and feed the hose in to the team of firefighters fighting the blaze. The blaze was centered in the kitchen, all the way in the back of the house, but they were going in too fast and repeatedly calling for more hose. They kept advancing as if toward an enemy pillbox. 'More hose!' they shouted, 'More hose!' I kept feeding it to them when suddenly the hose went taut and got real heavy. 'No more hose!' they shouted, 'No more hose! Grab the hose!' Knowing something was very wrong, I shouted for a replacement to anchor the hose and went into the house. When I got into the kitchen I saw that one of the firefighters had fallen through a hole in the floor and was hanging onto the hose. The other firefighter was trying to use the hose to pull him up, but he wasn't strong enough. Together, we pulled him up, saved his life. These were seasoned firefighters who had rushed into the room so quickly that they didn't know there was a basement that was flaming like holy hell down there, eating at the floor boards. The way to tell that is if when you step on the floor and it feels spongy, that tells you that the floor boards have burned away and all that's keeping the floor together is the tile or carpeting or whatever. Back out immediately if you feel this. These seasoned firefighters had been taught this, but got lazy. Well, they learned their goddamn lesson that day. Be patient and be careful."

With that, the Chief activated the holocube and a series of three-dimensional videos played on the surface of the conference room table. The first was a video of a firefighter in his bunker gear dousing a smoking ground car with a thick stream of water. He was standing in front of the car and the smoke was coming out of the hood. There was a sudden explosion and the firefighter disappeared from the scene. It looked like the camera shook, somebody cursed, and the cameraman switched the view from the smoking vehicle to the firefighter about twenty yards away. He was rolling on the ground screaming; he had no legs under both knees. A group of firefighters surrounded him and carried him to the ambulance. Somebody was shouting and the cameraman focused on a firefighter bending forward, pointing, and saying, "I found his legs." The holocube showed a pair of bloody boots, a pale white shin was sticking up out of each of them, the jagged end of bone stuck up out of those. Near the boots was the bumper of the car. A firefighter narrated what had happened: "Looks like the bumper blew off. I've seen this before. Bumpers are welded to the frame of a car by a pair of hollow tubes to make them stronger and lighter, but air gets trapped inside the hollow. When that air is heated, pow! The bumper blows off. I've seen a bumper sticking out of a brick wall. The energies released are amazing." Then a firefighter picked up the boots and rushed them to the ambulance, saying he hoped they could re-attach the legs.

There was a collective gasp of horror in the room when the video ended; Braden's was loudest. He'd never considered how seriously injured he could be. He also had never heard of a bumper blowing off a car. It showed him that he should always be observant when at an emergency scene.

The next video was of a firefighter climbing a ladder to get to the roof of a house. There was another firefighter heeling the ladder below, but he was doing this incorrectly and the ladder slipped out from his boots. The firefighter at the top of the ladder was like a weight on the end of a see-saw; the bottom of the ladder came up violently, dropping the firefighter at the top onto the roof like a slag of meat. He bounced once, rolled, and fell off the roof down onto the black-topped driveway. It sounded like a sack of unripe potatoes hitting the ground.

Next, the Chief played them an audio tape of an emergency call. It was a man's voice and he was panicking. A train had just derailed a block from his house and the train was carrying canisters of chlorine gas. He was coughing, the fear in his voice betrayed the fact that he knew they wouldn't get to him in time. "Please don't hang up on me! Please!" he begged the operator. His breathing sounded labored and scratchy, and he vomited. Chlorine gas, when in contact with water, turns to acid. The inside of the man's body (which is mostly water) was being burned away. "We're trying to get to you in time, sir," the operator said, trying to hold back tears. "Just hang on, sir! Stay with me!" "Please!" the man coughed. "Please." And that was it. The scratching of the man's breathing stopped. There was a thump, as if the phone hit the floor.

The Chief deactivated the holocube and its audio feature and sat down. He looked somber. Braden realized that he was testing them. Seeing if they had what it took to face situations like that.

"Still interested?" the Chief asked.

They nodded.

"Then, when this orientation is over this afternoon, I want you to concentrate on getting yourself in shape for the obstacle course test next month. The three of you will compete for the right to become a firefighter for Station 85. You will be allowed access to tour the course and to the exercise room. After that, I don't care how you prepare yourself and I don't care if you fail. I care about getting the best man in here."

Braden, Stan, and Roger traded glances. But Braden wasn't worried at all. He'd already planned to make use of the exercise room. He was also part of a stocking crew that was going to open a new Maynerds in Downers Grove. That meant a lot of lifting, pulling, and pushing. If he was going to beat the others out, he'd have to be in the best shape of his life.

~ * ~

Braden smiled to himself as he realized that he was now officially a cadet for Chicago Engine Station 85. And he was going to be a father. Amy wanted four kids, their own miniature Brady Bunch; that was fine with Braden. He wanted them, too.

He looked up at the skyway, which was already starting to congest. It hung above the city like a river of glittering diamonds in the sky. Sometimes, one of those diamonds would fall away from the main body, swoop down, land on an air-car pad atop a roof or melt into the traffic stream that hovered between the buildings. Other times, a diamond would rise up out of the shadow of the great city and join the streaming current of the river above. Braden was amazed that there weren't more air-car collisions than there were.

Computers were in charge of it all and were almost as intelligent as humans nowadays.

He looked back down at the city and smiled. He loved Chicago and he wanted to be a part of what made the city great. Of course, another Daley, Jack, was running it. The family could legitimately be considered a pharaonic dynasty, but that was all right. The family had done right by the city and would probably continue to do so. Jack had three sons and a young daughter waiting in the wings. The machine kept going.

The fresh air was beginning to work. Braden's mind was clearing. He was finally feeling drowsy. He'd been out there a long time thinking and the time had passed quickly. He went back in, leaving the screened door open to bring in some of the breeze, and lay in bed next to Amy. She stirred when he got under the covers. She put her arm on his belly and kissed his cheek.

"Are you all right, honey?" she asked through a yawn.

"I'm perfect, babe."

Five

Chicago Engine Station 85 was just like every other firehouse in the city: everything to run a firehouse and tend to the needs of the firefighters encapsulated in one efficiently designed seven-story building.

There was a floor devoted to any outward billing that was pertinent, and any income. Two floors were reserved for the obstacle course/training room. Another floor held a large exercise room complete with a half-sized basketball court, a full racquetball court, ten different kinds of computerized treadmills, a row of weight benches, a cleared and padded area for a virtual-reality aerobic instructor (they called him "Ahnold"), climbing ropes hanging from the ceiling, and a punching bag. All of this was crammed inside a five-lane running track. The sixth floor was a hospital, designed to meet the specific wounds a firefighter might have accrued during a job, but it was also a full service hospital for the station's family members with all the latest computerized equipment available, including nanobots. The top floor, covered by a huge, white retractable dome, was where the apparatus, kitchen, bunkrooms, game room, and the showers were. Braden spent the first week after becoming a cadet familiarizing himself with everything on each floor as he would be in contact with them at one point or another. He, like the rest of the station, was on one day and off the next (though the Chief worked almost every day). Station 68 covered for them on their day off.

Braden had to take a First Aid class to get certified in CPR. This was held in a conference room in the hospital and Dr. Payne was a patient, knowledgeable teacher. It wasn't an in-depth program, as all a firefighter was expected to do, because they were usually the first on the scene, was stabilize a patient and get them to the ambulance crew.

He also learned about nanobots. They were small, microscopic machines that could be injected into the body, drunk if mixed with water, or sprinkled over a wound, depending on what they were programmed to do. Some nanobots were programmed to flow through the blood stream and clean out illegal drugs and were ejected in the urine later on. Some repaired cellular damage internally, or if sprinkled on an open wound, externally. Braden was fascinated as Dr. Payne took a scalpel and cut his thumb open; next, a nurse came with a small bottle of what looked like cinnamon powder. She poured the contents on the wound. Braden could actually see the nanobots pull the edges of the cut together, heal it cleanly; in seconds it was as if there was never a wound. No scar was left behind.

When Braden wasn't taking the First Aid classes he was kept busy with training under the dome. Drills were a commonplace occurrence and Braden loved them. The bunker gear drill was his favorite. All the firefighters had a space marked out in tape on the floor just outside the entrance to the bunkrooms. He was so proud when he saw his name on the wall in the digital display hanging next to his jacket, even though the word "Probie" was in front of it. That made it official, he was going to be a firefighter. So did the metal passport hanging off the zipper protector on his jacket. It had his name, weight, height, what sex he was, date of birth, blood type, what station he was a member of, and his charge of duty. That was to identify his body in case he was injured in a fire or to identify himself and his station if more than one station was involved on a job.

A firefighter's jacket was made of a fireproof material called Nomex and it shone with horizontal reflectors. It had to stay clean and fully charged. Firefighters were expected to maintain their own equipment and keep it in proper working order. That meant checking a list of duties every day: the battery pack, the compressor, and the air bladders in the lining of the jacket for leaks, making sure the helm cam was working, along with everything else. The breeches were connected to the boots and were also made of Nomex, which stiffened them like starch so that the boots stood up on their own. The breeches were rolled down ontop of the boots so that a firefighter could just step into them and pull them up.

In the drill, the firefighter had to don every last bit of the gear in sixty seconds. First he had to step into the boots, pull the breeches up, and secure his arms through the overall straps. Then he had to put the jacket on, zip it up, slide his head into the flash hood, and throw on the helmet. He would put the gloves on last. Braden's first try was a minute, forty-three seconds. Incredibly disappointed, he practiced the drill at every chance he had; soon his fastest time was fifty-four seconds.

The most challenging aspect of the drills had to do with the hose. Braden was shocked at how heavy a dried and empty hose was; he was even more shocked at how hard a hose was to control when fully charged with water. That's why there was always a firefighter to control the nozzle spray in front and one behind him to add support and feed the hose.

One crisp, sunny morning, the Chief ordered the entire crew, with the exception of the ambulance crew, into their respective vehicles. A few minutes later they stood in their bunker gear in an abandoned, fenced-in lot just outside the city limits. The lot was surrounded by empty, harvested farm fields; there was a small, yellow-bricked warehouse in the middle that had apparently been burned out long ago. Braden could see the black sooty scars of smoke imprinted on the brick above the windows. Joni and Mo landed the apparatus in the backyard behind the warehouse and a giant metal tank sat in a cradle near the fence, fifty feet away.

"What's going on, Sam?" Braden whispered.

"You're going to learn how to fight a propane fire," Sam answered and smiled at him. Braden didn't like that smile at all.

The Chief went to the tank and stood by a small nozzle that came out of the top. Braden had studied fighting a propane tank fire in the giant seven hundred page manual he'd been given, now it was time to see if he'd learned anything.

"Thom!" the Chief shouted. "I want you to run two hoses from the hose bed in the Engine. Bring 'em out fifteen feet then stay back and tend the hose so it doesn't tangle."

"Copy that," Thom said. Immediately he began pulling a hose out of the hose bed. He dropped it on the ground fifteen feet from the Engine and went back to get the other one.

"Paul, you're the nozzle man for hose number one. Take Big George as your hose man."

"Copy that, Chief," Paul said. He and Big George hurried to the first hose and picked it up, Paul in front, Big George in back.

"Braden, you and Sam take hose number two. You're the nozzle man."

"Copy that, Chief," Braden picked the nozzle up just as Thom dropped it. Sam positioned himself behind Braden and pushed his shoulder into Braden's back. Braden felt like he was leaning against an oak tree. Being the nozzle man for hose number two meant that his job was to fog the air around the flame in an "X" pattern, trying to cool it down so that Paul could advance on the flame, douse it, then turn the valve on the tank off.

Thom activated the hose valve on the Engine. The hose went thick and heavy; it almost jumped out of his hands. Braden felt the power of the pressure inside and his heart raced. With a force of eight hundred PSI, a single stream of water could blow a hole through a brick wall. The Chief pulled out a lighter and held it up over his head. The others who weren't involved in this first drill stood back by the Engine and watched.

"Are you guys ready?" the Chief asked.

Braden couldn't take his hands off the nozzle or it would fly wild, so he shouted an "Ugh!" Paul did the same. The Chief quickly turned the valve on the propane tank and Braden heard a high-pitched hissing. The Chief lit the lighter, brought it down, quickly striking the tiny flame into the invisible jet of propane gas. There was a low roar. The Chief ran away as a narrow, triangular column of blue flame erupted into the air. Braden felt the heat on his face immediately. He nodded his head violently so that the blast shield fell and protected him. He couldn't believe how hot the flame was, and yet they were a good thirty-five feet away. But it was beautiful and mesmerizing, glowing brightly like a neon blue, forty-foot tall, electric ghost.

Paul opened his nozzle and was hurriedly swiping a mist of white water into the air near the flame. Braden did the same, turning the valve on the nozzle just enough to create a spray, or fog. Then, twenty feet apart from each other, they advanced, taking slow, deliberate, careful steps, never taking their eyes off the blue flame. The closer they got, the hotter it became. Braden felt tendrils of heat rising up from under his blast shield. He hated to think of what would have become of him if he wasn't wearing the bunker gear.

The digital display on his blast shield read two hundred forty-six degrees and they'd only gone forward five feet. He raised the nozzle up high, repeatedly penciling "X's" in the air, but the heat turned the mist into a hissing, steaming cloud of useless vapor. He feared the mist was too light so he turned the nozzle a little to the right, intensifying the spray. It worked; the spray was penetrating closer to the flame now. They moved forward as Paul concentrated his spray on the surface of the tank. He intensified his own stream when he and Braden traded targets, Paul cooling the air and Braden cooling the tank. They worked well together and were synchronized as if they'd done this a hundred times before. They were ten feet from the tank when Paul once again intensified his stream, attacking the flame itself. It seemed to dance away from the blasting water, writhing and shimmering like a mirage, but Paul's onslaught was relentless. It was as if the flame screamed out in agony and disappeared.

"Keep cooling the tank!" Paul shouted at Braden. Braden nodded.

Paul sprayed the air above with water as he and Big George reached the tank. If the flame re-flashed, they would be seriously injured. Braden sprayed the tank as Paul reached out, twisted the valve, cutting off the propane jet. Then he and Big George stepped back, targeting the tank along with Braden. A few minutes later the ambient air temperature was cool enough to shut the hoses down.

Everyone behind them was clapping as the Chief came up to them.

"That was textbook, gentlemen," he said. "Excellent. Now trade hoses and do it again."

Thom came up and reset the hoses on the ground while the two teams traded sides and waited for the Chief's go ahead. Braden, now in charge of dousing the blue flame and shutting the valve, did everything just as he'd seen Paul do it that first time. They had the same successful result.

"Great job, people," the Chief said through a smile. "Now let's create new teams and get the rest involved."

By late afternoon they were all hungry, exhausted, hot, and irritable. The Chief, satisfied with how well things went, decided it was enough for the day. He told them that he'd buy them dinner at the Hot Zone when they got back and had showered. That cheered everyone up as they emptied the hoses, re-bedded them, and cleaned things up.

As Braden went around the truck he saw that the yellow brick on the burned out structure of the warehouse that had faced the propane flame was still smoking from the intense heat. He took his glove off and pressed his index finger on a brick. It felt like he'd been stung by a bee. He put his fingertip into his mouth, shook his head in amazement, and then went up the ramp into the Engine.

As a cadet, Braden also had to keep the trucks clean, keep the cans (two and a half gallon fire extinguishers) on the trucks maintained, check the hoses and hose rollers for defects, make sure the deck guns worked properly, as well as the ladders, the sirens, the lights, and the anti-gravity superconductors. Sometimes Sam helped him but mostly he was on his own so that when they ran a drill over the city and everything worked perfectly, it reflected well on him and nobody else. The Chief called it "cutting your teeth."

Braden had to become familiar with the varied array of tools a firefighter used. The flat-head and pick-head axes, the pike pole, the Halligan bar, the spanner wrench (for opening hydrants), the Jaws of Life, the Personal Alert Safety System (PASS) — this went off with a manic ninety-five decibel shriek if a firefighter remained still for thirty seconds, and they were even allowed to use small blocks of C-4 if the fire was susceptible to that because fire needed oxygen to live and an explosion throws a vacuum that sucks oxygen right out of the air.

Then Braden's classes began. He took them on his *Off* days just so that he could finish them faster. They were held in the conference room in the station with the Chief instructing him. He had Hazmat training, WMD classes, and fire behavior classes going one after the other. He didn't see Amy or her ever-widening belly very much. One day in late November, just before Thanksgiving,

Braden was washing the windshield that took up the entire front of the Engine when the domed roof of the station suddenly began retracting. From closed to fully opened and locked, the giant dome retracted in under a minute. Braden had no time to protest as snow and sleet rained down on his newly cleaned apparatus. The kitchen door suddenly burst opened and Sam came out laughing riotously, followed by the Foam Tender crew. They seemed to be hyped up about something, especially Sam. Braden closed off the nozzle and dropped the hose he was using.

"Hey, Kid!" Sam barked, jumped on the side rail of the engine, and climbed the ladder to the top. The ambulance crew came out of the kitchen, applauding wildly. The Chief stepped out of his office and stood next to Braden, shaking his head. Wind and snow were swirling above.

Sam, still laughing on top of the Engine, knelt down and began fumbling with the control board. The whirring motor of the massive turntable ladder sounded and the ladder began rising. It went up slowly. When it was perfectly vertical, Sam pressed the control that extended the ladder. There were two fifty-foot sections, Sam extended both of them. Without a moment's hesitation, he jumped onto the ladder and began climbing.

"What's he doing?" Braden asked the Chief.

"A Church Raise," the Chief replied. "One of those yahoos must have dared Sam to do it."

"What's a Church Raise?"

"Watch and learn, my boy."

So Braden watched. Halfway up the ladder, fifty feet, Sam stopped. The ladder was swaying dangerously in the wind. A couple of times Braden thought it was going to come crashing down. Sam held his hands out and the Foam Tender crew began throwing him ropes with hooks on the ends, one at a time. Sam caught them and attached them to the outside beams of the ladder. The Foam Tender crew spread themselves out so that they had the Engine surrounded on all sides, then they began pulling the ropes taut. The ladder stopped its dangerous swaying immediately. Sam let out a pleased victorious howl and began climbing again. Up and up he went; they all held their breath when his right foot slipped on a rung and he almost fell. But he caught himself and made it to the top. He didn't stop there. Instead, he pushed himself up so that his upper body was beyond the tip of the ladder and he sat down on the last rung, slipping his feet through the back of a rung below so that he had some measure of grip. He looked down, put his arms out to his sides, lifted his face so he was looking up at the sky. He yowled, "Top of the world, Ma!"

Growling like a maniac at the top of his lungs, he shook his shaved, bald head free of the snow that had quickly gathered on it.

"And he called me a clock," Braden said in disbelief.

The Chief laughed. "He's one crazy sonofabitch, that's for sure."

Yes, he was. But it occurred to Braden that Sam was the kind of man he wanted to be partnered with. A man who would do a Church Raise was a man who would do anything. He was fearless.

After a few minutes it appeared that Sam had had enough of the driving wind and the swirling snow so he began climbing down. Everyone was cheering uncontrollably. When Sam got back down, they carried him into the showers, drowning him with hot water. Then Debbie made them all homemade pizzas and hot cocoa. Sam was still blue and shivering but said he considered it all worth it. No one would ever dare him to do that again.

Afterwards, just after dark, Braden went back out under the dome and had to clean the apparatus again. Chief's orders. It took him most of the night. When he finally finished, they were all sleeping in the bunkrooms. He got himself a soda and sat down at the large, rectangular kitchen table. He began thinking about Sam and wondering what would have happened if something had gone wrong, like maybe the ladder snapping, or Sam slipping and falling. He hadn't been wearing any protective gear, hadn't even tied off to anything. The ladder had been better protected than he was. Replacing a man like that was nearly impossible.

This brought Braden's mind to the suspicious things that had happened to him during the obstacle course test. He remembered that he was supposed to tell the Chief about the weights on Victor's ankles; he had forgotten after getting the news that he was going to be a father. Then his training began. It had been a while. Braden figured that before he woke the Chief up, he'd better make sure the weights were still there. He went out to the utility lockers. He opened

Victor's locker, knelt down, and rolled up the pant legs. The weights were gone. Victor hadn't been used since his test so somebody had come in and removed them. Now he couldn't tell the Chief of his suspicions about Stan. He'd look like a paranoid probie.

Braden frowned, stood up, and closed the locker. Nothing suspicious had happened since then, but could it be the lull before the storm? He hoped not. He turned and went back in to finish his soda.

G.C. Rosenquist

Six

A week after New Year's Day, 2070, a blizzard came down out of Canada and settled itself right over Chicago. Ground traffic turned into a frozen parking lot; anyone brave enough to use the skyway without radar was most likely suicidal.

All day Saturday the temperature had fallen. By nightfall it had stabilized at twenty-three degrees. The snow came down in large cotton-like fluffs and the wind coming off Lake Michigan kept the snow circulating in the air like the blades of a helicopter, so that by the time the snow hit the ground, it had had enough time to sponge what moisture it could from the air, becoming sloppy. As it sat there on the sidewalks and streets, it froze, and no amount of salt or heat treatment the city threw at it worked. This made things worse, in fact, by turning the ice to mush and then the mush froze right back again, creating rock-hard, uneven, jagged hills of dark ice.

Braden looked out the living room window in his apartment. He was relieved he was off on this particular Saturday. It was a mess. The Chief had told him once that Saturdays were the worst day for every station in the city. Crazies came out, fueled by liquor and narcotics; there was always someone who'd gotten himself stabbed or was lying face down, drunk and freezing to death.

Braden had gone with the Chief and the ambulance crew on a few "drive-alongs," seeing it for himself.

He went into the bedroom and lay in his soft bed under the warm comforter he and Amy had received from her parents for Christmas. It was lined with a material that was activated by a person's body heat and only got as warm as the person's exuding heat. He lay on his side, his hand on Amy's seven-month high, round belly, and slept deeply. Dreamlessly. Sometimes, though, Amy's belly would bubble out then roll violently. It would wake him up, and he'd fall back asleep by holding his hand there, feeling his little baby move under Amy's smooth, warm skin.

They'd found out from Dr. Payne, just after Thanksgiving, that they were going to have a girl. Braden was thrilled. He remembered how Amy had lain on the hoverbed in the hospital as two ultrasound paddles hung from a pair of robotic arms attached to the ceiling, gently sliding along the surface of her belly, throwing sound waves at the fetus. The result was an eerie, detailed, perfectly clear, three-dimensional representation of their baby that hovered in the air and spun slowly at the foot of the bed via a holocube in the ceiling. It had been clear from the beginning that it was a girl; Amy's eyes filled with tears. Braden felt just as emotional but he controlled his reaction. He imagined his daughter's first smile, her first laugh, her first words, her first steps. Her future was wide open and limitless. Braden couldn't wait to tell everyone he was having a girl.

They hadn't decided on a name yet but there were some lovely ones that had made it to the final four: Jennifer, Amanda, Maddie, and Braden's current favorite, Evangeline or Evie. But there were still two months to go so that could change.

Sometimes Braden would see Amy standing in her pajamas in the bathroom as she brushed her teeth, or doing whatever magic it was that she did in the kitchen, and her little belly would be sticking out under her sleep-T. He'd become overwhelmed with emotion, and it was all he could do to hold his tears in. He did more around the house for her, cooked for her when she was too tired, even cleaned the dishes away after a meal. Her cravings were not for pickles but for pickle juice so they had three full jars of pickles in the fridge with no juice. Sometimes Amy would wake him up and make him go get a fresh jar from the local convenience store. Yet her cravings didn't stop there. She had a distinct taste for anything with lemon in it and all things salty, mostly Slim Jims. It was as if her sweet tooth had fallen out, replaced by a salt demon. He did his best to ease her cravings, but sometimes he felt like a restaurant waiter, only without receiving a tip.

Once, when his mom and dad were over for dinner, Braden

did everything from cooking the meal to setting the table. His dad remarked how strange it was to see him so domesticated. It wasn't a rip on Braden; it was his father telling him in that subtle way of his that Braden was a man now and the torch had been passed.

And then there was his firefighter training. His classes were nearly complete. He was due to receive his certification from the Mayor in April. Amy was due in March. All he had to complete was the Fire Marshall test. With all of this coming to a head, the spring promised to be a busy one and Braden was looking forward to it. Maybe after that he'd finally get some rest.

An incessant beeping sound invaded his thoughts.

Braden sat straight up in bed and looked over to see his beeper going off like Chinese fireworks on the surface of his bed stand. The holo-clock hovering over the beeper flashed 1:35 a.m. It was the Chief rousing him for another night of drive-alongs.

The drive-alongs always seemed to be on his *Off* day and they always bled into the morning of his *On* day so, by the morning of his next off day, Braden was a worthless, exhausted shell of a man. It was hard on Amy, because sometimes he slept all morning while she was left alone to do whatever it was that she had to do that day. He promised her again that it wasn't going to be like this forever; once he was a firefighter, there'd be no more beepers rousing him for a drive-along. He hoped she believed him.

He reached over, shut the beeper off, threw his feet over the side of the bed as quietly as he could, and yawned long and hard. He had brought his bunker gear home and proceeded to do the drill: step into the boots, pull the breeches up, and so on.

He landed his blue, '66 Chevy Camaro on the station dock less than ten minutes later. The snowfall was terrible, pure whiteout conditions, but he had a state-of-the-art computerized, GPS auto-pilot put in just for this purpose. He'd also installed an extra powerful sonar emitter that made it easy for other air-cars to pick him up on their detectors. He was about as safe as someone flying a hundred feet above a major city in a snowstorm could possibly be.

He got out of the car. The Chief was standing with Debbie and Danny, the ambulance crew, by the ambulance. The Chief was in his bunker gear and the other two were in their official EMS blues underneath thick jackets and tight knit caps with Station 85 signage on them.

They all greeted him sleepily.

"What's on the menu tonight, Chief?" Braden asked.

"Stacey just sent us up a call about a possible overdose," the Chief replied as they made their way inside the ambulance. "I figured, since you haven't seen one yet, it'd be a good experience for you."

Braden nodded as Debbie and Danny made their way into the cockpit, sat down, belted in, and began powering up the vehicle. The ambulance was a sleek, shiny, red, shoebox-shaped vehicle with a wedge-shaped glass-enclosed cockpit. In back was a large, sanitary triage area capable of stabilizing and transporting up to six people. Every kind of medical apparatus a hospital had was either in the drawers, on the walls, or hanging down from the ceiling. It was fully stocked with nanobots, the latest synthetic painkillers, two Thumpers, four defibrillators, six respirators, and a complete IV set-up. All that was missing was the patient.

Braden and the Chief sat in their own seats in the back of the cockpit and belted up. Debbie switched the lights and sirens on as the cockpit darkened. Then she pulled back on the wheel and the ambulance shot straight up into the swirling blizzard above. Just like an air-car, speed was transferred to the superconductor jets underneath the ambulance by pushing a pedal down with the right foot that activated the magnetic accentuators, making the vehicle move. The farther down the pedal was pushed, the faster the vehicle went. The ambulance could stop on a dime, turn, dive, spin, roll, whatever Debbie wanted it to do. Once, Debbie sent the ambulance into the fiery mouth of a warehouse fire to not only save a civilian, but also the pair of trapped firefighters that had been sent in to rescue them. The commendation for that hung on the bulkhead behind Braden.

Debbie wasted no time, turning the ambulance to the north, gunning the jets. The dashboard was a dizzying array of radar, sonar, thermal, and visual monitors. Debbie knew how to use each one. A GPS screen kept her on course and warned her vocally of any course-wavering or oncoming obstacles. The speakers in the ceiling were alive with transmissions from the dispatcher. Stacey had the person who had called in the OD still on the line and they listened with great concentration. Braden noticed that the Chief seemed to be greatly troubled by what he heard. His eyelids were heavier than usual, Braden thought, not from being tired, but from being concerned.

"She's not breathing too well." the man said in a panic.

"Keep saying her name, sir," Stacey said. "Keep her awake. It's important that you do that."

And the man repeated "Brenda! Stay with me, Brenda!" until it nearly broke Braden's heart. He never understood why people took drugs. Drugs didn't make your life better. They just numbed you, tuned you out of an experience you had only one chance at, life. Why would someone want to miss that, no matter how sad their life was?

Debbie had the ambulance going at an incredible clip now. The sirens screamed outside like banshees, the lights painted the curtain of falling snow ahead with neon red and yellow. It reminded Braden of the confetti falling in the spinning lights of the Hot Zone when the clock struck midnight a week ago. What a great time they all had. Sam had managed to lose his shirt again.

"We're almost there!" Debbie shouted back at them. "Remember, you're just onlookers. Stay out of our way! If we need your help, we'll ask for it!"

Braden nodded.

The Chief saluted in the affirmative.

The front of the ambulance went down, as if they'd just fallen over Niagara Falls. The strap tightened around Braden's chest, locking him deeper into the seat cushion. He felt his stomach coming up but he swallowed hard to keep it down. Then the ambulance leveled off, turned a little to the right, and stopped with a sudden lurch.

Debbie hit the triage door release and unbelted herself. She got up, followed by Danny, and they ran down the narrow aisle between the Chief and Braden, into the back of the truck. By the time Braden and the Chief made it back there, Debbie and Danny were already down the ramp and in the house tending to the OD.

It was an old neighborhood they'd landed in, similar to the one Braden grew up in. Two or three story flats up and down the block, all covered in snow. Debbie parked the ambulance in the front yard a few feet from the front porch. The open front door allowed snow inside the house.

Braden followed the Chief down the ramp, through the snow, which was a good fourteen inches deep now, up the wood stairs leading to the snow-covered porch, where they stomped their boots clean before going into the house.

They were in the living room; Braden sized it up quickly. It smelled like sour milk and coffee and made him want to gag. The walls were painted a depressing shade of brown and an old chandelier hung from the ceiling, but only one bulb worked so there were harsh shadows everywhere. The carpet was a thick brown Berber, worn down to the padding near the kitchen entrance. There was an ancient, flat screen LCD television in the fireplace playing old Tom and Jerry reruns; on the floor near the far end of a tattered, stained green couch was a space heater, its grill white with heat. There were magazines lying perilously close to it. Braden pointed it out to the Chief. The Chief frowned and shook his head as he kicked the magazines away from the heat. Then he leaned over and pulled the plug from the wall.

Danny and Debbie were kneeling over a middle-aged woman with stringy brown hair; her skin deathly white. She wore a wrinkled red T-shirt and a pair of shorts that were two sizes too big for her. The bottoms of her feet were dirty, but her toenails looked freshly done in the French style. She just lay there unresponsive as the EMS crew did their work. She looked about as dead as someone could be.

Danny had a pulse-finder pressed against the jugular in her throat and waited patiently for the display on it to register a beep. But all he got was a long, whining, flat line. The sound cut through the air in there like an axe blade. Debbie was checking the eyes for dilation.

"I'm not getting anything," Danny murmured.

"Neither am I," Debbie said.

A sound burst from the shadows of the tattered couch like the howl of a coyote. Braden hadn't seen anything on it before, but there was a man there, sitting with his knees up to his face, convulsing as he was crying. It was the man who'd called the OD in to dispatch.

"Please save her!" he begged. "Please save her! She just took too much! She took too much!"

"We're trying, Mr. Bachard," Debbie said in a businesslike monotone.

Danny released the pulse-finder from the woman's throat and attached it to his belt.

"We need the Thumper!" Debbie shouted. "Go get it, Rathman!"

Braden turned and trampled his way through the snow, slipped as he went up the ambulance ramp, found the Thumper in a drawer near the number four cot, and then ran back into the house. Danny was injecting the woman with nanobots as he came in. Debbie took the Thumper, putting it on the floor next to the woman. After checking the woman's eyes again, she reached down, took hold of the woman's shirt, and ripped it open, revealing a wrinkled, saggy torso. It looked like the body of a seventy year-old woman.

The Chief must have seen Braden's shock. "The computer says she's only twenty-four, Kid," he muttered. "That's the toll *Trip* takes on the human body. The most addicting synthetic drug ever produced."

Debbie slid the Thumper around the woman's upper torso, attached the respirator mask to her face, and pressed the activator near the drum. The woman's chest trembled in response to the drumming; the respirator hissed like a startled snake.

"You've got to save her! You've just got to!" the man sobbed from the couch.

"All we can do now is transport her to the hospital," Danny said. "The nanobots are cleaning her blood; hopefully it's not too late."

The Chief knelt down, picked up a small square of foiled paper from the floor, and handed it to Braden. There were thirteen other pieces of paper just like it scattered around the room.

"It comes rolled up in this foil like a chocolate," the Chief began. "They even flavor it to whatever you like best. The user sticks it to the roof of his mouth and licks it so that the flavor makes him salivate, then it's swallowed, absorbed through the stomach wall, and into the bloodstream. The high is almost immediate and lasts for forty minutes, all the while destroying brain cells in the deepest part of the brain and eating through the stomach, causing ulcers that allow the drug to be absorbed faster with each hit. Of course, the faster the drug is absorbed, the faster it's diluted, and the more desperate the junkie is for a bigger hit. Vicious cycle. I once saw a young woman who'd used *Trip* for almost a year. By the time we were called she was bleeding through the pores in her abdomen. She had no stomach and precious little of her brain left. The autopsy showed that her body had been hollowed out."

"Why do they do it?" Braden asked as Danny went outside to get a floating stretcher.

"The high, Kid. It drowns the brain in a nirvana they say is indescribable. One hit and you're through. There's no rehab for it because there just isn't time. It kills too quickly."

Danny came in with the floating stretcher in front of him. He pushed the stretcher through the door and lowered it so that they could roll the woman onto it. Once that was done, Danny raised the stretcher until it hovered waist-high. Debbie strapped the woman in and followed Danny as he pushed the stretcher back out to the ambulance.

"Come on, Mr. Bachard," the Chief said. "You own a coat? You gotta come with us."

"In-in the kitchen," the man in the shadows said.

The Chief went to the kitchen, coming back a few seconds later with what resembled a flannel shirt. He gave it to the man and the man slipped into it gingerly, as if his whole body was in pain. Then he got up and found his boots by the front door. The man looked as if he hadn't eaten for a month; his hair was nothing but a patchy black mess on a scabbed white skull. There were red lesions all over his skin.

"You're in pretty bad shape," the Chief said. "Better have you looked over, too."

The man didn't say anything. He kept his head low and his shoulders slumped forward as he closed the front door, following them into the ambulance. Once they were all inside, Debbie raised the ramp. Mr. Bachard sat on a stretcher next to his dying wife. His eyes were red with tears as he stared at her, his face stubbled with whiskers.

Thankfully, it was a quiet trip to the hospital in midtown. By the time they reached the parking dock on the roof, the woman came out of her stupor and urinated freely onto the stretcher. The nanobots had done their job in time. Danny unloaded her off the ambulance as a male nurse came up, transferred the woman to a hospital gurney, and took her away; her husband, frail and thin, followed them. Danny gave the attending physician a verbal report. After a long conversation, they shook hands and he pushed the empty, soiled stretcher back into the ambulance. He covered the stretcher with protective plastic before they left.

Nobody said anything as Debbie sent the ambulance into the air, back towards the station house. There was an uneasiness among them. They knew that those two people were doomed; it was just a matter of time. A few days probably. Braden found it sad that nothing could be done for them. There had to be a way to cure people of *Trip*. There had to be.

An alarm came through the speaker system in the cockpit; Stacey's voice blared through.

"Chief, we got a call about a possible AVA. Police are already on the scene. Looks like there's at least one K involved."

Braden knew what a K was. A dead body. He hadn't seen a real one yet and didn't relish the thought of seeing one now. He'd already been made depressed enough for one night. He'd seen a part of this city he knew existed but had never witnessed close up and it looked like his journey wasn't through yet.

The Chief brought his hand up to his ear mic. "Copy that, Stace. Feed the coordinates into our GPS and inform the commanding officer we're on our way."

"What's an AVA, Chief?" Braden asked.

"An Air Vehicle Accident," the Chief replied. "Sounds like a couple of air-cars got lost in this mess. Probably weren't using their detectors. It's your lucky day. Your first K."

Braden didn't even try to force a smile.

They made good time to the location of one of the crashed air-cars. It was on the roof of an apartment building a few blocks south of the station house. There was plenty of room to park the ambulance on the southwest corner; Debbie landed it without a bump. When they came down the open ramp the entire roof swarmed with heavily coated police officers. Some threw bright red flares around the perimeter of the roof. The flares melted large holes in the snow and sent billowy, glowing red smoke into the sky. Braden thought that, to someone watching from afar, it probably looked as if the entire roof was on fire. Other police officers shoveled snow off the roof with small portable shovels and cursed that this wasn't what they became police officers for, that they could do this just as easily at home.

There was a big crane attached to the side of the building. A long boom arm reached across the roof, stopping in the middle where a huge drum-shaped object hung and rocked gently in the wind. Yellow warning lights flashed all along the boom. Under the huge drum was an impact crater about the size of a swimming pool. Braden looked into the hole and saw that it went down four floors; he could see people's kitchens, their bathrooms, and their bedrooms. The damage was incredible; debris was everywhere. Black electrical cables dangled down from each floor like those he had faced in the obstacle course test, only these had sparks of white-hot electricity spraying out whenever any kind of moisture hit it. And there was a lot of moisture.

At the bottom of the crater was the air-car. The police had spotlights pointed down into the hole and Braden saw that the air-car was on its side, crumpled like tin foil. It was a green antique Pontiac, so old it probably ran without radar or a detector. He saw a long bloody arm hanging out the driver's side window. Yeah, it was a K for sure.

Braden heard a low, rumbling voice behind him, "Nice to see you, Heany."

Braden turned around and saw the Chief shaking the hand of a giant black man. He'd seen the man before, on the holocube. He wore a long black overcoat and under his much decorated and snow-covered policeman's cap he sported tiny, circular glasses that clung to his nose without the aid of temples.

"Good to see you, Kelly," Heany said.

"It would take a crappy night like this for us to get together again."

"I wouldn't have it any other way, Kelly."

They laughed as if they'd been friends for decades.

"I want you to meet my new cadet, Heany. Fresh off a *Trip* run. We're on a drive-along."

The Chief brought the big man over and Braden stuck out his hand. The big man's hand swallowed his. "This is Cadet Braden Rathman. Cadet, meet Chief of Police Heany."

"A great pleasure and honor to meet you, sir," Braden said.

"You bet it is," Heany said and laughed. "Good luck to you. I'm sure we'll see each other again."

"Yes, sir."

Braden knew a lot about Heany. The Mayor had brought him on during the early days of his first term and Heany turned out to be the toughest Chief of Police the city had ever seen. Braden remembered an incident a few years ago that had run on the holocube for a solid month. It was a daylight bank robbery in the financial district; someone had tripped the alarm in the bank. In minutes Heany and half of his police force had the bank surrounded, and a hostage situation ensued. The negotiations were going nowhere so Heany offered himself up as a trade for five hostages. The robbers accepted this. Heany, unarmed but wearing that big coat and distinctive white cap of his, went slowly towards the bank, his hands held high. But, for some reason, the robbers had a change of heart and began firing at Heany through the glass facade of the bank. The initial onslaught threw Heany backwards to the ground, then the firing stopped and Heany just lay there, apparently dead.

Suddenly, like that evil robot in Westworld, Heany sat up, got to his feet, and began walking towards the bank, his hands up high again. People and news reporters in the crowds watching this screamed in disbelief as the robbers unloaded on Heany again, but this time he leaned in towards the bullets, lowering his head as if he was walking into a heavy wind. Sometimes the force of the bullets made him stumble but he kept walking forward, slowly, an unstoppable juggernaut, fearless in the face of gunfire. When he reached the doors, he reached behind, under his coat, and pulled a sawed-off shotgun from a hidden holster on his back. He blew the glass doors in, went inside, then an unbelievable melee followed. No one inside the bank had a camera so all people outside could see were flashes of white light, all they could hear was what sounded like the thunderous throes of a world war. The ground shook with each blast, there were screams coming from inside, until finally there was silence. A few minutes later, a line of men and women came running out of the bank with their hands in the air, the hostages. Heany was the last to exit the building. He waved a group of his men into the building to clean up.

Braden remembered the interview Heany gave to Kathryn Gold afterwards, with a big unlit cigar sticking out of his mouth. All the robbers, twelve of them, were shot dead, but all the hostages were unharmed. The most amazing thing was Heany himself. He showed Ms. Gold his cap, obviously bullet proof. It was speckled with craters; in some cases, the bullet was still lodged in the crater, nothing more than a flat, round slug. His coat, vest, and breeches were the same but he hadn't suffered a single wound. Ms. Gold called him "Chief Meany" and after that crime in the city fell fifty per cent. No one had robbed a bank since.

Braden and the entire city considered him a living legend. An old time Sheriff in a modern, dangerous world. His popularity closely rivaled that of Mayor Daley's. Braden wondered if Heany could do things like that because he was unmarried, had no family to speak of, and was a loner.

He also wondered if all this fame made him lonely and bitter. Fame always had a heavy price.

Heany had everyone move back so that they could power up the gravity-magnet and pull the air-car out of its crater. Braden overheard other policemen talking and learned that they'd kept the body in the car so as not to disturb the scene. Once everyone was clear, Heany gave the order. The gravity-magnet hummed like a million bass singers in a choir. Snow was shooting off the surface of the big vibrating drum like popcorn. Then it seemed to catch onto something and became perfectly still.

"We got it!" the engineer running the machine shouted. He was in a weather-protected cockpit and his voice came out of a speaker attached to the outside.

The crossbars on the boom over the roof moaned against the weight of the air-car but they remained strong. Suddenly, out of the crater came the air-car. Every single inch of the body of the vehicle was dented or mangled. The top of it clanged against the magnetic drum like a bell. The engineer swung the boom around slowly and lowered the air-car to the roof, well away from the crater.

"Block that hole off! Make sure no one goes near it!" Heany

barked at a group of officers who were standing near the lip of the crater. The engineer powered down the gravity-magnet and the air-car pinged free, wobbling on the roof like a giant egg.

A police photographer immediately began taking pictures of the air-car, inside and out. When he was finished, Heany threw that dangling bloody arm back into the vehicle, grabbed the frame of the door, and pulled. It came off like a pop tab under Heany's strength. He just let it drop into the snow on the roof.

"He's all yours, Kelly," Heany said.

Danny and Debbie brought a stretcher forward. It was a grisly task pulling the dead man out. That dangling arm came off the man's body as if it had been attached with Velcro and Braden had to swallow his stomach again. The man was in so many pieces Braden had lost count. Danny and Debbie had to carefully place the parts on the stretcher so that they wouldn't fall off when moved. They did this quickly and efficiently.

When it was completed, Danny covered the body parts with a sheet and pushed the stretcher into the ambulance. The next stop was the city Coroner. Heany leaned into the mangled vehicle, pointing his flashlight inside. He waved it around as if looking for something specific and then switched the flashlight off.

"Just as I thought," he said.

"What is it?" Chief Kelly asked.

"It's pre-radar. One of the first models ever made."

"How can you tell for sure, Chief Heany?" Braden asked.

Heany waved him over, pointed the flashlight into the vehicle, and showed him. The dash, with the exception of a speedometer and altimeter, was bare as a baby's bottom. There were no radar or sonar displays. There wasn't even a portable GPS unit. "Completely illegal to run these things nowadays. This idiot never should have taken it out tonight. Pity."

"I have another question, Chief Heany," Braden said.

"Fire away."

"Where's the other car?"

Heany let out with a rumbling, low laugh and pointed southeast. "At the bottom of Lake Michigan, Kid," he replied. "About half a mile straight out from the Shedd Aquarium. Divers won't be able to reach him until the weather breaks, poor bastard. He was bringing ice cream home for his pregnant wife when this idiot tagged him. Didn't see him coming on the detector until it was too late."

"Jesus..." Braden whispered.

"No, his name was Steve Arnold. He was a mailman. Now he's fish food. Damn shame, but that's life, Kid. Welcome to life in the city of Chicago."

With that, the radio unit on his shoulder went off; another call was coming in. He started for his cruiser while listening to the dispatcher. His boisterous, rumbling laugh ceased and he piled into a police cruiser and darted off into the air before Braden could say goodbye. Braden knew how Heany had all that information on Steve Arnold. All air-cars were licensed and tagged with a beacon that runs through the city's traffic computer. The city knows how often a person drives, where they drive to, if they're speeding, where they live and work, and whatever other personal information a government entity can legally acquire about someone. It was all in the name of safety as it could easily be a free-for-all up there hundreds of feet above the city. The city had to know what was going on, who would have to pay in case something happened. But Heany didn't rattle off any details about the traffic offender, or idiot, as he called him. Braden wondered why. Maybe it was an anger coping mechanism.

The Chief came over. "Are you all right, Kid?" he asked.

"Yeah," Braden answered. "I'm just tired. It's been a rough night."

"I'm tired, too. We're through for the night, Kid. It's just 4:00; you'll be able to get a couple hours of sleep before you're on duty."

Braden was thankful for that. He was exhausted, mostly mentally, though. Sometimes that was worse than being exhausted physically.

"Well, I'll be a Flaming Rum Punch," the Chief blurted out.

"What is it, sir?" Braden asked.

"It's stopped snowing."

And it had. Maybe it was a good omen.

They loaded into the ambulance and dropped Braden off at the station before they went to the Coroner's office. Braden got into his Camaro and headed home. When he got home he shed his bunker gear at the door and slid into bed with Amy, trying not to wake her. She breathed deeply, sleeping peacefully. He wanted to kiss her, he wanted to touch her belly again, feel their child moving inside of her. But his lips and his hands were still too cold. He'd not only wake her but she'd be angry about it.

So Braden lay on his back. He thought about that poor bastard, Steve Arnold, and his pregnant wife. Braden had done many midnight runs for Amy; it could have been him lying at the bottom of Lake Michigan. He wondered what his own report would tell Heany if he should die in an AVA someday.

He never got back to sleep.

Seven

One night a year, Chicago Station Number 85 held a fund raiser to squeeze a little more cash from the community, also giving the public-at-large a chance to tour the firehouse, meet the station crew, and have their picture taken in front of the massive fifty-eight foot Engine. It was held on the first Saturday of February and was a welcome respite for everyone involved from the terrible mid-winter weather doldrums that had fallen over the city like a dark curtain. Every station in the city held a yearly fund raiser but only Station 85 held theirs during the winter, which insured, of course, a heavy crowd eager to party.

The roof under the dome was lined with food and beer vendors (who gave eighty percent of their profits to the station). It smelled like a meat lover's dream. Italian beefs and Chicago style dogs were the most popular items on the menu, although pizza, burgers, brats, and corn on the cob were also sold. It was similar to the yearly Taste of Chicago.

On a stage in the southwest corner of the roof was a local Led Zeppelin tribute band called Black Dog and they rocked like the original band did a century before.

The members of the crew of Station 85 were each in charge of a particular event. Debbie and Danny were in charge of showing people the apparatus and Joni, the Engine driver, took pictures of people in front of it (five dollars each).

Sam, for obvious reasons, ran a group of people down the elevator every twenty minutes and escorted them through the exercise room. It showed the public that the firefighters of Station 85 took their health seriously.

Paul Rose and his Foam Tender crew drew the short sticks and were stationed at the entrance of the Hot Zone seven levels below, welcoming people in and showing them to the elevator.

The Chief functioned as an ambassador more than anything else. He went around, introduced himself to people, laughed at their unfunny jokes, shook hands, kissed babies. Braden swore he was running for office.

Braden, wearing the official Station 85 navy blue T-shirt with the station crest on front and the words CADET spelled in big white letters on the back, was in charge of walking around selling raffle tickets. Already he'd had to turn in two moneybags to Old Mary Perry, the station's 90-year-old chief accountant. All the cash would go into a pot and a lucky winner would receive half of what was in it at the end of the night. Mary said there was already over a thousand dollars in the pot.

His parents, Gene and Zoey, arrived a little after seven. They were having a beer and talking with Amy and her parents. They seemed to be having a good time and in fact, the four of them got along wonderfully. With Braden's dad in architecture and Amy's dad in construction, they had much to talk about. Amy and the two mothers talked about the wonders of the station house, so this freed Braden to continue to sell more raffle tickets.

He got a kick at how proud his dad was of him. Gene was always telling someone that "Braden is the first true hero in the family". Braden always felt as if he had to live up to that statement. But that was all right with him. It was what he wanted and he felt capable.

Braden turned in a third moneybag while the band jammed. As he melted through the crowd, trying to fill a fourth bag, he ran into Stan Winslow and Roger Kelly. Stan's right shoulder seemed fine as he shook Braden's hand; Roger wasn't limping anymore.

"How's it going tonight, Braden?" Roger asked.

"Like a Vegas casino," Braden replied and they laughed. Stan's laughed seemed forced.

That day on the obstacle course seemed a hundred years in the past but the results of it weighed heavily in the here and now. Braden still felt guilty about beating them out. It didn't seem strange to him that Roger, the Chief's son, was here but Stan was a different story. He seemed to always be hanging around with Roger and Braden wasn't even sure what Stan did for a living, if anything. All Braden knew was that Roger was working as a freelance electrician (a skill he learned in the military) and that Stan gave him a bad feeling in his gut. He was thankful that he was too busy to stay and have an actual conversation with them. They said their "See ya' arounds," as Braden was swallowed in the crowd.

At ten o'clock, Black Dog was in the middle of another song when they suddenly stopped. A spotlight was thrown on the closed door of the elevator. Everyone turned and waited to see who came out. The anticipation was as heavy as that blizzard just after New Year's. Somebody coughed. Somebody sneezed. Then the doors slid open and Black Dog's singer said into the microphone, "Ladies and gentlemen, please welcome the Mayor of the great city of Chicago, Hizzoner, Jack Daley!"

The crowd burst into applause and whistles as the Mayor stepped out of the elevator, followed by his aides. He wore an immaculate gray three-piece suit with a black tie; the whole ensemble must have cost in the thousands of dollars, but it was worth it—he looked sharp. He waved at everyone and they waved back. Jack Daley was a portly, middle-aged man of normal height. He was almost a dead ringer for his grandfather, Richard M. Daley. He also had all the charisma and political sense of his grandfather. Because of this long, great dynasty of Daleys running Chicago, everyone called him Pharaoh Daley. They loved him and he knew it. He also knew how to run a city of ten million. It was what he was born for.

The Mayor made his way through the crowd, shaking people's hands, laughing at their unfunny jokes, kissing their babies...that made more sense to Braden. This man *was* running for office. After a few minutes of this, Black Dog began playing "The Song Remains The Same". The Mayor's aides led him to the Chief where they shook hands and exchanged pleasantries. Flashes from reporters' cameras lit the room up like the Fourth of July; the two of them playfully posed for the photographers. The funniest moment was when the Chief gave the Mayor his white helmet and the Mayor put it on. The flashes lasted for many blinding minutes on that one.

The Mayor didn't stay long enough for Braden to work his

way through the crowd to meet him. Pharaoh Daley was, like his Chief of Police, a busy man. But this was a great photo-op for him, reelection next year to his fourth term practically assured. Everyone in the Chicago Democratic Party was either too scared to run against Daley or owed him something, and seeing a Republican challenger in Chicago was as rare as seeing a tumbleweed rolling down Lakeshore Drive. Also, with a Democrat presently in the White House, government pork was rolling into the city faster than in the old stockyard days. A right-leaning columnist from the Tribune called it "Hog Heaven."

At midnight, Black Dog closed with a perfect eleven minute version of "Stairway To Heaven," complete with the sparkling disco ball at the end, then the singer announced the raffle winner. Someone named Oscar Catman won the thousand-dollar pot (which meant that there was two thousand dollars actually in it). He said he was happier than Jack Daley on Election Day, jumping and screaming joyfully.

Gradually, as low house music came over the speakers and Black Dog began breaking their stage down, the roof began to empty out of people. It was a successful night for the station as far as Braden could see and he was confident he'd done his part. He would do anything to keep this station functioning. He felt a hand on his shoulder; turning, he saw his mother and father standing there.

"We're going to leave now, Son," his father said. They embraced.

"Have we told you how proud of you we are?" his mother said as she hugged him.

"Only a capillion times!" Braden said.

"Well, make that a capillion and one times," his mother said and kissed him.

As they were walking away, Braden heard his father asking his mother what the hell a *capillion* was. That was when an idea struck Braden. He turned and ran over to them.

"You wanna sit in the Engine?" he asked his father.

Gene's eyes became large as baseballs and fell upon the great, yellow hulk of the vehicle and its giant, bulbous glass cockpit.

"That would be amazing," he said and Braden led him to the Engine.

He saw that Gene was awestruck. He'd had his and Zoey's

picture taken in front of it earlier but he'd never been inside. Braden watched as Gene noted how it floated eight inches above the ground; he said it was still hard for him to believe something that weighed a hundred tons could do such a thing. Braden showed his father the niches where they stored the Jaws of Life and even let him hold them. Gene said that they weighed much more than he'd thought. Then Braden hit the release on the side of the Engine and the ramp came down. It was like the Bat Cave inside: dark and flashing with all sorts of little but important lights. It smelled lemony clean.

Braden led Gene in, through the staging area where he and Sam sat in seats that folded up to the bulkhead, around the padded corner and into the heart of the beast, the cockpit. Gene said it looked like an old airplane cockpit on steroids. Braden told him that the Chief sat in the seat on the right and it was the command center of a job when they were on one. Then he pointed to Joni's seat, the pilot's seat, and told him to sit down in it. Gene hesitated for a second, remarking that it seemed almost a sacred thing to even be standing in the Engine's cockpit. But with Braden's urging, he overcame that and eagerly sat down.

The seat swiveled left to right and was deep and comfortable. The wheel hung there in front of him, begging him to grasp it; he did, exclaiming that it was thrilling. Braden watched as Gene looked around at the sheer technological complexity of the dashboard: flashing lights, deactivated view screens, buttons and switches, levers and keys, dials and LCD displays, meters and speakers. Braden wondered if he was imagining himself piloting Braden and the Chief to a five-alarm fire and how amazing it must have been to come down on a burning building from the sky: all those lights, the smoke, the chaos.

"I'll be learning how to drive this thing in a few weeks," Braden said. "We all have to learn to drive it."

Gene just sat there, his eyes wide and far away.

"You all right, Dad?" Braden asked, waking him from his daydream.

"You know I am, Son," Gene said. Braden smiled, sat in the Chief's chair, and they both closed their eyes, immediately immersing themselves. They were a father and son on their way to fight a mythical, burning high-rise of the imagination. It blazed bright and yellow, like a gargantuan funeral pyre. Gene swung the Engine around so that Braden could aim the deck guns at it. Braden beat the flames down like a prize fighter and now they could both see that there were people on the roof waving at them, women and children with their pets, all desperate for rescue.

They traded confident glances and went in. And much, much later, they were coming back heroes.

Eight

It was a Monday night in mid-March, only a few days from Amy's due date. Braden's mind wasn't on the Foam Tender he was washing down with a two-inch hose. Amy had been having shadow pains, false labor, for the last few days. Dr. Payne told her that she could go anytime. To keep his mind off things he funneled all his energy into his station duties.

Everyone else was in the game room playing pool or watching the news on the holocube. They all had a crush on the local blonde news anchor, Kathryn Gold. Thanks to the nature of the holocube, they could check her out in 3-D from all sides, even as she sat behind the desk. They all made bets on what kind of shoes she'd be wearing before the newscast began. Sam was the winner again with his nomination of three inch, strapless, black sandals. Joni and Debbie couldn't figure out how he always knew what shoes Kathryn Gold wore. But if they had asked, he would've told them that he and Kathryn had been living together for the past two months. That also would have explained to Braden why Sam had stopped seeing that red-headed waitress from the Hot Zone.

Big George Jackson, though, wasn't in there with them. He was trying to shake a case of the flu that Braden thought resembled an exorcism. He lay in a cot in the bunkroom sleeping off his cup of DayQwill. This worried Braden. George was the workhorse of the Foam Tender crew. He was the kind of man who, if he couldn't think of a way through a problem, would use his brute strength to create a solution. Braden had heard his temper had, on more than one occasion, saved each of their lives. He hoped there wasn't a job that day. It didn't seem as if there would be. The city was as quiet as George was in his cot.

Braden decided to take a short break and relax in the game room. When he went in he saw Mo Zwan, the Foam Tender driver, and Thom Brandt arguing. They stopped once Braden walked in. Then Thom cursed at Mo as he turned and hurried out of the game room. Mo sighed heavily and invited Danny to play some virtual ping pong. Danny accepted. They took up the electronic paddles and activated the holocube. Immediately, a holographic ball appeared on the table. Mo picked it up and served but Danny parried, returning it quickly, catching Mo off guard, winning the point.

Braden saw Sam sitting in a chair in the corner reading the *Tribune* on a sheet of electronic paper. He sat down in the chair across from Sam.

"What was that all about between Mo and Thom?" Braden asked.

Sam lifted his eyes, focusing on Braden. "Ol' yellow knees. It's a long story, Probie," he answered.

Braden remembered Sam talking about yellow knees at the Hot Zone. He'd had been curious about it ever since. "I'm on my break; I have time."

Sam stared at Braden. After a moment he folded up the paper and leaned forward. Braden waited patiently for Sam to start the story.

"It's like this, Kid," Sam began, speaking very softly, "Thom's in his early forties, he's been a firefighter for twenty-two years. He's developed a severe psychological condition we all call 'Yellow Knees.'"

"Yellow Knees?"

"That's right. About a month before you arrived we had a job at the Pier, big grease fire at the Bier Garden restaurant. It was a real bad one; fire spread like the flu in January. There were people inside and it was Big George and Thom's job to get them out. Problem is, just as Big George goes into the blaze, Thom freezes up worse than an icicle. Big George got trapped with the victims and Mo had to cover for Thom, barely got them out alive."

"But why did Thom freeze up like that? He's been on the job forever," Braden asked.

"With only three years to go before he could retire on full benefits, Thom has recently decided to consider the risk to himself before going into a burning structure. That's a career killer if you're a firefighter. I've been told that it's a subconscious form of self-preservation. He doesn't realize he's doing it until afterwards when we review the job on the holocube. Then he's mortified, embarrassed, and apologetic. But by then it's too late."

"Can anything be done? Can he see a counselor?"

"Not really. He's a good man, Kid. He does have a wife and five kids, after all, but his yellow knees render him almost useless in a fire. You can't trust him to watch your back. It concerns Paul the most as Thom is part of his crew and he often asks the Chief if they could put Thom on early-retirement at full bennies, but the Chief always refuses. He believes it's a privilege to be a firefighter and one has to earn what they receive."

"That is a problem," Braden said, sitting back in his chair.

"And with Big George temporarily out of the game, Thom's condition concerns Paul even more. So Mo made it clear to Thom that there better not be a job until Big George gets healthy or he won't let Thom on the Tender."

"Can Mo do that?"

"No, Kid," Sam replied. "Only the Chief can make that call. Those are just words. It was more to make a point than a threat."

"Thom has to feel horrible," Braden murmured.

Sam shrugged and went back to reading his newspaper.

Braden left the game room, searching for Thom, thinking that maybe he'd want to talk about it, but he found Thom lying in his cot in the bunk room, his arm over his eyes. So Braden went back out to finish washing the Tender. The whole time he was thinking about himself. What if he developed yellow knees? He had a wife and soon a child. It was conceivable he'd feel the way that Thom did at a certain point in his career. When he finished he called Amy on his cell phone. She seemed groggy as if he'd woken her up.

"I'm just calling to see how you are, babe," he said. "I miss you."

"I'm fine, hon," she answered in a garble. "I'm just really, really tired."

"You have the number of the station house on the speed dial, in case you go into labor?" he asked.

"Yes, honey. We've already gone over this."

"Sorry, babe. I'm just concerned, that's all."

"Well, don't be. I'm fine. Really."

"All right. I'll call you later."

"Love you."

"I love you, too," Braden said and hung up.

Braden stood there under the dome next to the shiny, clean apparatus. He shook his head. He didn't like how quiet it was. That always meant a storm was coming.

It came an hour later.

The alarm broke up the quiet of the station house like a tornado. Everyone ran to their bunker gear and began suiting up.

Big George came stumbling out of the bunkroom door like a mummy, his dark skin pale and sweaty, his eyes barely open.

"Retreat, Jackson," the Chief ordered.

"But, Chief—"

"I said retreat. You're no good to us in your condition."

"But who's gonna take my place?"

"Rathman," the Chief answered. "He's familiar with the Foam Tender and its duties."

Jackson lifted his drowsy eyes up to focus on Braden, who was already suited up. Jackson nodded, turned, and went back to his cot.

Braden ran up the ramp after Paul, Mo, and Thom and strapped himself into Big George's seat. He wasn't feeling confident about being teamed up with Thom, especially after what Sam had told him, but he pushed it from his mind.

The entire cockpit of the Foam Tender was enclosed in a bulbous sheet of fire resistant plasteel; Braden could see in almost every direction. The basket of the ladder hung over the top of the cockpit; it was the only thing that hindered his line of sight. Mo sent the Tender up and stayed behind the great flashing yellow Engine as it arced and turned in the night sky, its sirens wailing. The ambulance crew was behind them.

The Chief's voice came over the radio. "I've got some bad news for everyone," he said. "Our destination is the Mayor's residence. Don't be alarmed, he and his family made it out but it looks like we've got ourselves a Class A. Our goal is to save and salvage everything we possibly can without killing ourselves."

Class A, Braden thought. *That was a fire involving combustibles such as wood, paper, and other natural materials. Pretty straight forward. I've drilled on this until my hands cramped.*

Being that it was the Mayor's residence, the place would likely be surrounded by police cruisers and other fire units were probably on route. But the Chief made it clear that Station 85 was the Incident Commander. Everyone was to report to him. The Fire Chiefs from the other stations radioed in and agreed with this. The cooperation impressed Braden. Competition for the Mayor's favor was usually intense. It was a good thing the Chief was in good with the Mayor.

The Tender listed to the left as the historic thirty-story condo that the Mayor lived in came into view. He was right, police cruisers had the place surrounded and their spotlights lit it up like the Washington Monument.

"We're going to approach the Mayor's residence from the west," the Chief said.

Mo barked his verification and the other stations, who hadn't reached the residence yet, did the same.

As the Tender fell in line with the Engine, Braden saw flames spewing out of the windows of the thirtieth floor. Everything on the balcony on the east side was awash in fire and smoke. The Mayor would have to buy a new porch set.

In front, the Engine edged up to within twenty feet of the building then its two driver side water cannons turned and began spraying water on the flaming west windows. They scarred the air with alternating heavy streams and fine sprays, laying the groundwork for the primary search to begin. But the flames were stubborn; the water didn't seem to affect them. They came out in long, flailing trails of solid yellow and red heat. It looked to Braden as if they were boldly swatting at the water cannons.

Sam's voice came over the speakers. "Minus a thousand gallons."

The Engine held five thousand gallons of water; after that was used up they'd have to patch into an external source like a water tower or the building's main water line.

"Minus two thousand gallons."

"Why isn't the fire going out?" Mo asked.

"There's gotta be something else going on here. Maybe it isn't a Class A," Paul said, leaning forward in his seat as he watched.

The cannons kept the pressure on. Finally, the flames were dying down, retreating back into the building.

"Minus three thousand gallons."

Thick smoke billowed from the windows.

"Looks like we've got containment enough for a primary," the Chief said and the side ramp came down from the Engine, falling against the small sill of the window. Braden watched as Sam and the Chief ran across with a hose in the textbook "two-in, two-out" procedure. They would do the primary search, making sure the fire was put out, and then he'd let the other crews come in and mop up after they were clear. Three other Engines had arrived; they were hovering above the building, waiting.

The Foam Tender's dash screens showed what Sam's and the Chief's helm cams saw. The damage was fierce. Smoke still clung to the ceilings, what was once a piano was now just a charred mass of wood and twisted wire. The wire frames of a couch appeared on the screen, its upholstery completely burned away. The walls were blackened; pieces of drywall had peeled off the studs and were sheared back like tortured bodies from the intense heat.

Sam and the Chief went through the kitchen, the dining room, the main bedroom. Everything seemed to be under control. They sprayed everything down just to make sure.

"Thom!" the Chief shouted.

"Copy, Chief," Thom said into his ear mic.

"I want you and Rathman to do a secondary," the Chief ordered. "You've done them before. Show him what to look for."

"Yes, sir," Thom said. He waved Braden out of his seat and to the landing ramp.

Once Sam and the Chief were out of the building with the hose, the Engine moved away so that the Foam Tender could move in and drop ramp. Thom went in first. They had their blast shields down and Joni had sent a GPS through so they could follow it. It smelled like burnt wood in there and the floor was under an inch of water, making it sound like they were slogging through a swamp.

They sloshed into the kitchen where they came across an electrical box that was sparking wildly inside a broom closet. Thom froze as he watched the sparks bouncing off the walls of the closet. It didn't take Braden long to remember that live electrical wires and people standing in water weren't a good combination. He backed away slowly.

"We've still got live wires here, Chief," Thom said.

The Chief's voice came through their ear mics, "Impossible, Thom. The power in the entire building has been shut down."

"Just telling you what I see."

"I'll check it out, stand by."

Thom looked at Braden, "Stay clear. I don't like this at all."

Braden nodded.

The Chief's voice came through on their ear mics again, "Uh, I've just been informed that we have another problem, gentlemen. The Mayor's daughter, Jillian, is unaccounted for. It's entirely possible she's in there somewhere." His voice was low and concerned.

Jillian's picture appeared on their blast shields. She was eleven years old, ninety pounds, long brown hair, a very beautiful little girl. She resembled more the mayor's wife.

"I thought the entire family was cleared," Thom said, his voice starting to waver.

"That's what we were told. There was some mix up in communication."

Braden saw that the black smoke on the ceiling was banking down and growing. Something was feeding it.

"Is this normal?" Braden asked, pointing his glove at the creeping smoke.

"No," Thom said and looked around. "Chief, I think we got a Class C. Seat of the fire is the kitchen electrical box. Better have Paul and Mo ready with the frosting."

"Copy that, Thom. Now go find the girl!"

Class C was an electrical fire and it was dangerous to use water on it. The Foam Tender's chemically treated "wet water" was designed specifically for Class C fires.

Before Thom could take a step, the box in the closet blew up, throwing him across the wet floor of the kitchen. Thick arms of white flame slapped the air above him. Braden got onto his knees and crawled in to get him.

Thom reached out, Braden took his hand and pulled. He helped Thom get to his feet after he got him into the dining room. They both watched as the oak cabinets in the kitchen suddenly erupted in flames. Braden had read about this in one of his training manuals. It was called a *flashover*. It was a near-simultaneous ignition of all the combustible material in an enclosed area. It was rare and only happened if the conditions were right.

Braden reached into his jacket pocket, pulled out his SCBA mask. He quickly took his helmet off, strapped the mask to his face, put his helmet back on, expecting Thom to be doing the same. But Thom just stood there, his eyes staring at the raging inferno in the kitchen, his pupils large with the terror of a man who knows he's going to die.

"Thom?" Braden said. "Thom?"

"Christ! What's happening in there?" the Chief asked.

"Brandt? Rathman! Answer me!" the Chief sounded panicked now.

"We've got a flashover, Chief," Braden said. He looked up at the smoke crawling down off the ceiling of the dining room. The dining room table, already burnt beyond recognition and wet, erupted in flames anyway. The display on the lower left corner of his blast shield said that the temperature was 209°F. "I need the foam crew to flood the kitchen and the dining room. Thom isn't responsive."

"Is he injured?"

"No, Chief. Just seems scared."

"Copy that," the Chief said. Suddenly, thick streams of white foam were flying through the dining room window. Once the foam hit something, it thickened like a loaf of bread in the oven and strangled every flame it touched. There was a crash and Braden saw that they were foaming the kitchen through the window above the sink.

The foam in the dining room had knocked down the fire enough so that they both could safely reach the window and the ramp.

"Thom!" Braden shouted. "Thom! You've got to get out of here! Thom!"

It was no use. Thom was like a mummy. Braden threw him over his right shoulder and carried him to the ramp. Paul rushed out of the Tender, took Thom by the hands, and dragged him onto the ramp.

"Go get me a Halligan!" Braden shouted.

"Why? Where are you going, Kid?" Paul asked.

"To find the girl!" Braden shouted.

After dragging Thom back into the Tender, Paul reappeared in the doorway of the Tender and threw Braden the Halligan. The Halligan, named after the first Deputy Fire Chief in New York City, Hugh Halligan, was a multipurpose tool for prying, twisting, punching, or striking.

Braden, with the Halligan in hand, turned and disappeared into the building again. The smoke was so bad he could barely see a foot in front of him. The temperature on his blast shield read 325°F. He could cook a Thanksgiving turkey in here.

"Joni," he called. "Light up the GPS again on this residence."

His blast shield flashed. The animated schematic of the apartment appeared on the plastic. He was in a hallway just past the kitchen. It went straight for twenty feet then split off to the right and left like a "T". The room on the right was the master bedroom; there was another room to the left. That had to be Jillian's. Sam and the Chief had already checked these rooms; she must have been hiding.

He ran down the hallway, carrying the Halligan in front of him, and stopped where the hall went left and right. He saw light coming from underneath the master bedroom door; the fire had somehow found its way in there, whatever was in there was cooked. He looked at the door to the other room and didn't see a light in the crack. He tried the doorknob but it was locked. He wasn't going to try to run the door down; there wasn't enough room to gain any kind of momentum. He knocked on the door heavily and shouted Jillian's name but didn't hear any response. But if no one was in there, why was the door locked? He lifted the Halligan and shoved the pick-end into the door jam. Once it was embedded deeply, he began pulling the Halligan back and the doorknob popped off under the pressure.

As Braden pushed the door open, the master bedroom door exploded, and fire blasted out into the hallway. Feeling the heat coming up from under his jacket and under his helmet, he quickly ran into the room, closed the door behind him, and jammed it tight with the Halligan dug into the carpet. He was effectively trapped. The only way out was the bedroom window.

It was a girl's room for sure. The lights on his helmet and jacket illuminated a giant unicorn and flowers painted on a pink wall. The room seemed undisturbed. The dresser had a mirror and little elf knick-knacks ontop, the closet door was closed, and the bed was still made. Braden called out Jillian's name again as he checked under the bed. Nothing.

She has to be in here!

Smoke was beginning to come through the missing knob hole and under the door. Braden pulled the blanket from the bed, stuffing it tightly in the crack under the door. He opened a drawer in the dresser, found a T-shirt and stuffed that where the doorknob should have been. It would hold long enough, he hoped.

"Jillian!" Braden shouted. He heard a noise coming from the closet. He ripped it open to find Jillian sitting on the floor underneath a row of dresses. She had her knees up to her chin and her hands clasped tightly to her trembling legs. She looked up at him, he saw that same fear in them that he'd seen in Thom's eyes.

"It's all right," he said as he knelt down. "I'm here to help you. I'm gonna get you out of here."

She didn't say anything. She just stared at him.

"It was very smart of you to hide in the closet with the doors closed," he said. She smiled.

"I've found Jillian, Chief!" Braden said into the ear mic. "She's fine, just a little scared."

"We see it on your helm cam," the Chief muttered in relief. "It looks like you're in her room. Can you get out of there and make it back to the entry point?"

"Negative, Chief. The master bedroom just went up and the hallway is frying bacon."

"What can we do to help you?"

Braden looked around. There was only one window on the east wall. He glanced back at the door, the T-shirt he'd stuffed in the doorknob was smoking.

"Get someone to Jillian's window on the east side fast. We

don't have much time."

"Copy that."

Braden stood up and tried to open the window. But it was one of those safety windows that only went up a few inches. There was no way either of them could squeeze through. He grabbed the Halligan and used it like an axe to smash the window to pieces. He scraped the frame, making sure no pieces of sharp glass were left. He ripped a blanket off the bed and laid it over the bottom of the window frame just in case. The pressure built up by the fire in the hallway suddenly blew open the door; fire and smoke flowed in like an avalanche. Jillian screamed.

Braden dropped the Halligan and stuck his head outside. He didn't see any kind of vehicle coming to rescue them but there were plenty of police cruisers throwing light down on the situation.

"Chief! We've run out of sand! We gotta go now!"

"Copy that, Rathman. Debbie and Danny are on their way! I repeat, the bone box is on its way!"

Braden ran to the little girl in the closet. He took her hand but she didn't want to come out.

"Jillian," he said. "You've got to trust me. There's only one way out of here."

She looked at him, at the window, then at him again. She understood.

"That's right," he said. "But I need your help. Can you be a strong girl for me and stand up?"

She nodded and with his help stood up. She was wearing a blue pajama top and shorts decorated with Pegasus. She was going to be cold once they got outside.

"Okay! Now, I promise you, there will be someone out there to catch us, do you understand?"

She nodded.

Fire and heat blasted into the room. Braden watched it singeing and curling the ends of Jillian's brown hair. His blast shield display read 388°F. He looked through the window again but still didn't see the ambulance. There was only one thing he could do.

"Hold your breath, honey," he said.

Jillian closed her mouth and her eyes as Braden activated the helium bladders in his fire jacket. The compressor hissed; he felt the jacket get thick. Then he swooped the little girl up in his arms and leapt through the window just as air in the room reached flashover point and exploded.

Nine

As they fell, Braden held Jillian to his chest as tightly as he could. The air was freezing cold and saturated with beeps, screeches, and wailing sirens. But Jillian was true to her word; she didn't cry or scream. Instead, she clung tightly to him, her arms around his torso, her head buried in his coat, even as Braden turned his body so that when they landed, it would be on his back.

Braden felt the air friction violently pushing on his helmet. If it wasn't for the strap around his chin, it would've been blown away in the first second of the descent. He wasn't an especially religious man but he prayed anyway. It couldn't hurt.

Thoughts of Amy and his unborn child raced through his mind. He promised that if he made it through this, he'd avoid any *unnecessary* risks in the future. This was an exception though; it was either jump out the window or be burned alive. He'd chosen the lesser evil. Hopefully, Amy would understand that and forgive him. He had a feeling that she'd been watching the holocube which meant she had seen everything as it happened. She would be on the phone with her mom; her mom would be trying to calm her down.

It seemed to Braden as if time had slowed. That he and Jillian had been falling for a good two minutes. In reality, the fall lasted only a few seconds. Then they hit something hard and flat; the weight of Jillian's body knocked the air out of him, despite the fully filled bladders in his jacket. The heels of his boots slapped against the hard surface and bounced up only to land again, but softer this time. What had they landed on? It couldn't have been the ground; they were still alive. He held onto Jillian and she clung to him in a death grip as he struggled to force air back into his body. It felt as if his guts were kicked out, that he was going to die. Finally, he was able to breathe again. Sweet, cold, breathable air. And that terrible pain in his gut was fading away.

A woman's voice rang through his ear mic. "We got you, Kid! Just hold tight, we'll be on the ground in a sec." It was Debbie. They must have landed ontop of the ambulance. He lifted his head up, adjusted his helmet with his left hand, and confirmed this. The black windows of the condominium he'd just jumped out of were right in front of him, only a few feet from the ambulance. The bone box was going down. He grabbed one of the roof railings with his free hand for added security and held Jillian with his other hand.

"I told you we'd be okay," he told her, exhaling in relief.

She looked up at him and smiled.

The ambulance carefully swept around the east side of the building. Braden lifted his head to see over the edge of the bone box; they were heading towards a brightly-lit clearing in a parking lot on ground level. The light bars of countless police cruisers flashed red, white and blue, filling the parking lot with a throbbing chaotic burst of colored lights. The ambulance leveled off, slowed, and landed like a feather in a clear part of the lot. Braden heard the buzzing of the superconductors powering down; the long ride down was finally over.

He and Jillian lay on top of the ambulance quietly, waiting for their rescuers to come get them. He stared up at the building and saw the thirtieth floor completely surrounded by Foam Tenders from four different stations. Their deck guns were filling every open window with "wet water". They had turned the flames into thick black columns of smoke that swirled around above the building. The Mayor's apartment was a total loss.

Let them mop up, I'm done for the day.

Braden let out a long sigh of relief and heard the ramp hiss open below. The running footsteps of a herd of people coming towards the ambulance grew louder. Their voices were excited and concerned and he could make out certain people's comments.

"Where is she? Where's Jillian?" "Is she alive?" "Who was it that jumped out of that window with her?" "How did the fire start?" There were a million other questions; all had different voices.

Braden assumed they were reporters. There were TV news vans hovering in the sky over them. He saw the shiny, glassy lenses of cameras being aimed down at him; their flashes lit the sky like atomic-powered fireflies. He also saw the Engine and Foam Tender from Station 85 gliding down out of the darkness, landing in an area of the parking lot not far from the ambulance.

He heard Debbie running interference below, answering people's questions and keeping them back with the help of a line of police officers, while Danny climbed the ladder to the roof of the ambulance. He knelt next to them and tried to lift Jillian but she wasn't loosening her grip on Braden.

"You're safe now, Jillian," Danny said as he pressed the pulse-finder to her throat. It registered fast.

"She's still scared," Braden said.

"Hey, I'll take a fast pulse over a missing one any day," Danny said.

Their concern relaxed Jillian. She loosened her grip on Braden's jacket and raised her head.

"That's a good girl," Braden said. "It's all over now."

Danny leaned over and stroked her hair. "Your mommy and daddy are here, honey," he said. "Let's go see them."

Jillian's eyes widened; she held her arms out to him. Danny took her and when he stood up there was a round of applause and boisterous cheering usually reserved for a Cub's game. Braden, through a barrage of aches and pains, stood up also. The applause grew even louder. An army of policemen, reporters, and bystanders surrounded the ambulance. Spot lights from the various TV news vans fell on them as they climbed down from the roof.

There was a disturbance at the far end of the crowd. The Mayor and his wife were being escorted through the crowd by a line of policemen. Danny carried Jillian to them. Once the family was reunited, the place turned into a chaotic, off-the-chart, cheer-fest. Flashes were rifling off from every direction; reporters were tripping over each other as they asked the Mayor and his wife questions.

It was through this interviewing that Braden learned that the Mayor had been at City Hall when the fire broke out. His wife had gone down to the condominium convenience store on the first floor to get a gallon of milk and some toiletries when the alarms went off.

Before she could go back up and get her daughter, security people rushed her out of the building. No one touched on the miscommunication concerning Jillian's whereabouts; they probably didn't even know about that yet. The Mayor's PR people would handle it when or if it ever came out.

It was cold. Braden's knees were weak so he went inside the ambulance and sat on a stretcher. His back was burning with pain; his neck was tender if he turned his head to either side. Other than that, he sensed no permanent damage. He was lucky and he realized it now as he thought about what had just happened. *What if the ambulance had been a foot or two off its mark? What if it never even came?* He pictured the gruesome image of his and Jillian's bodies splattered all over the black top of the building's parking lot. Such a picture would have been in every e-paper and on every newscast the following day. At least Amy and their baby would have had his full bennies. Yes, he'd been lucky.

In his ear mic he was listening to the Chief coordinate the secondary search with another station unit. Finally the words, *"Secondary search, all clear!"* rang out. He took his gloves and helmet off, putting them on the stretcher beside him. Danny came in shaking his head and pressed the pulse-finder to Braden's jugular.

"Normal?" Danny said. "After what you just did, your heart rate is normal? What are you, a robot?"

Before Braden could reply, there was more applause outside. From where he sat, he could see Joni, Paul, Mo, Sam, Thom, and the Chief making their way through the crowd under a halo of flashes, fielding questions as they walked. Braden was glad the reporters hadn't approached him yet. He was too spent to deal with them. Besides, he didn't do what he did for fame and recognition. He did it because it's what he does. And if he made the news, he'd have to treat his stationto ice cream.

It took them a few minutes, but his co-workers finally edged their way through the crowd and filed into the ambulance. They slapped him on the shoulders, messed his short-cropped hair, gave him fake punches to the gut (Sam). They were just plain relieved he'd come through that ordeal alive.

Braden tried to modestly push it off on Danny and Debbie, telling them if they hadn't picked him and Jillian up, it'd be a different story. But none of them were buying that. He'd done something amazing and it also made them look awfully good. Braden figured he had a few apparatus-cleaning reprieves coming.

The Chief, though he didn't say anything, kept a proud smile on his face. He stayed in the background, watching everything unfold on its own.

"Jeezus," Sam said. "You look like an underweight turtle in that jacket." Then he picked up Braden's glove from the cot and pressed a button, deactivating the compressor in Braden's jacket. It deflated like a balloon until Braden looked normal again.

"That's better," Sam continued. "I can't have all those reporters out there thinking you're bigger'n me."

Everyone laughed, but their celebration was interrupted. Someone whispered "The Mayor's coming," and the crew parted down the middle. The Mayor, his wife, and Jillian came up the ramp and stood in front of Braden. They were wearing big, blue thermal blankets, glistening tears sparkled on their faces. News cameras were forced into every possible crevice.

"I want to thank you, firefighter," the Mayor said and held out his hand. He seemed sincerely grateful, not like the calculating politician he really was. At this moment he was just a human being, a father. "I want to thank you for saving my daughter's life."

Braden eagerly took the Mayor's hand and shook it. "You're very welcome, sir," Braden said. He glanced down at Jillian. "Jillian's quite a girl. Didn't complain once."

The Mayor smiled. "She takes after her mother."

The Mayor's wife bent over Jillian and whispered something into her ear. Then Jillian went up to Braden and kissed him on the cheek. Braden was nearly blinded by camera flashes. Heartfelt "Aws!" flowed around the inside of the ambulance like the wave at a ball game.

The Mayor motioned everyone to be quiet and looked at Braden again, right in the eyes. "With firefighters like you, this city is in the best of hands," he said. "My family, and the entire city, are indebted to you and your colleagues this night."

"Thank you, sir," Braden began and suddenly felt as if he had to set the record straight. He didn't want it going out over the news flood that he was a full-fledged fireman. "But I'm still a cadet.

I graduate next month."

The Mayor looked at the Chief. The Chief nodded.

"Not anymore, son," the Mayor said. "You and all of Station 85 are to appear before me at City Hall this Wednesday morning where you will officially receive your firefighting license and a commendation for bravery. But unofficially, as of right now, you are a firefighter for the city of Chicago!"

Everyone cheered. The Mayor shook Braden's hand again; more flashes erupted. Finally, the family went down the ramp, followed by the mob of reporters. The Mayor took the time to answer more questions and joke with them. The politician was back.

"I think I'll have a banana split, hero," Sam teased.

Braden's head was spinning. In all of his wildest fantasies he'd never dreamed of a night like this and it all began with him filling in for Big *Sick* George Jackson. He hoped Big George wouldn't be too mad at him for stealing what should have been his glory.

A half hour later, Braden was in the cockpit of the Foam Tender sitting across from Thom in the back row. They were finally on their way back to the station house. Thom hadn't looked at him since he froze up there in the Mayor's residence, which was fine with Braden. He was so upset that he didn't want anything to do with Thom. Yet Thom kept starting to say something and stopping short. Again, he took a deep breath, gained some courage, turned to Braden, and spoke.

"I'm sorry I let you down up there, Braden," he said. "You didn't need that crap ontop of everything else that was going on."

"It's all right, Thom," Braden said. "What's done is done."

"No, it's not all right. It's never all right to let your partner down, especially in the middle of a job as dangerous as this one. I could've killed both you and Jillian—"

"But you didn't," Braden interrupted. "Things worked out this time. But you're going to have to go deep inside yourself, Thom. You're going to have to decide if finishing out your last three years is worth the risk. You're going to have to decide if you can look at yourself in the mirror every day and tell yourself and your kids that you're a firefighter...and mean it. No one can do that for you."

Thom glanced quickly at Braden, dropped his head, and

looked away.

Up ahead, Braden watched as the huge dome of the station house opened up like a giant white mouth. The Engine in front of them veered to the left, positioned itself for approach, and landed in its specially marked area on the roof. The Foam Tender landed next, followed by the ambulance. Then the huge white dome closed overhead.

As they piled out of their vehicles, Big George appeared; his nose had a Kleenex sticking out of the left nostril and he had a hot steaming towel wrapped around his neck. He went up to Braden, holding his right hand out. Braden went to take it but then remembered how contagious the flu was.

George realized it himself and pulled his hand away, embarrassed.

"Sorry about that, Kid," he said. "I just wanted to tell you what a great job you did tonight."

"Thanks, Big George. You're not mad?" Braden asked.

"Mad? Mad about what? You stealing the glory that should've been mine?"

Braden nodded.

"Nah. Fantasy and fairy tales, Kid. I ain't like that. If I was there tonight instead of you there would be no glory for me or any of us in the station and that little girl would've died. There's no way I woulda thought to do what you did. I may be big but I ain't crazy. No, it was like God or whatever power rules the Universe made me sick so you could go and save that girl. I, for one, am glad about it."

Big George's eloquence surprised Braden; it touched him deeply. He held out his hand and they shook.

"Good," the Chief said. "Now that that bit of sugary shit is out of the way, back to bed, Big George, before you make everyone else sick. And don't forget to take your NightQwill."

Big George saluted half-heartedly, turned, and dragged his feet back into the bunkroom where a nice warm cot waited for him.

Braden went into the washroom and washed his hands. Thoroughly.

Ten

The man was furious. He lay naked on the bed of the darkened hotel room watching the rescue of the Mayor's daughter on the holocube. His stomach cramped and groaned. It had taken him weeks to plan and execute the fire in the Mayor's apartment, but many things had gone wrong. The Mayor was supposed to be there and he was supposed to die. But the Mayor wasn't there for some reason. Rathman was supposed to fail in his effort to save the Mayor. He was supposed to be publicly humiliated, his path to becoming a certified firefighter for the city of Chicago delayed if not halted. But Rathman swooped in to save the Mayor's daughter, during a live holo for Christ sakes! Rathman was a certified hero now. It was on every local channel and was starting to be picked up by the international channels. If an election were held tomorrow, Rathman would be elected Mayor of Chicago in a landslide.

The man had underestimated Rathman again. He desperately needed a beer. He needed a whole case of them. Then he needed time to think of a new plan, one that included Rathman's mortality. The man had the resources, the connections, and the will. If the plan was conceived properly, everything would fall into place. The man would get what he'd always wanted. What he'd always deserved.

There was noise in the bathroom. It was the faucet going full blast. He saw the white light coming from the space under the closed door; a thin shadow was moving back and forth. It was the girl he'd picked up at the Hot Zone. A pretty, red-headed waitress with a pair of legs he'd love to use as toothpicks. With the failure of his most recent plan, he'd completely forgotten about her, but he wasn't in the mood now. He was supposed to watch the fire on the holocube, see the Mayor die, Rathman get humiliated, then he was supposed to celebrate with a night of wild, uninhibited sex with a girl he hardly knew. Rathman had spoiled his entire night.

The door opened. The redhead turned off the bathroom light as she came out. In that brief moment he'd seen her with the light still on he knew she was naked and ready to rock. In the light from the holocube he could see her toned abs, firm breasts, and those long fingers with the red fingernails. She had a swing to her hips that had made him salivate when he saw her walking in the Hot Zone. She was a teenager's wet dream. It seemed such a shame to waste a perfectly good body but there could be no romance this night. He got out of bed before she got in and picked up his pants. He started digging through the pockets.

"What's up, lover?" the redhead asked playfully.

"Nothing," he mumbled, still digging through the pocket. Ah! Finally, he found what he had been searching for…his wallet. He flipped it open, reached into the flap, pulled out a series of bills. He didn't know how much it was but he knew that it was enough. He threw the cash at the red-headed girl. It fluttered off her belly like falling leaves in autumn.

She stepped back, surprised, and knelt down to see what she'd been hit with. She had all the cash in her hands in seconds. She stood up again, holding it in front of her like a bouquet of flowers. Her hand was shaking.

"What the hell is this?" she asked. Scorn scratched her voice.

"Your tip," the man said. "Now get out."

He saw the gears inside that cute little head of hers turning. A switched flipped and suddenly she understood. Her eyebrows came together and her mouth fell into an ugly frown.

"You sonofabitch," she muttered, throwing the money back at him. "I didn't come here with you for this." She began darting around the small room, scooping up her clothes, getting dressed. He ignored her and fell back down in bed. He stared at the images of the Mayor's burning condo fluttering on the holocube.

The redhead was like an angry cat, hissing and spitting as she dressed. After she put her shoes on and grabbed her purse, she said, "You know what? You're a real hole." Then she ripped the door open and slammed it behind her. A few moments later he heard her ground car start up. Her tires squealed away into the distance like a wounded dog.

Now that that was over, the man could watch the holocube in peace and think. The next plan had to be sophisticated and foolproof.

The Mayor was talking to Rathman. *"You and all of Station 85 are to appear before me at City Hall this Wednesday morning where you will officially receive your firefighting license and a commendation for bravery..."*

The bloated windbag. Making that punk an official firefighter for the city before he even earned it? Such a thing had never happened in Chicago before. It was like Rathman was the second coming of Christ. The man's stomach tightened up and twisted violently. He felt like throwing up. But he held it back and watched the news coverage alone in the dark of the small hotel room. He watched it until the birds started singing outside and the first hint of dawn outlined the thick, plaid curtains. By then he had a new plan all thought through from beginning to end. It was perfect. He would start implementing it later that night.

He brought the sheets up over his naked body and slowly fell into a deep asleep. The holocube played the morning local news program on WFLD. Braden Rathman saved the little girl again and again and again.

Eleven

Braden received the commendation and his certification at ten sharp on Wednesday morning. Much to his surprise, the ceremony took place on the marble steps outside of City Hall on North LaSalle Street.

Thankfully, it was a mild, late winter day. The sun was warm and shone in a crisp blue sky. In a carbon copy of Monday night, every reporter from every local TV station and e-paper was in attendance. Hundreds of cameras recorded the event. Braden credited Mayor Daley for recognizing the photo op, even if he had had to create it himself.

Braden stood on the top step next to the Mayor during the Mayor's speech to the throng of people standing below on the steps. Amy stood next to Braden. Even under a long, heavy coat, her advanced state of pregnancy was obvious. Braden's parents stood next to her; Gene was beaming so brightly it looked as if he'd swallowed a uranium rod. The crew of Station 85 stood behind them in their dress blues, watching the ritual silently, respectfully. The Chief stood to the left of the Mayor, wearing a bright, white cap that gave him a solemn dignity

"...And this man standing next to me," the Mayor said, putting his hand on Braden's shoulder, "has shown that same courage. He is a perfect example of what it means to be a firefighter in this great city. What all firefighters in this city should aspire to. He is selfless, brave, intelligent, and resourceful. He is the future. It is with great respect and honor that I bestow upon Braden Rathman today two things: a commendation for bravery in the line of duty and his official certification as a firefighter in the city of Chicago. Congratulations, young man, and thank you."

The Mayor shook Braden's hand, then gave him two certificates. The crowd erupted with applause and whistles, cameras flashed.

Braden knew he was expected to make a speech. He'd spent his *Off* night trying to write one, but nothing he wrote down felt honest. He'd finally decided that he'd say whatever came to his mind.

"Thank you, Mr. Mayor," Braden said into the microphone. "It is with great respect and a great honor to accept these awards from you."

The crowd applauded again; the Mayor feigned modesty.

"It has been a lifelong dream of mine to become a firefighter," Braden continued. "And now that I am a firefighter for this great city, I promise you, I will fight for it with all the strength I have in my body and with all my heart. The city of Chicago has and always will be my home. I promise, I will never let it, or you, down."

More applause and handshakes. More flashes and whistles. The Mayor waved at everyone, then he and his aides led the crew of Station 85 into City Hall for a small private luncheon in a dining room near the Mayor's office on the top floor. Security was tight; there was a police offer stationed at every door they passed. Braden wondered if it was like that every day or just for today's celebration. Everyone filed into the dining room and sat around one long cherry table, the Mayor being at the head, Braden and Amy to his right. Filet Mignon and potatoes were served, a treat for Braden, who'd never had filet mignon before. He loved it. It went well with the Pinot Grigio that was served in tall, round glasses.

The Mayor was a gracious and funny host (the story about playing "Craps" with the President in the White House bathroom was a riot.) and spent time with everyone, including Braden's parents, who were thrilled beyond belief to be sitting and talking with the Mayor. He talked in more detail about the fire at his residence. Old wiring was the cause. In fact, his wife had contacted two electricians to get quotes on updating the wiring in the apartment a few days before the fire. They had just chosen the electrician when the fire broke out. They were now living temporarily in a luxury apartment near the Loop until they could decide where to live permanently.

The luncheon lasted two hours. The Mayor took his leave after that. They were escorted out of City Hall by the Mayor's Chief of Staff, a small, little, round man with glasses named Patrick Perry.

Mr. Perry shook their hands as they went down the wide, long, empty flight of steps in front of City Hall. It was Station 85's *On* day so Braden said goodbye to his parents and kissed Amy. She went with his parents, looking tired, her skin flushed. It had been an uneventful but long pregnancy, and he knew that Amy was exhausted. Little Evie couldn't get here soon enough.

The Mayor had brought the crew to City Hall in a white stretch limo. That same vehicle waited for them at the bottom of the steps. They piled in and the limo took to the air. It was a five-minute ride back to the station house; once there, Braden noticed that the digital display on the wall next to his jacket didn't flash *Probie* anymore. Instead, it just read *B. Rathman.*

"Well, we can't call you Probie anymore, can we?" Sam asked, playfully slapping Braden's shoulder.

"Everyone in the conference room," the Chief ordered. Apparently, it was back to business as usual.

The Chief stood at the head of the table, took his white cap off, and looked at them.

"It's been a good day for the station," he began. "In an effort to try to keep these good days going, I've restructured the duty assignments a little. The ambulance crew are exempt from this."

Debbie and Danny traded relieved glances.

"First order of business is that Braden here will be partnered permanently with Sam in the Engine crew."

Sam whooped and hollered and high-fived Braden. "Two in, two out!" he shouted.

Ever since that day when Sam did the Church Raise, Braden had hoped he'd be partnered with Sam.

"Also," the Chief said, "I've talked to Thom about this already and he's agreed to switch places with Mo. Thom will drive the Foam Tender and Mo will now be Big George's partner. It's a solution I thought would be best for everyone. Once Thom retires, Mo will go back to being the driver again."

Mo and Big George nodded respectfully. They seemed at peace with the idea.

Then the meeting went onto other less important things like re-certification of the Fire Marshall test and who was due for it. Firefighters had to pass this test every six months or they couldn't go out into the field. Big George, Joni, and Paul Rose were up for re-certification; the Chief gave them their study guides.

After the meeting the Chief had them complete a series of hose drills blindfolded. Braden thought it was the funniest thing to see Sam and Big George blindfolded on their hands and knees on the floor as they tried to find and roll a dozen flattened hoses that were scattered all over the room. It looked like playtime in Romper Room. But he didn't find it so funny when he had to do it with Paul. It was harder than it looked. After that, their time was their own. The game room awaited.

Around nine o'clock, the Chief received a phone call and informed them that they had been given special permission by the Mayor to go *Off* early. The plan was to go down to the Hot Zone to celebrate Braden's promotion. Sam, of course, was hyped about that.

Braden called Amy and invited her. She still sounded tired, and told him to have a good time. She'd see him when he got home.

Wednesdays were a slower day at the Hot Zone than the rest of the week. That was fine with the crew of Station 85. They got their beers faster and all the Virtual Reality games were open. Mo was in the middle of an animated Karate battle with a VR fighter named "Striped Tiger" before he even got his first beer. The rest of them sat around the table, drank their beers, and had a good time commiserating. Again, Braden wasn't allowed to buy a single drink. But he bought one for Thom anyway as a show of forgiveness for what had happened at the Mayor's residence. Thom thanked him. Braden thought the Chief was a good man to let Thom stay on after that blunder. The Chief could have fired him with half bennies. Now all he had to do was drive the Foam Tender, no more fire walking. His wife would probably be ecstatic about that.

By ten o'clock none of them were feeling any pain. Even Debbie, who usually refrained from drinking, was lit like a forest fire. She told the dirtiest jokes and laughed at them when the others didn't. When her husband called to say he wouldn't be home that night, her mood changed. She broke down in tears at the table. Joni took her to the ladies room to talk privately.

But Braden was the worst. They'd been keeping a long, uninterrupted stream of beers and shots open to him all night. Something called a "Jager Bomb" did the most damage. He made two trips to the bathroom. Sam went in with him and laughed when Braden, in his drunken stupor, refused to get on his hands and knees to upchuck into the toilet bowl. The maintenance people did their best, but they couldn't always keep the bathroom floors in the Hot Zone clean.

The Chief left a little after ten, nursing a pretty powerful buzz himself, saying he would sleep it off in his office. Braden felt sorry for him. Even though the Chief hid it well, Braden knew he was lonely and missed his wife, Jaclyn. She'd been dead over twenty years now and he still loved her with the kind of deep, obsessive passion Braden hoped he'd have for Amy when they were the Chief's age. He had an apartment on the west side, the same one he lived in with Jaclyn all those years ago, but he rarely went home anymore. It was either too convenient just to bunk down at the station or there were too many memories for him at the apartment. If that was the case, Braden wondered why the Chief always renewed the lease. No one had the balls to talk to him about it so no one really knew what the true details were.

At eleven, they'd all decided that Braden had had enough so Sam told everyone to pile into his car. He'd drop everyone off. He had drawn the short stick earlier, making him the designated driver so he'd been drinking cola all night. Braden had seen him emptying a flask of rum into his cola now and then, but it didn't seem to be affecting him at all. They filed into the elevator, took it up to the roof, and wobbled over to Sam's '68 Cadillac. It was white and almost as big as the limo they'd ridden in earlier. But it wasn't big enough for all of them. Braden found out too late that there wasn't room for him so he made a fuss.

"Hey!" he protested. "It wash my pardee!"

"You know what?" Sam asked. "You're right, Kid." He went to the back of his car and popped the trunk. It was deep, carpeted, plenty big enough for Braden.

"Thash what I'm talkin' about," Braden said and shook Sam's

hand. "You're a good friend. A good friend."

Sam helped him into the trunk then slammed it closed. It was pitch black inside but there was plenty of air.

"You all right in there?" Sam asked.

"Yesh, Sam the Manly Man. Less go!"

Braden heard Sam get into the car and slam his door. He heard the motors that open the dome humming and he felt the car lurch into the air. He was hoping that, since it was his night, he'd be the first to be dropped off. He lost that hope when the drive home seemed to take an inordinately long time. The car rocked and dropped at uncommonly fast speeds. He could hear them in the back seat screaming and laughing. Sam was taking them all for a joy ride. Braden bounced around the trunk like that worm inside a Mexican jumping bean.

"Hey!" he shouted. "Shlow down! It's bumpy back here!"

That only seemed to make the ride faster and bumpier. The car did a long fast turn. Braden was pinned by the gees into the left side of the trunk where he bumped his head on the trunk lid. They giggled and screamed some more. He wondered if they could even hear him.

But it was what he heard that stopped his heart. A siren blared somewhere behind them and was getting louder. He heard someone in the back seat say, "It's the coppers! Cheese it!" Braden began to panic. He heard them swearing and yelling at Sam. Someone told Sam to land; someone else told Sam to pull a Superman and fly. That apparently was the option Sam preferred. The car accelerated. Braden was pinned to the ceiling of the trunk as it dove, then pinned to the floor as the car rose. He did his best to control his thumping around but the force and speed of the car were too great. The violent jostling was upsetting his stomach. A few times he burped, feeling like he was going to throw up, but thankfully he never did. Sam wouldn't have been too happy if he puked back there in his nice clean trunk.

"If they catch us and find Braden in back, the Mayor will pull Braden's feathers out. He'll be toast and never work in this city again." Braden recognized that as Joni's voice; she started weeping. She was right. Everything he'd worked for would be lost. He'd be back working at a Maynerds in some off-the-chart town like Fox

Lake, managing the paint department. He didn't know what else to do but lay there quietly, hoping Sam lost them. But the siren was louder now and he heard an angry man's voice coming from what sounded like a loud speaker telling them to stop the car immediately.

Braden wanted to kill Sam. He could've gotten a cab ride home and probably would've been soundly sleeping by now, but no, Sam had insisted that he drive them all home. He had insisted that he hadn't had a drink all night but Braden knew better. A drunk driving offence, especially for someone who worked for the city, was a career-ending mistake. There was no second chance. And the charge could apply to everyone who was in the vehicle. If they were caught it would resemble the St. Valentine's Day massacre.

"There!" Sam shouted. "Down there! We'll land on that roof and run. If they can't find us they can't blow us for alcohol."

"But what about Braden?" Joni wept again.

"Tell him to stay still and don't make a sound. They won't look in the trunk. They'll tow the car to an impound lot and we'll have the Chief go get him."

Joni yelled through the seat cushion and the trunk wall, telling Braden everything Sam had told her to say.

"Okay! Okay!" Braden replied. He felt the car suddenly slowing down. Then it stopped; he heard the doors open and the sound of heavy footsteps quickly running away into the night. The siren seemed right ontop of him now; suddenly it ceased, and he heard a man's deep voice talking into a radio.

"Yeah, dispatch, I got a group of runners heading down the fire exit of an apartment building on the lower west side of Wacker. Need back-up to corral them."

"Copy that, JR-One. Units are on their way."

Braden lay there in silence. Every muscle in his body froze with fear as he heard the police officer walking around the car, as if inspecting it.

"Dispatch. Plate number of the offending vehicle is FyreMan1."

"Copy that, JR-One. Sounds like a firefighter."

The police officer mumbled something inaudibly then opened the driver side door. "Get a forensic team up here also, Dispatch. Looks like viable prints on the steering wheel and door handle," he said.

"Copy that, JR-One."

Braden heard the police officer's ran down his forehead, but he didn't move. If the police officer opened the trunk, Braden's life was over.

"Dispatch. I think I hear breathing in the trunk. Permissionto open and check it out."

"Permission granted, JR-One."

You sonofabitch, Sam! Braden thought. *Leaving a partner when he needs you the most. You're worse than Thom. I'll get you for this!*

There was a knock on the trunk. "Anyone in there?" the police officer asked. Braden swore he heard the metallic cocking of a gun.

Braden remained silent, not knowing what to do. He felt like throwing up or pissing his pants, whichever came first. Now he didn't care what Sam's reaction would be.

"Answer me! I know you're in there!"

"All right! All right!" Braden shouted. "I'm in here and I'm unarmed!"

"I thought so," the police officer said. "Keep your hands up so I can see them when I open the trunk."

"Yes, officer," Braden said and raised his hands up. What was his father going to think about this? And Amy? Jeezus! She was going to kick him out. He'd be back living with his parents.

He heard a clicking sound in the lock gear of the trunk. The latch sprung and the trunk opened. Braden closed his eyes and swallowed deeply.

"Two in, two out, hero!" he heard. But it wasn't one voice. It was a group of voices and they were snickering loudly.

Braden, his hands raised high, opened his eyes and saw the entire station crew looking down at him, laughing. The Chief was in the middle, his hand on the wireless radio transmitter from the nearby ambulance. He was the police officer. Stacey was probably on the other end, pretending to be police dispatch. They were still on the roof of the station house and Braden wondered if they'd even left the dome at all.

Sam bent over and kissed him on his sweaty forehead. "Welcome aboard, hero," he said, and they all laughed riotously.

"Sonofabitch!" Braden said, dropping his hands.

"Gotcha good, didn't we?" Paul asked through delirious snorts.

"Tied and fried," Sam heaved and fell over in a fit.

"Tossed and frosted!" Paul shouted, joining Sam on the floor of the roof. Both were convulsing hysterically. Braden let them laugh as he got out of the trunk. At first he wanted to kill them all but then he realized that every firefighter had to go through a rite of passage. This idiotic prank was his ticket to the big show.

Braden's legs were still shaking with fear but he was immeasurably relieved. Yes, they'd gotten him good. After calling them a few more colorful names, Braden began laughing and didn't stop until Sam dropped him off at home. He hadn't been drinking at all, he told Braden on the way home, saying there'd been nothing in the flask. Sam just wanted Braden to think he was drinking to heighten his terror when the police started chasing them.

Still giggling in relief, he went into the bedroom, nearly stumbling over Harley, their cat. He found Amy sitting up in bed wearing a pink nightgown. One hand was on her belly; the other was holding the phone. Her head was slumped forward; her forehead was pale and glistening with sweat. She inhaled and exhaled in short, explosive bursts.

Braden sobered up quickly.

"I've just called Dr. Payne and the ambulance," she said when she saw him. "I'm in labor."

Twelve

On the way to the Station 85 hospital, Braden called his and Amy's parents. They arrived in the waiting room not long after Amy was admitted.

Amy's room was small and dimly lit, consisting of nothing but the large, caged, hover cot, a small closet, a single plasteel chair, and a window that was hidden behind a long gray curtain. A series of six colored graphs and numbers hung suspended in the air above Amy's head, projected by a line of holocubes in the ceiling. Six coin-shaped sensors were stuck to the skin on Amy's right arm. These relayed specific body functions to the holocubes above. Braden recognized the pulse rate graph—that one was easy because there was an animated heart pumping in the top left corner and a pair of numbers, one ontop of the other—the rest were beyond him. He wasn't even sure it was English he was looking at. The words that puzzled him the most were *Abruptio Placenta, Cephalopelvic Disproportion Risk,* and *Perineum Elasticity.* He wanted to ask the doctor for a dictionary.

Dr. Payne came in at regular intervals, checking Amy's blood pressure and the timing of her labor pains. He found that the contractions were still too far apart. She was a few hours away from giving birth. A quick ultrasound told him that Evangeline's head was in the correct position and had stretched Amy to three centimeters. Dr. Payne told him that that was a good thing and all was normal, it should be a regular, run-of-the-mill delivery (was there ever such a thing?).

So, to feel as if he were part of the process and doing his

part, Braden lay quietly next to Amy in her hover cot. He held her hand when another round of labor pains came. This gave her something to squeeze and vent the pain through. At times it felt as if the bones in his hands were going to break. It looked to Braden as if she was being tortured and he hated to see her in such pain. When Dr. Payne came in to check on her again Braden sat up.

"Isn't there anything you can give her for the pain?" he asked.

The doctor shook his head. "No can do, Braden," he replied. "It's still too early. We'll have to wait until she's about to give birth. She did request an epidural, didn't she?"

Braden nodded even though he didn't know exactly what an epidural was. Maybe it was Dr. Payne's way of saying *painkiller*. Amy was too practical to go for that natural birth hype. He remembered when Dr. Payne gave her the option of giving birth in a portable swimming pool, one of those small plastic pools with pictures of fish and sea weed on the bottom that a parent spent an entire afternoon blowing up for their child on a hot summer afternoon. Amy would have to scrunch down, completely naked, her waist under the warm water, spread her legs, and give birth while sitting up. Braden had never heard Amy laugh so hard.

The doctor patted him on the shoulder. "She's almost there, son," he said. "Just keep comforting her and I'll be back when it's time."

"Thanks, Doc," Braden said as Dr. Payne left the room.

At this point Braden felt the chilliness of the room; his fingertips were going numb. He noticed Amy was sweating. He realized that one of those many coin-shaped sensors that was stuck to the skin of her forearm was probably relaying her body temperature to the climate control generator that hung down out of the middle of the ceiling like an upside down toaster. If Amy's body temperature went down, the climate control generator would sense it and the room would heat up. Another one of the miracles of modern technology.

When the pains were finally just a few minutes apart, Dr. Payne came in with a nurse and told them it was time. He'd been watching things closely on monitors in his office down the hall. He and the nurse whisked Amy away while Braden did as Dr. Payne had told him. He slipped into a long, green hospital tunic he found hanging in the closet. On his way to the birthing room, he stopped in the waiting room to tell the concerned grandparents-to-be what was going on. He found Sam there waiting with them.

"Thanks for coming, Sam," Braden said in surprise, shaking Sam's hand.

"No problem, hero," Sam said. "The others weren't feeling too well but they send you their good wishes."

Braden understood and nodded.

"How are you feeling?" Sam asked. "You look a little pale."

"Yeah," Braden whispered. "I picked the wrong night to quit drinking."

Sam laughed. "That's my boy. Keep that attitude and you'll survive this night to drink again."

Braden smiled. He turned his attention to his and Amy's parents.

"It's time, everyone," he said. Their eyes widened with expectation and glee. "I'll let you know how things go."

They kissed and hugged him before he went into the birthing room.

Evangeline Grace Rathman was born at three in the morning, perfectly healthy and screaming her welcome to the world. Once the nurse cleaned her up, she wrapped Evie in a white blanket and gave her to her exhausted, but grateful mother. It was the most beautiful thing Braden had ever seen. He could already see the bond the two of them shared. Amy began crying, then Braden joined her and they cuddled together, living fully in this wonderful moment. They were holding their child, their future, their legacy to the human race, in their arms.

"You still want more children?" he whispered.

"Of course, honey," she said. Her voice was strong and he knew she was relieved that it was all over. "But give me a few years to spoil this one."

"It's a deal."

Eventually Braden went into the waiting room and was crushed with delirious hugs when he told them the good news. He brought them to the waiting hall outside the infant-care unit where they could see through the thick pane of glass, Evie lying in her hover crib. She'd stopped crying and everyone's heart was melting, even Sam's, as she slept quietly. Once in a while, something would startle Evie, a dream maybe, and her whole body would spasm but she'd fall back asleep immediately, as if nothing had happened.

"She's so beautiful," Amy's mom, Barbara, whispered as Dennis held his arm around her. Gene was doing the same thing with Zoey.

"Seven pounds, twelve ounces," Braden said proudly.

Both sets of grandparents ogled at Evie for a few more minutes then decided to get some coffee.

Braden thought that was a great idea; he needed a cup of coffee more than anyone in the room.

"It's been a long, long day, make mine black," he said. The grandparents went to the cafeteria, but Sam stayed with Braden, staring at Evie quietly. Braden thought that Sam seemed to be a million miles away.

"Why is it that babies are always born after midnight?" he asked. It looked like he truly wanted an answer. "Did you ever notice that?"

"Good question," Braden said and shrugged his shoulders. He had, in fact, noticed that, but he had no answer.

There was a long silence. Braden suspected Sam was troubled about something. Then Sam coughed gently and spoke softly.

"My sister, Julie, was born at 1:30 in the morning," he began. "Looked just like your little Evie there. I was only five but I remember everything. She had this thick tuft of curly white hair right in the middle of her head—give her wings and she'd look just like one of those baby angels."

"Cherubs," Braden said.

"No really, she did," Sam countered.

Braden tried not to laugh and wanted to tell him what a cherub was but he changed the subject instead.

"I didn't know you had a sister," Braden said.

"Yeah," Sam replied. "I don't talk about her much. Hurts too bad."

"Why? What happened?"

"She died when she was six. I was eleven. It was in late June a long time ago—our house caught fire. Something to do with a faulty heater unit in the basement. She was in the basement playing with the *Barbie Dream Home* she got for Christmas. You know, the one where you pull a string and the elevator goes up? It was the coolest thing. Just between you an' me, I used to put my *Sky Cop* guys in it and play with it whenever Julie was gone. I always used to make Officer Nelson arrest Barbie and then he would *accidentally* push her off the top floor so Ken could run her over in that silly, dune buggy thing. Good times. Anyway, Julie never had a chance of escaping once the fire broke out. The rest of us were watching the holocube upstairs in the living room when we heard her screams and smelled the smoke. I remember seeing the firemen taking her out of the house on a stretcher; her body was covered in a white sheet but I can still remember the smell. Once you smell burnt flesh, you never forget it, Kid. My mother was never the same after that. She died of a broken heart a few years later."

"God, Sam. I didn't know. I'm so sorry."

"Don't be," Sam said, trying to control his emotions. "It's because of Julie that I'm a firefighter, and a damn good one. In my mind, with every person I save from a fire, she lives on, like it's my tribute to her. It makes something good out of her senseless death. I know that sounds corny but it's how I feel. She was a good kid and didn't deserve to die that way. I miss her a lot." He looked down at the floor, closed his eyes, and his face turned red with emotion.

Braden was an only child and couldn't truly feel what Sam was feeling. But as he stared at his little girl, helpless and small in that hover crib, her whole life in front of her, he knew exactly how he'd feel if something like that happened to her. It was way too dark a thought to dwell on for very long, so he threw it from his mind quickly.

"Sometimes life seems so senseless," Braden said.

"Yeah. You're right. Nothing's more senseless than the Chief's wife's death," Sam said.

"She die in a fire, too?" Braden asked.

"Nah," Sam replied. "*Trip* got her just after Roger was born. She still had residual pain a few months after the birth so one of her close friends told her to try *Trip*. This was before anyone realized how dangerous it was. She tried it once, to dull the pain. Well, it did that and more. She was dead in less than a year."

That explained why the Chief seemed so upset on that last drive-along, when they went to that house where those two *Trip* users lived. Braden remembered the Chief telling him about that woman whose insides were eaten away by *Trip* and suddenly he realized the Chief was talking about his wife, Jaclyn. Braden understood the Chief's blind dedication to his job now and it was the saddest thing in the world to him. Everyone had their own reasons for becoming a firefighter, Braden was learning that most of those reasons were based in sadness and a deep need to trade that sadness in for something good. Yet Braden didn't have that sad background. Was that drive, that need, that sadness, imperative to have if one wanted to become a good firefighter?

"You ever seen a picture of his wife?" Sam asked.

"No, have you?"

"Yeah," Sam replied, his voice going low as if telling a government secret. "He keeps a big picture of her and Roger in his desk drawer. She's holding Roger on her lap; they're in a park or something, and it's a gorgeous sunny day. Roger was still just an infant, maybe a few weeks old at the most. But you wouldn't believe how beautiful she was."

"Yeah, I would," Braden murmured and looked away.

"I'm sorry if I'm being a downer, Braden," Sam said. It was the first time he'd used his proper name. "This is supposed to be a joyous night. We should be celebrating."

"No. It's all right, Sam," Braden said, glancing over at his big, bald partner whose heart was as large as his body. "It's good that I know this stuff. I can understand things better that way. The world makes more sense."

Just then, the grandparents came through the swinging doors, each holding a tall cup of steaming coffee. They were laughing, and Braden was soon inebriated by their happiness. But deep in the back of his mind he wondered if he'd gone so high that the only place to go now was down.

Thirteen

The Engine came down on the burning boat, circling it once, slowly. It was a chilly but sunny early June day and the choppy waves of Lake Michigan knocked the hulk around like a toy. Smoke and flames were bent sideways against the wind, making it look like a Viking's funeral barge.

They'd made it to the job in less than five minutes from Stacey's contact, just as the Chief always preached. But as Braden watched the fury below he didn't think it would matter this time. The damage was done. It was a salvage operation now instead of a rescue, save what they could and then go home.

"Doesn't seem to be anyone aboard, sir," Joni said as she completed the Engine's slow circuit. "This is real spooky."

The Chief frowned. "I don't like it either, Joni. Something doesn't feel right about this," he said and waved for Sam to begin the salvage operation. Sam leapt from his seat, making for the control panel on the passenger-side bulkhead cabin door. The Chief looked at the rear monitor on the dash board and saw Debbie and Danny hovering in the ambulance a quarter of a mile back, to the south, waiting for further orders. Then he looked out the window at the smoking chaos below.

It was an older but well-kept, cream-colored, twenty-foot cruiser with the name *King Joshua* painted in red cursive letters on the starboard aft side. Most of the inside of the boat was in flames.

"This doesn't make any sense...what would an unmanned boat be doing out here on fire?" the Chief asked.

Lake Michigan had very little surface boat traffic anymore

thanks to the advent of air-car technology but there were some old "hangers-on" who still enjoyed the contact of a boat on water. It was mainly the middle class who bothered to purchase a boat; some even rode in large, beautiful white-sailed cutters powered by the wind, just like the old days. The filthy rich, in contrast, preferred the smooth ride of a hovering, streamlined, fifty-foot sea cruiser rather than dealing with a choppy surface, like it was on this day. There were plenty of them skimming above the surface of the lake many miles out; they looked like rocket ships. Somebody on one of them must have called the fire in.

Since there was an unlimited source of water nearby, the procedure was to draft water from that source instead of tapping the Engine's tanks. Sam opened the ramp and pressed a button on the control board on the bulkhead wall. Outside, a hatch on the Engine's rear passenger side blew. A long, four-inch thick hose with weights on the end slithered out, plunging into the violent waves below like a needle into skin. Once it was deep enough, Sam pressed another button and the hose stiffened with water pressure.

Braden leaned out to visually check the hose. "All set for drafting, Chief!" he shouted. Joni aimed the deck guns down on the flaming boat and watched the pressure gauge on the dash rise to full, meaning the deck guns were charged. She opened up the nozzles of the deck guns. Thick white streams of water battered down on the fire below, sucked from the inexhaustible body of Lake Michigan. The boat listed to the right under the pressure but kept itself righted somehow, even as it slammed against the rolling mountains of oncoming waves.

"Just a little more, Joni," the Chief said.

Braden could see the White Cap restaurant far, far in the distance. It hovered black in the haze above the heaving white-capped swells and deep, dark valleys of Lake Michigan like a giant UFO studded with thousands of lights. It was an ultra-expensive restaurant/hotel/casino only the very elite rich could afford to eat at. On top, a beam of yellow light flashed like a pulsar, underneath, luxury air-cars went in and out of its belly like bees in a beehive.

Below, the deck guns kept their relentless pressure on the boat. Joni fogged them, then streamed them in cycles, which seemed to work. The fire made a last attempt at life, then was thrown down like an unconscious wrestler. She deactivated the deck guns; their streams weakened to slow drips until they stopped all together.

"All clear, Chief," Joni said. "Fire's out. Scan shows the structural integrity of the boat is still 100%."

The Chief expressed his surprise at that fact. It looked like a hellish fire had gone on down there. Hellish enough to burn the hull away and sink the boat.

"Great job, Joni," the Chief said. "Secure the deck guns and pull the plug. Rathman, it's your turn on the Moon."

That meant Braden was up for the primary search of the vessel. Sam had done the last one and it had been a cakewalk. Nothing more than a small grease fire at an auto shop downtown. He had thrown a little sand on it, given the owner of the shop a citation, and they had lunch at the Hot Zone a few minutes later.

Braden stood in the cabin, his left foot on the ramp. He held the ceiling strap tightly as Joni brought the Engine over the smoldering boat and edged next to it so that the ramp touched the top side of the boat's hull.

"Camera check?" he asked the Chief.

The Chief glanced at the monitor on the dashboard. Perfect picture and sound. "Camera check a go," he said. Braden went across the ramp and carefully dropped himself into the flooded depths of the boat.

It was his job to make sure there weren't any "K's" on board and then make a complete visual record of the hulk with his helmcam. Everything was pretty much affected by the fire: the seat cushions, the plasti-glass windshield, and the deck boards. The damage was considerable but not total. He saw dark, splotchy patterns on the deck just below the water; these looked as if something had been poured and then lit. That meant some kind of accelerant was used. Nothing else could cause such damage so unevenly or as quickly. The steering wheel was just a crispy, smoking ring on the end of a sizzling, smoking stick. Thankfully, so far, no sign of a human victim.

Stranger and stranger. This didn't feel copacetic to Braden at all. The Chief was right. To his left was a door in the forward bulkhead that led to a sleeping compartment. It was closed and, miraculously, had avoided any contact with the inferno only a few feet away.

"Going down, Chief," he said.

"Just be careful, Rathman. There could be a backdraft."

"Right, Chief," Braden said, then slid the door lock to the left. It clicked as it unlocked. He pushed it in slowly and a wisp of brown smoke feathered out. It was dark inside. A good sign. He pushed it farther in, still couldn't see anything. He activated his forward helmet light and leaned his head through the opening. There was a small flash; suddenly the inside of the sleeping compartment was bright with fire. He saw something on the bulkhead. Something that didn't belong. Out of place. Square gray bars of some kind...clay? They were duct-taped in long lines to the bulkhead, resembling a pack of giant firecrackers. The light from the fire burned so bright he only had a second to see this, then he jumped away from the door screaming "Reflash! Reflash!" and turned towards the ramp. He saw Sam standing there, his gloved hand reaching out towards him; his eyes were bulging, staring at the flaming doom behind Braden.

There was a sound like two air-cars colliding and Braden felt his body spinning through the air.

Fourteen

Braden felt like he was riding a tsunami as he spun through the air, pushed on by the force of the blast. Sam, who'd had his hand out to grab him, instead had become a safety net. Braden barreled into him and both were flying backwards into the Engine crew cabin. Their bodies untangled, falling to the floor with violent thumps.

"Christ!" the Chief said as he looked back at them from his cockpit seat. "What the hell was that?"

Before Braden or Sam could answer, there was a horrible sound, like a whale screaming out. Suddenly, the rear of the Engine fell down into the swirling waters of Lake Michigan. All Joni could see was the clear blue sky and the menagerie of warning lights flashing impatiently on the dashboard.

"We've lost the rear superconductor rack...trying to compensate!" she shouted.

"Our ass end is too heavy...can you dump the tanks?"

Joni was fiercely pushing buttons and flipping switches on the dashboard. "Negative!" she shouted. "The tank bleeds aren't responding! Must be a blown fuse or something!"

"All power to the forward racks," the Chief ordered as the Engine lurched violently to the right. If not for the seat belt, he would've been thrown out of his open window and into the soup below. Joni managed to pull out of the turn but the Engine's front end still stuck up at an angle.

"If I overload the forward racks we risk a blowout, Chief—"

"I know! Just do it!"

Joni cursed, fighting to keep control of the hundred ton

vehicle. The Engine started turning again and the sky outside was spinning now. She saw the ambulance getting closer with each spin.

"Stay clear of us, Deb," she said into her ear mic. "At least until I can tame this fricking horse."

"Copy that, Joni."

The Chief, fighting the force of the spin, managed to look back towards the rear of the cabin. Braden and Sam struggled to secure themselves. They flopped uncontrollably on what should have been the rear bulkhead of the crew cabin, but it had been turned into a floor.

"Grab something!" the Chief shouted.

"We're trying!" Sam exploded; his face was red and snarling as his hands searched wildly for anything to grab.

Joni was frantically punching buttons and flipping switches, trying to effect the switchover to the front superconductor racks but the force of the spin was weighing on her, too, making it difficult. She was wondering why the Chief had told her to overload the front racks. He knew damn well that that would blow the magnetic thruster jets out, leaving the Engine crippled. Then it made sense to her. Blowing out the thruster jets would stop the Engine from spinning like a tornado. They'd be dead in the water, like a buoy, but at least they could get towed back to the station. The man was a genius.

Braden and Sam had their own dilemma. Normally, the ramp would close automatically once the Engine's gyros picked up an irregularity in the leveling of the vehicle, but the ramp had taken most of the blast and was now a warped, useless slag of plasteel. It repeatedly went up a few inches then crashed back down before finally giving up the ghost. The hinges that it rolled on were also probably damaged so the ramp remained down and the cabin remained open, threatening to vomit the two of them out. By some miracle, Sam managed to grab a ceiling strap and even though his feet were dangling in the air, he was secure. Braden wasn't so lucky. He'd been thrown into an area of the cabin where a ceiling strap was out of reach; there was nothing else but Sam to hold onto. At the moment, Sam's right boot was working just fine. But for how long? Already Braden felt his hand slipping and his feet weighed on him like buckets of cement, pulling him towards his doom.

The gray white-capped water of Lake Michigan spun below him, and with it, the smoldering remains of the *King Joshua* as it sank under the waves. There was smoking debris all over the surface of the water around the dying boat. The destruction was complete. For the police technicians, evidence would be hard to find.

With a valiant effort against the heavy gee spin of the Engine, Joni forced her right hand up, pushed the energy modulator forward, transferring all power to the forward racks. The Engine stopped suddenly, with such a lurch that Braden lost his grip on Sam's boot. He was hurtled out through the ramp opening but managed to grab the bent corner of the ramp on the way out. Using his momentum, he swung around, falling against the rear passenger side rails on the outside of the Engine. He hit the rails hard but his grip held firm. Thankfully, the Engine was static, just hanging there, frozen at a steep angle. He looked down; its rear end was submerged a few feet under the boiling waves. The Engine itself was bobbing up and down with the swelling of the water.

Sam's head poked out the cabin exit, which was now above Braden. "You all right, partner?" he asked.

Braden was too shaken, too exhausted, to say anything so he just tiredly waved at him. Sam gave an "Ugh!" as his head disappeared back into the cabin. Braden's eyes focused to the right. He saw how the violence of the blast had warped the plasteel of the two-inch thick ramp. The end of it was turned up, its edges burned and sheared. It made him realize how lucky he'd been to survive the initial blast. He looked back towards the rear end of the Engine; his body stiffened with horror. The water was up to the rear hose bed doors. They were sinking. The five thousand gallons of water the Engine held was weighing it down, making it too heavy for the remaining superconductors that still functioned to stabilize her.

"Chief! Chief, do you copy?" he stammered into his ear mic.

The Chief thrust his head out through his open window.

"I-I think we're sinking!" Braden shouted.

"I know it, Kid. But as usual, you're way ahead of us!" he said.

"W-what do you mean, sir?" Braden asked.

"Whaddaya mean, what do I mean? You're making your way to the turntable ladder on top of the Engine where you're going to catch the winch hook from the bottom of the ambulance and attach it to the eyelet underneath the ladder. That way Debbie can pull our asses out of the water and drag us home." The Chief winked after he said this.

"Oh, yeah," Braden said. "Right."

Braden saw the ambulance dropping slowly over the Engine. Debbie waved at him from the cockpit. He took a deep breath, loosened his grip on the rail, gave her a thumbs up, and climbed to the top of the Engine. Once inside the rails of the ladder he saw the huge hook of the ambulance's bottom winch coming down. It was on the end of a chain massive enough to haul well over the hundred tons that the Engine weighed. All the station's vehicles had powered winches placed on the bottom, front, sides, and rear of the vehicles, but they all handled different weight limits. The bottom winch was rated the strongest, two hundred fifty tons. The person who designed this feature into the apparatus must have had a similar experience and knew it would come in handy.

The ambulance itself was only ten or twelve feet above him when Braden took the hook in his gloved hands; there was plenty of slack in the chain now for him to do what had to be done.

"Okay, Deb, we're good." he said. The winch above him stopped turning in its protective hollow. He looked down at the thick iron eyelet sticking up through a rung in the Engine's ladder; He reached down, attached the hook. It had a locking arm and it clicked solidly. "We're hooked, Deb."

Debbie snickered playfully into his ear mic. "Don't let your wife hear you say that, Tiger."

"Or your husband," Braden countered.

"Ha! He wouldn't care one way or another, hero."

Braden blushed and climbed over the side of the Engine, back to his place on the side rails. He didn't want to be anywhere near the hook if it should snap free under the tremendous weight of the Engine. It probably wouldn't happen but he didn't want to take the chance. Once clear, Debbie began reeling in the winch. The chain snapped taut. Suddenly, the weight of the entire back half of the Engine was being supported by the chain and the ambulance's superconductors. Slowly, the rear of the Engine stopped sinking and lifted, an inch every few seconds. In a few minutes, the Engine was righted enough so that Braden could make his way safely along the side rails and back into the crew cabin. Sam helped him in and they went into the cockpit to watch the video on the external monitors. The rear of the Engine came up out of the lake, shedding streams of green water and white foam, until it was level. The winch continued to turn, bringing the entire Engine up. The two vehicles shuddered when their bodies came together.

"It's almost like watching a porno, isn't it, Kid?" Sam asked and guffawed.

"What kind of porno's do you watch, partner?" Braden said, laughing back.

Joni and the Chief sat back in their seats, sighing in relief. He took off his white helmet and wiped the sweat from his forehead with the back of his hand.

"Good call on the overloading of the superconductor racks, Chief," Joni murmured through a smile.

The Chief smiled back at her. "I wasn't sure it would work," he said. "I read it somewhere in a safety manual a long time ago. It was under a chapter named *Things You Should Never Do With Your New Engine Apparatus.*"

Joni looked at him, wondering if that was a joke. But he wasn't laughing. She burst out laughing instead, shaking her head in disbelief.

There was the sound of a small explosion. They turned their attention to the column of brown smoke coming out of the water below. It looked like a plane had crashed into the water. Smoking debris was scattered over a half mile radius.

"Jeezus!" Sam muttered in disbelief. "Seems like someone really wants you dead, Kid."

Braden, surprised, looked at Sam and nodded. He'd thought he was the only one who'd thought that. He didn't feel so paranoid now.

"Now, don't get all conspiratorial on me, Sam. You either, Rathman. It may look mighty suspicious but it's way too early to make that judgment," the Chief said. "When we get back to the station I want to go over the video from Braden's helm cam. Maybe we'll see something we missed. Until then, everyone relax and strap in."

Braden and Sam went back into the crew cabin, sat down in the cushioned bulkhead seats, and strapped themselves in as the ambulance lifted them into the air, heading west over the lake, back towards the station house. The sky in front of them was dotted with flashing lights, an orchestra of sirens chorused in the distance. The lights were getting brighter and the sirens were growing louder.

"Heany's men," Sam said. "Late as usual."

The vehicles came at them at a blinding speed then broke pattern, allowing the ambulance and the Engine through as they rushed by.

"I don't think they'll find much of anything left," the Chief said. "But I'm not going to stop them from trying."

Braden nodded, knowing that the only likely evidence they had was saved in his helm cam video. He hoped it was enough.

Fifteen

The big Engine, safely back in the dome of Station 85, hovered eighteen inches in the air over a portable mat of reversed polarity superconductors. The entire crew stood alongside it, shaking their heads in disbelief. The driver's side ramp was hanging down like a burned, broken, and warped metal jaw. The light bars under the rear half of the vehicle were either blown out or melted, along with the rear superconductor rack. There was also a great deal of paint damage. It was disheartening for Braden to see something he thought nearly indestructible hovering before him, looking so crippled, so helpless. It reminded him of his own mortality; there was no way he was going to tell Amy about this. She'd overreact, equate his own mortality to the damage, and make him quit.

The Chief called in a specialist, Mike Perry. In a smashing example of nepotism (he was the twin brother of the Mayor's chief aide) Mike was the lead mechanic for the city of Chicago. Even though he'd clearly landed the job by being Patrick Perry's brother, he was also the most talented, skillful mechanic in the city and well deserved it. He was the man responsible for the technological advances in their jackets and blast shields, especially the sound dousers, the helium bladders, and the wirelessly linked GPS feature. He always came up with new, exciting tools for the firefighters of the city to use. His most recent idea had been to install a poisonous gas detector in the rim of their helmets so that if they walked into a room filled with carbon monoxide or some other toxin it would flash a warning on the blast shield, alerting the firefighter.

Like his brother, Mike Perry was a short man, but he had a

blinding shock of bleached white hair over a face that, even in the winter, seem suntanned. He had a temper that matched his face. He came out of the elevator with a group of three tall assistants, all wearing dirty, grease-stained blue coveralls and boots. They stood over him like the towers around a castle, each carried a thick leather tool bag, tools jangling around inside as they walked. For a second there, Braden almost confused Mike with Santa Claus. All Mike needed was a beard.

The Chief came out of his office and met Mike just as he and his assistants reached the wounded Engine.

"Glad you could make it on such short notice, Michael," the Chief said and they shook hands.

Mike smiled cordially and nodded. He was one of those people that could look at a person without actually looking at him; his eyes were either up in the sky or off somewhere in the corner of a room.

"No problem, Chief," he said, and released the Chief's hand. "When I got your call and heard what happened, I dropped what I was doing and rushed right over. I couldn't believe it. I had to see it for myself."

"I hope what you were doing wasn't important," the Chief said.

"No, no," Mike replied. "I was just watching the original 1921 silent version of Robin Hood on the holocube. In glorious black and white and starring Douglas Fairbanks. Ah, they don't make them like that anymore."

"No, they sure don't," the Chief agreed. Everyone focused their attention on the Engine.

"Okay, let's see what wonders you have for me today," Mike said through a grin. He reached into a pocket in his coveralls and pulled out a pair of small, round glasses. He put them on so that they clung perilously close to the edge of his bulbous nose, then he rubbed the stubble on his chin and slowly walked around the entire vehicle like a man inspecting the core of a nuclear power plant. He made a low growling noise whenever he spotted something interesting. His three assistants placed their big, worn leather bags on the floor at their feet, watching him silently. Mike stopped at the rear of the vehicle, kneeled down. He took a large mirror from his bag and angled it in his hands so that he could see the bottom of the Engine. The light bars and superconductor racks underneath were designed to be easily replaceable; the station kept extras in the supply shed near the elevator. The only problem was the warped ramp. It couldn't be fixed. They'd need to fly a new one here from the main warehouse downtown to replace it. He stood up again, placed the mirror back in his bag, and continued his inspection.

When Mike came back around to where everyone stood, he glanced up at the dome and said through a series of blinks, "Three and a half hours, four tops."

"Perfect, Mike," the Chief said. "If you need anything, let me know."

"Will do, boss."

As Mike and his men began working on the Engine, the Chief told his people to hit the conference room. They filed in, sat in their seats, as the Chief closed the door behind them. Braden noticed that the Chief's eyes looked more tired than usual. He was concerned. The Chief didn't sit, but pushed his chair back out of the way so he could stand at the head of the table.

"I've gathered all of you here because I want to go over the video of what happened out there today—it concerns all of us," the Chief began. He glanced up at the black holocube in the ceiling. "I've already looked at it and want to know if you see what I see. Your input is important, so don't be shy."

They stared at him.

"The video is from Braden's helm cam," the Chief said as he picked up the remote and pressed a button. A three dimensional image appeared over the center of the table. It showed the white, flooded hull of the *King Joshua* from above because Braden was still on the Engine's ramp as they came down over it. It was bobbing low in the gray water of Lake Michigan, partially flooded from Joni's deck gun attack. Other than that, it seemed harmless enough. Then it was clear that Braden had jumped down into the boat and was doing the primary search. The fire damage was intense, widespread. The dark ghostly shadows of the accelerant that was poured all over the deck was plain to see. This was clearly arson. When Braden got to the door in the forward hull, the Chief slowed the image down.

"What I want you all to see is coming up. It's just after Braden opens the door and the fire begins. I'll stop it when it appears."

The door opened in slow motion, there was a flash, something hanging on the inner bulkhead was illuminated. The image froze and they all leaned forward in their seats.

"Chief!" Thom erupted. "That's C-4!"

"Yeah," Joni chimed in. "I remember seeing it when you had the Army come out a few years ago to familiarize us with the various explosives terrorists might use against the city."

Braden listened with interest; he hadn't been there but they remembered it well.

"Looks like five bars, maybe more, taped to the bulkhead," Sam said. "Seemed like a lot more when it went off."

Braden agreed.

They stared at it in horror; each knew what the implications were.

"It was a set-up," Paul said, his eyes wide with fright.

The Chief let the image hang there in front of them.

"Yes," he said. "The boat was rigged to blow. The fire was just a reason to get us there in the first place. But why? And who was the target? Braden seems to think he's the target. He's brought up some suspicious things concerning his obstacle course test and Victor, the Victim. He's claimed he was being sabotaged. We don't know by whom, or why. I'm still looking into it."

Everyone's eyes fell upon Braden. He met each of their glances, shrugged, and glanced back at the Chief.

"I ran the chemical tester over Braden's fire jacket when we got back. It picked up trace amounts of high-quality explosive resin. It wasn't your normal C-4 that almost killed Braden out there; it was pure, military grade C-4. A teaspoon of the stuff can blow an air-car to air-car Heaven. Leaves a whole lot of nothing behind."

"Jeezus," Sam murmured.

"Who called the job in?" Joni asked.

The Chief shrugged. "We don't know. I contacted Stacey and she said the caller was anonymous. As we speak, she's trying to triangulate the location where the call originated. It may not lead to anything, but at least it's a start."

"What else can we do?" Big George Jackson asked, frustration cracking his voice.

"I've contacted Heany about all of this," the Chief answered. "I sent him a copy of this video and everything else we have, including the results of the chemical test on Braden's jacket. He's running down the registration info on the *King Joshua*. Once he finds anything out, he'll let me know. Then I'll let you guys know."

"What about their evidence sweep? Did they find anything?" Sam asked.

"Nothing yet, but I believe they're still out there. It may be a while."

They all traded worried glances with each other.

"People!" the Chief shouted. "Focus! I need you to stay alert! You see anything suspicious anywhere, whether it's on a job or not, tell me. Does everyone understand?"

They nodded.

"Keep this to yourselves for now," the Chief ordered. "If the press gets hold of this it could ruin our chances of catching this maniac."

Braden looked at Sam, realizing that would be a hard task for his friend as he was dating Kathryn Gold, local Channel 7 evening news anchor.

"Any questions?" the Chief asked.

"I have one," Debbie said. "Should Braden be put on some kind of leave, for his own protection?"

The Chief shook his head vigorously. "No. Not until we find out that he's definitely the target."

Sam sat back and looked at Braden. "I don't see a target on you, pal," he said.

"Sure feels like one is, though," Braden said.

With that, the meeting was over. They filed back out of the conference room, but the haunting image of those gray bars of C-4 taped on the bulkhead wall of the *King Joshua* remained, hovering above the table like a bad memory.

Sixteen

By late June the weather in Chicago had warmed and the thunderstorms that came with that warmth were powerful. Explosive. This night was no exception. The rain was coming down like medieval arrows during a battle; lightning lit the sky in blinding flashes. It was as if the world was ending.

Through this turmoil, the loud multi-toned alarm of the station blared. Everyone rushed to their assignment cubicles. As they secured themselves in their bunker gear, the Chief told them that another anonymous call had come in, placing a fire at an oil recycling warehouse two blocks from Union Station. Oil, fire, and lightning: Braden knew no good could come from it and was extremely suspicious about it.

The Chief was, too. "Keep your eyes open, people!" he shouted as they boarded their respective vehicles. "I don't like this one at all!"

Sam, though, didn't seem upset at all. In fact, he was more animated than usual. The Chief had to tell him twice to stay strapped in until they arrived at the job. Sam sat there in the seat in the back of the cabin, his eyes dancing around like Fred Astaire, his fists opening and closing nervously, his legs rocking up and down. It looked as if he was high on *Trip*.

"You all right, partner?" Braden asked him.

"I'm frosty, my man!" Sam replied, shifting in his seat. "I can't wait to lay some hose down! OOOOOOOOOOEEEEEEE! We'll show that fire who its masters are!"

Braden wished he could share his partner's enthusiasm.

Long black rubber wipers, molded to the rounded shape of the glass cockpit swept the rain away in a blink; Joni had them going full speed and it still wasn't fast enough. Braden saw, through the intense splattering on the windshield, a flickering yellow light in the crying darkness, small at first but growing exponentially; it seemed to be moving and alive, like a threatened dragon trapped in its cave.

As Joni brought the Engine down on it, Braden and Sam did a camera check and made sure their SCBA masks were in working order.

"This is a three-story structure built in the latter half of the twentieth century," the Chief said into his ear mic, looking back at Sam and Braden. He pressed a button on the dashboard, a schematic came up on their blast shields. "The first floor holds vats of untreated and treated oil used for lubrication or whatever outdated machine still uses gasoline nowadays. The second floor is where the oil is treated; there are eight, huge filtering machines. The floor manager has informed us that they are all full of oil. The third floor, where the fire is currently raging, is primarily office space. There are two sets of washrooms and a cafeteria that lays in between the outer foyer and the office area. The seat of the fire is in the back in the office area where a series of cubicles stand. The number one object here is that we have to stop the fire from getting to the lower floors. If it does, the whole block will become Hiroshima. It's too early to tell if this is an electrical fire or if an accelerant of some kind was used. We'll figure that out later. Sam, you go in first, set up an anchor point in the lobby, then Braden will go in to do the sweep with you."

"Check, Chief!" Sam shouted. "Let's rock and load! OOOOOOOOOOOEEEEEEEEE!"

Braden shot a glance at Sam, frowned with worry, then saw the Foam Tender and the ambulance in the rear view screens on the dashboard; they looked like ghostly smudges in the pouring rain, their light bars flashed as if weapons were discharging.

Joni skillfully lowered the Engine to the glass facade of the upper lobby on the third floor and released the shiny new ramp Mike Perry had installed a few weeks earlier. Sam got up, stole an axe off its perch on the rear bulkhead wall, stomped across the ramp, and threw it into the glass of the lobby. This shattered easily and black smoke fluttered out into the heavy, wet sky.

Braden was on the ramp also, unlocking the driver's side hose bed. He pulled the three and a half inch hose by the nozzle with both hands and it unreeled smoothly. But before Braden could take up position behind Sam to give him the hose, Sam had entered the building. He was supposed to create an anchor point; you couldn't do that unless you wet everything down first.

"Sam!" Braden called. "Where the hell are you?"

"I'm inside, Kid!" Sam replied. "Bring that hose in, willya?"

"The Chief said—"

"I know what the Chief said! It's not as bad in here as we thought! But I thought I saw somethin'! Just charge the hose and bring it in!"

Braden knew that the Chief could hear them through his ear mic but did as Sam asked anyway. He wasn't sure he could handle the strength of the hose by himself. Normally it took two firefighters, one, the nozzle man, and the other, the hose man, to control a hose. But Sam wasn't playing by the book now. Braden decided he'd do the best he could. He activated the valve in the hose bed, the flat hose went round, thick, and heavy in the space of a breath. He held the nozzle in front of him, pointing it forward; the hose jerked roughly. It felt like a giant struggling python in his grip, almost throwing him off the ramp where the ground lay three stories down, but he managed to tame it and entered the building.

The ceiling of the lobby was crawling with black smoke that was coming down a hallway at the far end of the room. This hallway went past the washrooms, the cafeteria, and finally into the office space where the cubicles were. He could see bright, glowing yellow flames there; they licked at the air like an army of pointed devil tongues.

He saw Sam halfway down the hallway.

"Sam!" Braden shouted. "Wait for me!"

Sam stopped, looked back at him; Braden's helmet lights showed Sam wasn't wearing his SCBA mask.

"Start layin' it down, Kid!" Sam shouted as he turned back down the hallway.

"Where's your mask, Sam?" Braden shouted.

"I tripped over a chair; it fell off," Sam replied. "Don't worry 'bout me, Kid! I got leather lungs!"

This made it all the more urgent that they put the fire out. Braden secured his feet, opened the nozzle, and began spraying the walls. Even with leather lungs, there was too much smoke. Sam knew this and stopped at the far end of the hallway, just before it widened into the office space.

"I'm going to ventilate!" he said, reached into his coat pocket, turned, and displayed a small pen-sized laser in his right hand. The beam that came out of this was only ten feet in length, unless you put in a more powerful battery. Then its maximum length was twenty to twenty-five feet. That was deemed too long and dangerous in the tight space of a building by the local firefighter union so firefighters weren't allowed to "jack" their lasers up. Thankfully, Sam obeyed this rule, but he either had forgotten or ignored, another important rule. He raised the laser, activated the thin, red beam, and drew a large smoking circle on the ceiling.

Braden watched in horror.

Before a firefighter cut a hole in the ceiling, he was supposed to confirm with an external crew if there was anything on the roof above the spot he was cutting. There was a loud *CRACK!* and a circular section of the ceiling fell down into the hallway. Something had fallen with it...the air conditioning unit. It tumbled down through the ceiling hole Sam had made, fell like a boat anchor, and went crashing through the floor to the level beneath. The black smoke went up through the hole in the ceiling, clearing the lobby almost immediately. But now Sam had cut off his only escape route and had opened a route to the second floor. The fire now had a way to reach the huge filtering machines below, machines that were filled with low temperature flammable oil. The only consolation was that rain was coming down through that hole in the ceiling in a thick, hazy column, drenching everything on the second floor. That gave them a little more time.

"Sonfabitch!" Sam cursed, staring at Braden.

"Christ, Sam, what are you trying to pull here?" Braden asked. "You've got to slow down and follow the Chief's plan."

"Sorry, but I can't, Kid."

"For Godsake, why?"

"There's someone in here. A man. I saw him sitting in a chair in the office as I broke through the glass of the lobby."

"Can you see him now?"

Sam turned back towards the fire. "Yes. I can see him. He's still sitting in that chair."

"Can you reach him?"

"I think so. Wait—" Sam made a move but another section of the opened roof shifted, moaned, and came down, landing ontop of him. He disappeared in a cloud of smoke and debris.

"Sam!" Braden shouted desperately. "Sam!"

Braden quickly shut the hose down, dropped it, and ran into the hallway. He stopped at the wide, gaping hole in the floor, looked down, and saw the reason for the second ceiling collapse. Another air conditioning unit lay dented and smoking on top of the first one. The hole Sam had made probably weakened the roof beams. Braden looked closely, making sure Sam wasn't down there with it. Finding nothing that resembled a human, he glanced back up into the hallway looking for Sam, but all he saw was a pile of debris just beyond the hole in the floor. All of this reminded him of the obstacle course. It seemed too coincidental that he should be facing the same elements again.

"Sam! Do you read me? Sam!" Braden's answer was a long, deafening screech, like the sound a tire makes when it stops too quickly on pavement. The tone rose higher and higher, his heart skipped when he realized what the sound was. Sam's PASS device. It activated when a firefighter didn't move for thirty seconds. It was coming from underneath the pile of debris. He had to get to Sam quickly.

Braden could jump over the hole but he couldn't make the jump back carrying Sam. There was nothing he could use on the walls to grasp onto and climb over. He thought of using the sound dousers to throw the debris off Sam, just like he did in the obstacle course, but he wasn't sure how the human body reacted to such a powerful stream of sound.

The Chief's voice blared through his ear mic. "Braden! Can you locate Sam? We're hearing his PASS device!"

"I can locate him and I can reach him. There's a hole in the floor. I can span it but I won't be able to jump it with Sam on my back," Braden answered. "How are his vitals?"

A few seconds later, the Chief replied, "The detectors in his jacket show he's still alive but his heart rate is slowing. His breathing apparatus is failing. I think he's suffocating."

Suffocating. Damn you, Sam! Braden thought. *Why didn't you stop, pick up your mask, put it back on?*

Braden went back into the lobby, looking for anything that he could drop over the hole to make a bridge. There was a small, kidney-shaped, glass desk, a rolling chair behind it. There was a set of small chairs and a green leather couch against the wall; a square table with magazines on it stood in front of them. Near the elevator door was a fake plant in a plastic pot. Some uninteresting artwork on the walls. Nothing! There was nothing he could use. None of it was long enough.

"Your heart rate has doubled, Kid! You still frosty?" the Chief asked.

"Yeah...I'm still in the game, Chief," Braden answered. His eyes fell upon the hose he'd dropped. In his haste, he hadn't closed the valve off all the way and the water was still coming out of it in a thin, weak stream. He looked out through the broken glass of the lobby façade; the Engine was still hovering there, the ramp down and waiting. He saw the deck guns ontop and the cable winch below the hose bed. Then he turned his eyes back down the hallway.

It's a straight shot. It could work. he thought.

"Chief, I know a way to get Sam out of here."

"Lay it on me, Kid."

"Sorry, no time to waste."

"Affirmative, Kid. You pull this off and live, I'll nominate you for President of the United States."

Sam's PASS device blared like a dying bird now.

Braden ran onto the ramp, stopping at the winch. He unlocked it and pulled the hook free. Then he attached the hook to a metal ring that hung on his breeches where a belt buckle would normally have been. He hoped that the ring was strong enough to hold both his and Sam's weight. After locking the hook, he went back down the ramp and into the lobby. The whole time the winch unrolled a metal cable; it fell loosely behind him on the floor.

Sam's PASS device was whimpering now.

Once he reached the edge of the hole, he turned around and inflated the helium bladders in his jacket; that would make him a little lighter. He went back to the entrance and steadied himself. The storm raged outside. He turned around, stared at the gaping hole for a moment, then he broke into an all-out sprint.

When he made the edge of the hole, he jumped. It all was up to gravity now.

Seventeen

The next few seconds were a blur. He hit the floor but there was a blinding morass of chaos and pain. Something caught his boot as he was rolling over backwards on a wet, but warm, carpet. He slid to a stop, lying there in a daze. Fire and smoke whirled all around him but his muscles didn't seem to work. There was a man's deep voice screaming at him in his ear, but Braden couldn't understand what the voice was saying. Was he dead and was that God yelling at him for stupidly throwing his life away?

No. He was alive because every muscle in his body sizzled with pain. He'd heard that there was no pain in Heaven.

His stomach ached; his back throbbed with fire. He moaned as he tried to catch his breath. Slowly, he was coming back. His mind was coming out of that hazy netherworld where reality and fantasy met like ghostly puzzle pieces.

"Rathman!" the voice yelled. "Rathman! Are you still there? Did you make it?"

Braden recognized the frantic voice finally; it was the Chief. Braden shook his head, blinked his eyes, and sat up on his elbows. He was well into the office space, fire lapped at him like a drinking dog. The air was hot and thick, smelling of burning plastic. He saw the high pile of debris that Sam lay under about twenty feet away from him. He could see one of Sam's boots sticking out at the bottom. The temperature display on his blast shield read 311°F.

"Rathman!"

"I-I'm all right, Chief," Braden said through his teeth as he rolled to his side and slowly stood up. "Be ready with the winch."

"Copy that."

As Braden limped to his buried partner, he looked back to see if he could see the person that Sam had been so sure was there, the whole reason he was now saving Sam's life. He scanned left then right until he saw the blackened figure of a man sitting on a chair in front of a desk. He was silhouetted against a bright flaming backdrop. There was something strange about him, though...he was covered in blue flames and charred beyond recognition, yet he just sat there, straight up in the chair as if he were working on the day's billing. That didn't seem right. Whoever the man was, Braden decided it was too late for him.

Save the living first, that's what he'd been taught.

He turned his attention back to Sam and made it to the pile of debris. Sam's PASS had long since expired. All Braden could hear was the deathly snap and roar of the fire. He began throwing debris off the pile, down through the hole in the floor; torn pieces of drywall, studs with nails in them, sheared electrical conduits, and jagged pieces of tarred roof. Rain was coming down in long curtains, flooding the second floor. That was a good thing, as long as the air down there didn't warm up.

It took him a few minutes, but he finally made it down through the pile to Sam. He dragged his partner away from the hole in the floor by using the drag rescue device, a strap that protruded from under the jacket collar in back.

Sam's body was limp, but it was heavy, over two hundred thirty pounds. Braden's back hurt even more as he pulled him along the wet floor away from the hole. When they were clear, he dropped Sam to the floor and kneeled over him. He pulled an extra portable air pack mask from his jacket pocket and strapped it around Sam's face. Almost immediately, Sam's eyes opened, blinked a few times, then closed again.

"I'm getting a stronger reading on Sam's vitals, Braden," the Chief said.

"Yeah, but he's still not able to help himself. I'm gonna throw him onto my shoulders and I'll let you know when to activate the winch."

"Copy that," the Chief said. "Station 22 has arrived. They're going to start spraying through the office windows on the north side of the building. Better hurry."

It would be like a hurricane in there once they started spraying. Not good. Braden grabbed Sam's wrists, pulled him forward and with one great effort, he brought Sam up onto his shoulders. His legs felt like spaghetti noodles but he fought through it, managing to stand up. He took a step closer to the hole in the floor and saw the metal cable of the winch hanging limply across the hole. There looked to be about five or six feet of slack. Hopefully, that was enough.

Sam weighed down on him, heavy as a house, and Braden knew he couldn't hold him much longer.

"Pull it, Chief!" Braden ordered. "Full on!"

The cable quickly slithered up out of the hole in the floor and rose up towards him, its thin metallic body straightening. He took a few steps forward, felt a violent tug on his waist and leapt forward, letting the powerful motor of the winch do most of the work. His body snapped backwards and he almost lost his grip on Sam, but the flight over the hole was so quick that when he did lose his grip, they were both rolling on the floor on the other side of the hole. The winch was still pulling at Braden's waist, though, he had to tell the Chief to stop the motor. He was halfway out on the ramp by the time it stopped.

Braden unhooked himself and ran back into the lobby where Sam lay face down, his legs and arms spread wide. He heard glass shattering, the hiss of multiple streams entering the building. Station 22 had wasted no time. He and Sam had escaped from there just in time.

"Chief!" Braden cried. "Get the bone box down here. Sam doesn't look too good."

Braden watched as the Engine disappeared from the shattered window of the lobby. Red and blue flashing lights suddenly filled the dark rainy sky outside. The red bulk of the ambulance appeared from above. When its ramp opened he saw Danny standing in the entryway.

"Time to leave this party, my friend," Braden said. He took Sam's drag rescue device in his fist again and dragged him out of the lobby, up the ramp, rain lubricating the way. Once inside the ambulance Danny helped Braden lift Sam onto a stretcher. The ramp closed behind them.

"We're going to land at the staging area in the parking lot," Danny said. "It'll give us a better chance at stabilizing Sam."

Braden felt the ambulance swerving down through the sky. But before they landed, Sam suddenly came to life, thrashing around on the stretcher. He threw his helmet and air-pack off and cursed like a man possessed. Danny held him down. Sam's eyes searched until they found his partner.

"Did you get him, Braden?" Sam asked, his eyes were narrow and desperate. "Did you get that man out?"

"No, Sam," Braden answered. "It was too late. By the time I got across he was charcoal."

"Damn. Damn," Sam muttered and threw his fists down into the cushion of the stretcher.

"Take it easy, Sam," Danny said. "Or I'll have to give you a tranquilizer."

"Won't work on me, Danny boy," Sam muttered. "I'm too mean."

Braden half believed him.

"Relax, Sam," Braden said. "We tried but we can't save them all."

Sam glanced at Braden angrily. "You just don't get it do you, man?"

"Get what? Tell me, Sam."

Sam dropped his head back onto the stretcher and began crying in desperate, painful sobs. He threw his gloves off then covered his face with his hands.

"What is it, Sam?"

"It's—it's the anniversary of my sister's death," he whimpered.

Now it all made sense to Braden...why Sam had been so hyper all night, why he'd rushed blindly into the lobby, his carelessness about the SCBA mask, his valiant effort to save the man in the fire. Sam failing to save that man meant that the promise he'd made to his sister all those years ago was for nothing, especially on the anniversary of the tragedy.

"I'm sorry, Sam," Braden said. He put his hand on Sam's shoulder.

Sam was saying, "I'm sorry. I'm so sorry" underneath his sobs; it broke Braden's heart.

The ambulance landed and the ramp opened. It was still raining like crazy outside. The Engine and the Foam Tender were a few yards away in the parking lot. Suddenly, they were all running out of their vehicles, towards the ambulance. The Chief's white hat seemed to be glowing with its own light. They came up the ramp and stopped at Sam's stretcher. Rain was falling off their helmets onto the floor.

"How is he, Kid?" the Chief asked.

"Pretty bad, Chief," Braden replied. "Did you know it's the anniversary of his sister's death?"

"Yeah," the Chief answered. "This is always the worst day for him."

"I wish somebody told me about it," Braden said.

The Chief looked up and stared him right in the eyes. "Why? Would you have done anything different up there, Kid? Would it have changed anything?"

Braden thought about it and shrugged. "Maybe not. I don't know."

"You did everything you could up there...and more," the Chief said. The others nodded in eager agreement. "You can't take up his cause, Kid. That's his package to carry. Tonight, it almost got him and you killed. He's got a lot of thinking to do. I may have to put him on suspension."

Braden knew the Chief was right.

The Chief looked down at Sam. "You back with us, Sam?" he asked.

Sam had stopped crying and was wiping the tears from his eyes with his hands.

"Yeah, Chief," Sam said. "Sorry about this. You too, Braden. I don't know how the hell we got out of there but I'm sure it was spectacular."

"Just wait until you see the holocube," Paul said, staring in wonder at Braden.

"Yeah," Big George Jackson said. "Your partner comes up with a new wrinkle at every job."

"Lucky for me," Sam said, winking at Braden. "Thanks,

Kid."

"Just live long enough to pay me back sometime," Braden said. He patted Sam's shoulder.

Just then, there was the sound of splashing outside. They all turned to see two firefighters from Station 22 running towards them. One of them was the Chief and the other was carrying something in his arms. It was too dark and rainy to see exactly what it was.

The Chief came up the ramp, shook Chief Kelly's hand.

"Thanks for the backup, Roy," the Chief said.

"No problem," Chief Roy Clifford said. "We got the fire contained and we pulled something out I think might be yours. Found it secured to a chair with duct tape."

"Ours?" the Chief asked. The firefighter behind Chief Clifford made his way through them and dropped something on the empty stretcher next to Sam. Everyone gasped at what they saw. Sam sat up to see for himself.

It looked like a human body: arms, legs, hands, feet, head, but it was charred black and the hair had been burned off. On its left foot was one shoe, apparently untouched by the fire. There were bubbles and blisters in the skin, giving the distinct impression that it wasn't really a human being. In fact, sand was coming out from one of the blisters.

"What the hell?" the Chief said.

Sam leaned forward so he could better see.

"Is this what you saw in the fire?" the Chief asked Sam.

"Sure looks like it," Sam answered.

The Chief went over to the stretcher and lifted one of its feet, the one with the shoe. He took the shoe off, revealing a perfectly pink and healthy foot. He looked at the bottom of the foot and his eyes went large with surprise. He turned the foot so that they could all see it: *Property of Chicago Engine Station 85.*

"It's Victor, the Victim!" Joni exclaimed, fearfully stepping back, her mouth open in fright.

Braden inspected it for himself. He knew that both of Victor's feet were stamped with that in case one of the feet fell off and was lost. The other foot was too badly burned to read. He recognized the red ink and how the "y" in *property* was missing because of Victor's arch.

"What the hell is it doing here?" Paul Rose asked.

"And how did it get here?" Mo asked.

They all shook their heads.

Braden thought about it; this job was phoned in by another anonymous caller. Someone had illegally gained entrance to the station house and stole Victor, or had they? Braden didn't think Stan Winslow had balls enough to do it all on his own. He needed help. Was it possible there was a mole in the station, someone working with Stan? Braden glanced at each one of them carefully but they betrayed no sign of suspiciousness. They each seemed genuinely upset about what had just been revealed. But what if he told them of his suspicions about Stan and one of them was a mole? He couldn't trust anyone yet, not even the Chief. Braden decided to keep it to himself until the right time presented itself.

"Looks like we've been set-up again," Thom said.

"Yeah," Chief Clifford said. "There was a barrel, apparently brought up from the first floor, found open, lying near one of the desks. It didn't take us long to figure this job as arson. Residue stains are everywhere around the room."

News vans from every local channel were rolling into the parking lot now like some modern caravan; their tires were squealing. The weather was too rough for flying so they were roughing it. Braden saw the Channel 7 News van and flashed a concerned look at his partner. Sam saw the van too but shrugged it off.

"What are they doing here?" the Chief asked impatiently, everyone shrugged in ignorance.

Braden ignored the spectacle outside and just stared at the charred, smoking remains of Victor. He'd truly become a victim. It made Braden's stomach churn. Finding Victor here in the fire was obviously a signal to him. Whoever this madman was, he *was* after Braden.

"Poor bastard," Sam said, staring at Victor.

"Yeah," Braden murmured, his mind still deep in thought, very upset at where it was taking him.

Reporters and cameramen were running through the rain towards the ambulance. The Chief's face turned red.

"Looks like the cat's out of the bag, people," the Chief said. "Let's hope we have nine lives."

A beautiful blond ran up the ramp. She wore a heavy, red wool coat and galoshes. It was Kathryn Gold from Channel 7. The Chief put his arm out but she struggled to get past.

"I can't let you in here, Ms. Gold," the Chief said.

She stopped and looked up at him. Her eyes were glazed over with tears, her mascara was running down her cheeks in long, thick black streams.

"I'm not here as a reporter, Chief," she said in a low, barely controlled voice. "I'm here as a concerned…" she looked at Sam, "friend."

The Chief stood there, confused and speechless.

Sam jumped off the stretcher. "Let her through, Chief," he said. "She's here to see me."

The Chief glanced back at Sam and then his eyes brightened as it all became clear to him.

"My apologies, Ms. Gold," he said as he stepped aside.

Kathryn Gold ran past him and into Sam's open arms as a flood of reporters appeared in the parking lot outside. They came on like a tidal wave, Chief Kelly and Chief Clifford blocked the entry way off so that they couldn't see one of their own in the arms of a possible story. Conflict of interest came to Braden's mind but he wasn't sure of the rules that journalists had to abide by nowadays. There were so few of them, bias not being one of them anymore.

Braden watched as Sam and Kathryn kissed. Everybody else in the back of the ambulance glared in shock.

"I was listening to the scanner and heard what was going on up there. I was so worried, knowing what day it was," she whispered, trying to hold back tears. Braden hadn't known that they were so deeply involved with each other. He thought that because of their busy lives, it was just a casual sex thing. Apparently, it wasn't.

"You're not supposed to hack into our bandwidth, Kath," Sam said. "It's illegal—"

"Shut up, lover," she said and kissed him long and hard this time.

Braden, feeling a bit uncomfortable, made his way around the two lovers. He, Danny, and Debbie went forward into the cockpit to give them some privacy. But Victor, The Victim lay on the stretcher near them, black, charred, and silent.

Eighteen

The man was wet and exhausted. He'd been running through the heavy downpour, taking the well-rehearsed path through the darkened alleys and little used back streets, trying to stay invisible. So far, everything had gone as planned. The only thing that kept his exhaustion from stopping him was the excitement of watching the holocube when he got home.

If Rathman made it through this one, the calling card the man had left him should unnerve him enough to scramble his thinking, make him jump to the wrong conclusion. Then he could put his backup plan into action. He almost wished Rathman had survived, the backup plan he'd conceived sounded deliriously fun and worth the effort. But there was little chance Rathman had survived. The warehouse was a bomb primed to blow.

The man was almost home now. He sped up his pace. As he came out of an alley and hurried down the empty city street, he threw the small disposable, untraceable cell phone he'd juiced up into an open garbage can. He heard it splinter into a thousand useless pieces. He remembered that, as he left the warehouse, he'd upped the ante, calling in the three major news networks. He gave them his name, the *Chicago Fire Man*. It just came off the top of his head and he was delirious about it. He'd be known as the Jack the Ripper of arsonists. He knew that the police were trying to keep what had been going on quiet as they tried to catch him, but the man had outsmarted them. The reporters should've been at the scene by now, pestering everyone to no end. He smiled at the chaos he imagined he'd created. And the frustration. He knew that they felt helpless and clueless, not knowing the why's, where's, and who's. It made him want to scream out in joy. He could do anything he wanted. They'd never find him!

His apartment was up ahead. He turned down the alley, went around back, and used the rear door. Instead of taking the elevator (there were security cameras in there), he took the fire stairs. It was eight floors but that was nothing to the man; he could do it without legs. Even though his feet felt heavy and his coat was drenched with rainwater, he treaded lightly, making little noise. He left large, wet footprints on the linoleum tile but that didn't matter to him. No one who'd see them would connect the prints to the *Chicago Fire Man.*

Once he made it to his floor he cautiously peered through the small square window near the top of the door. He'd unscrewed the security lights at both ends of the hallway before he left. No one had seen this yet; the hallway was still dark. He brought his left wrist up, pressed the illumination button on his watch, and discovered he'd been gone less than an hour. He was ecstatic. That was better than the three rehearsal drills he'd completed.

There were seven other apartments up here besides his and he'd planned accordingly. As quietly as he could, the man opened the door, slipped through. The door made no sound because he'd oiled the hinges after the first rehearsal. Before, the squeals from the door sounded like mating dolphins; he couldn't have that. Instead of letting the door close itself under its hydraulic arm, he grabbed the knob and held it firmly, closing it himself so that the bolt made no noise. Then he slowly crept down the hallway, keeping as close to the left wall as possible because the floorboards there made no sound. He'd left his apartment door unlocked; it was a risk, especially in this neighborhood, but it was a risk he had to take. He went in, gently closing the door behind him. It was dark and it didn't seem like anyone was in there with him.

He'd made it! His body trembled with goose flesh as he threw his coat off and went into the kitchen to grab himself a beer. That's all he ever kept in the fridge because he always ate out. No need for anything else in there. When he opened the fridge he saw that he was down to his last three beers. He'd have to go out tomorrow, remedy that. But first things first...

The man popped the tab and took a long satisfying pull from the can; it was a celebration, after all. After stretching his arms, he sat on his couch. He kept the room darkened while he found the holocube remote on the cushion next to him. He picked it up and turned on the Channel 7 Nightly News. Kathryn Gold's beautiful face hung in the air before him. She was interviewing Chief Kelly in the rain about the *Chicago Fire Man*.

The man took a deep swallow from the can and grinned pleasantly.

"Just who do you think the *Chicago Fire Man* is, Chief Kelly? A disgruntled firefighter? A sick teenager who likes matches?" she asked.

"I couldn't comment on that, Kathryn. I have no answer for that," the Chief replied.

"Why do you think the *Chicago Fire Man* chose this warehouse?"

"Don't know, Kathryn, maybe he's got something against recycling oil."

The Chief was good at deflecting the questions Kathryn Gold bombarded him with, feigning ignorance of the *Chicago Fire Man,* successfully throwing the attention back to his loyal and brave firefighters who'd again saved hundreds of thousands of dollars of property from another unfortunate fire. Then, to the man's unending frustration, Kathryn Gold turned and began interviewing Rathman.

He was still alive!

As she talked to him, the further exploits of Braden Rathman filled the air in the man's living room using video from Braden's own helm cam; the rescue of the Mayor's daughter from the Mayor's residence...*yep, that was me!* The boat that exploded on Lake Michigan...*me again!* And tonight's dramatic warehouse fire...*Bingo, moi! But that spoiled little bastard was supposed to die in those fires. He was supposed to die! The kid had more luck than a rabbit's foot in a field of four leafed clovers.*

The man knew that they'd found Victor by now and he knew Braden was smart enough to take it as the warning it was designed for. But he also knew that the kid was thinking things through and had come to a particular conclusion. He was asking himself *how did Victor, The Victim disappear from his comfortable little locker in the station and get here? Was there an inside man?*

Yes, Rathman is smart, the man thought. *But I have the*

element of surprise. He doesn't know what's coming next.

The man looked on the floor by the bedroom door. The gear for his next adventure sat there neatly stacked: night vision goggles, a SCBA unit he was given by his oblivious inside contact, a black fireproof body suit, black boots, black gloves, a tightly packed black parachute, four cans of military smoke cover, and a small canister of cyanide.

This next one is going to be fun. I'll be there, face-to-face, to kill him. I'll make sure of it this time. I'll watch him die and then I'll escape and they'll never catch me.

A file interview with Braden appeared in the flickering three dimensions of the holo. It was an interview taken right after Rathman saved the Mayor's daughter; his face was dirty with black soot and he still seemed a little shaken about jumping out that thirtieth floor window... "Just doing my job," he said. "That's all any of us ever do: our job."

The man snarled and threw the beer can at Braden but it went right through the holo, smashing into the wall beyond. He stood up and marched angrily to the window. The thunderstorm had finally washed over the city; all that was left of it was the faint rumblings of thunder and sharp white flashes of lighting far to the east. He saw the brilliantly lit white dome of the station in the distance. He squeezed his fist so tight that his knuckles popped.

Just doing your job, the man thought. *My ass. You're in it for the fame and glory, Rathman. Fame and glory that should've been mine. That'll all change next time, pal...believe me.*

The man stared at the drenched, black, sleeping city below and grinned again. He imagined all of it a tinderbox aflame, people screaming and jumping out of windows, children and pets burning like kindling...but he'd save them all. It was his city, after all. It was his rightful glory. He'd save them all.

Nineteen

When they got back to the station, the Mayor's Chief of Staff, Patrick Perry, was standing outside the door to the conference room. He was dressed in a brown suit and tie; even this late at night he looked pressed and clean. He held a palm-comp in his left hand while talking into an ear mic as he watched them all getting out of their vehicles. His face was a mass of worried wrinkles.

The Chief moaned. "The Mayor is here," he said aloud.

"Probably Heany, too," Braden murmured.

"Yeah, and he's probably real happy about the media coverage we got on that last job," Sam said sardonically.

"Or about your secret relationship with the city's top news anchor," Braden countered playfully.

"I'm getting a really bad headache," the Chief murmured as he rubbed his temples.

Patrick Perry hurried towards them, his little legs chugging so fast you couldn't see them moving. Then he stopped in front of the Chief and shook his hand.

"Hello again, Chief," he said. "Nice work tonight. The Mayor and Chief of Police Heany are in the conference room. They want to talk to all of you."

"Just let us gear down; we'll be right in, Patrick," the Chief said.

"Of course. Thank you, Chief," Patrick said and scuttled through the door into the conference room.

"I don't need this tonight," the Chief mumbled as they stood in their gear assignment cubicles and began stripping down.

"None of us do," Braden said.

"What do you think they want?" Paul Rose asked.

"I'm sure they're not too happy about our Mr. Chicago Fire Man," Sam answered, staring Braden down, daring him to bring up Kathryn Gold again. But Braden only smirked, remaining quiet.

The Chief moaned again.

They had stripped down to their gray T-shirts, shorts, and socks. They all needed showers but the Chief nixed that.

"Mayor first, showers later," he said.

This didn't go over to well with them. They smelled of burning oil and soot and were still sweating from the exertion of the job. But they went into the conference room anyway, finding the Mayor and Heany standing where the Chief usually stood, at the head of the table. They were whispering to each other, as if planning the play that would win the Super Bowl. Patrick Perry stood against the wall in the back of the room watching everything carefully with his little beady eyes through thick round glasses. His arms were folded and he tapped a finger nervously.

Braden sat down in his seat and glanced at Heany. With his long overcoat off, Heany looked even larger than he had on that snowy roof back in January. Heany and the Mayor straightened themselves up, then nodded at them. Everyone could see the consternation on their faces.

"First of all, good work tonight, people," the Mayor said. "Especially you, Mr. Rathman. You never fail to surprise me."

"Thank you, Your Honor," Braden said.

"Mr. Maxwell," the Mayor said, his eyes firmly on Sam. "It has come to our attention that you are quite close with a certain city news anchor. Is that going to become a problem in the future?"

Sam shook his head. "No, sir," he answered. He knew that there were policies against such a thing, conflicts of interest and legalities he never understood. But it looked as if the Mayor was giving him a break and wasn't going to dwell on it.

"Good," the Mayor said. "Make sure that it doesn't."

Sam nodded respectfully.

"Now, I am here with Chief of Police Heany tonight because the situation with this so-called Chicago Fire Man has gotten out of control. Because of the recent press coverage, the people of this city are scared, on the brink of riot, and I have to be in on everything about it so I can figure out how to deal with it. If we can't stop this sick bastard and pandemonium breaks out, there aren't enough firefighters in the city to put the flames out. So, just forget that I'm here. I'm one of you tonight, listening and learning. Heany, the floor is yours."

Heany smiled nervously. "Thank you, Your Honor," he said. He looked out over the table; his eyes narrowed as he focused. "Obviously, the Mayor and I weren't pleased at the media coverage of the event tonight—"

"We had nothing to do with it, Heany," Chief Kelly interrupted, his voice on the verge of red-hot anger.

"We know that, my friend," Heany said. "The Chicago Fire Man called it in to the press himself. Apparently he feels like he isn't getting enough credit. That makes this man extremely dangerous."

The Chief cursed under his breath.

"Can't you trace his phone calls?" Joni asked.

"He uses a disposable cell phone. He's mobile when he makes his calls to your station and to the press. That way, by the time we triangulate the signal and find out where he called from, he's gone. In fact, when he called in the boat fire, your dispatcher, Stacey, quickly traced it back and discovered that the Fire Man made the call from the boat itself just before he set it on fire."

"But it was in the middle of Lake Michigan and we were on scene in minutes. No one was around," Braden said.

"Yes," Heany said. "He is either an experienced diver or had some kind of underwater travel device. Probably a military frog-sub or something along those lines. Your evidence of military C-4 used in that blast set us in that direction, Rathman. In fact, every bit of evidence we've accrued suggests that the Chicago Fire Man is an ex-military man. Unfortunately, there wasn't much left of the *King Joshua* to process; most of it is still in little pieces at the bottom of Lake Michigan. This man knows what he's doing when it comes to covering his tracks."

"But what's his motive for all of this? Is he crazy?" Debbie asked.

"His motive could be anything. We don't think he's crazy. We think he's very angry, especially at Station 85."

"But why? What have we done to him?" Joni asked. No one answered her.

Braden wanted to answer her. He wanted to tell them that he knew it was Stan Winslow. He knew it in his bones but he couldn't speak up about it. Not yet.

"We did manage to trace the *King Joshua* back to a man named Greg Tornquist. He owns a boat and yacht selling business named *Boat & Float Forever* in Lake Forest. During our interview he told us that a man in his mid-twenties bought the *King Joshua* back in April. But there was something strange about him. Mr. Tornquist said that the man was wearing a cheesy disguise, messy black wig, fake mustache, even dark make-up put on unevenly. It was really obvious. If it wasn't for the fact that the man, who referred to himself as Peter, bought the boat with cash, he would've called the police."

"How much did he pay?" the Chief asked.

"Seventy-five thousand dollars."

Everyone gasped. Who paid seventy-five thousand dollars cash for a boat anymore? Everything over the cost of a lunch was credit nowadays. The answer was; *someone who didn't want to be traced.* Cash left no footprints.

"Didn't that amount of money make the business owner suspicious?" Sam asked.

"It did, so he asked this Peter what he did for a living. Peter told him he was a software developer. Of course, knowing how much a software developer makes and how eccentric they can be, well, all the red flags blew away in the wind. Tornquist took the money and ran. I guess he's got a mortgage to pay."

"So, this Peter lead is a dead end?" the Chief asked.

"I'm afraid so," Heany answered.

"All right, so what we have here is a rich, angry, ex-military man in his mid-twenties with an axe to grind against us," Sam said. It wasn't a question.

"Yes," Heany said. "Now does anyone here have anything else we can work with? Maybe something strange you saw in one of those arsons?"

The Chief, with Braden's permission, told Heany of Braden's concerns about being sabotaged in the obstacle course.

"You think you may be the target, Rathman?" Heany asked.

"It's possible, sir," Braden answered. He had to be careful not to give it all away. "I mean, it seemed like I was the one the C-4 on that boat was meant to kill. Even Sam thought so. Whoever set that trap knew it was my turn to lead the primary search and he knew it would be Station 85 responding to the call that day. I also believe finding Victor, the Victim in that fire was a clear signal to me. It was supposed to be a lure or a warning, but it snagged the wrong fish," Braden looked at Sam.

"That's not much to go on but at least it's something. We'll look into it," Heany said. "Anyone else?"

No one moved.

"Thank you for your time," Heany said, putting his coat back on. "I'll keep the Chief informed if we find anything else. Take care of yourselves."

"All right then, people," the Chief began, taking a position next to Heany and the Mayor. "I've ordered Stacey to route any anonymous calls up to me personally so I can filter them myself. It's up to you guys to stay safe. You're the best the city has to offer but it's getting dangerous out there, so be careful."

They all followed Mayor Daley, Patrick Perry, and Heany out of the conference room. The Chief led the Mayor and Patrick Perry to the elevator and went down with them while everyone else hit the showers. While the others were in the showers Braden took his cell phone from its perch on the shelf in his gear assignment cubicle and called Amy. He missed her voice and wanted to see how little Evie was doing. When she picked up the phone, Amy sounded frantic. She'd seen the video of his rescue of Sam on the news and wasn't pleased.

"You promised me you wouldn't be taking as many risks, Brad," she said.

"I know, babe. But I had to this time," Braden retorted. "Sam would be dead—"

"I know. I know. But what about us, Brad? What if you do something really crazy next time and don't make it out? Will you be lucky enough to have someone save you? Do you think Evie wants to grow up without a father? Do you think I want to be a widow?"

It was a horrible thought. He realized that Amy had been

thinking about this a lot lately. There was really nothing he could say to her except that he was a fireman, had always wanted to be a fireman, and this was the only way he knew how to be a fireman. Thankfully, she didn't know the full details on what had really been going on the past few weeks.

"Look, honey, I know where you're coming from but I'll be fine, no matter what happens."

"How do you know that? Are you psychic? Are you invincible? Are you really this Superman the news makes you out to be?"

"No, but—"

"Then don't tell me that you're going to be all right. This is the real world and people die in the real world."

She was right, of course. Braden didn't know what else to say to her. Amy went onto talk about terrible things like what life would be like without him, that she and Evie would have to go on somehow and live, that it was always harder for those left behind. Then the anger in her voice suddenly gave way to sadness and she began weeping. Braden tried to comfort her, but finally the conversation had reached its inevitable end. They said their *I love you 's* and hung up.

Braden went to the showers to cool off.

Twenty

It was midnight on Sunday, a week after July 4th, when the station's alarm sounded throughout the bunkroom. Its multi-toned blare rattled their bones to the marrow. They leapt out of bed and raced to the assignment areas where their bunker gear lay waiting.

It had been a lazy, calm evening in the station house; all of them had fallen asleep early and easily because of it. Now, as they struggled to put their gear on, that heavy sleep was difficult to shed. Braden felt clumsy and sluggish as he put his feet into the boots, nearly falling over forward, not quite fully awake yet. Sam kept a squeeze bottle full of water on his shelf for just this situation and briskly squeezed the cold contents onto his face.

Braden saw this and thought it was a great idea.

"Hey! Give me some of that, willya?" he asked, holding his hand out.

Sam shook his head, throwing splashes of water everywhere, squeezing what was left of the bottle into Braden's startled face. Water went up Braden's nose, into his open mouth, and all over his face. When the bottle was empty, Sam laughed, dropped it to the floor, and began gearing up.

"Thanks, jerkoff!" Braden said through wet coughs, but he was awake now.

"Be careful what you ask for, my friend!" Sam said. They both laughed.

The Chief, stumbling out from the bunk in his office, stopped in his assignment area and began suiting up.

"Looks like we've got another anonymous tip, people!" he

shouted impatiently. "Better wake up quicker than that! You think our Fire Man is sleeping? Hell no! He's been up all night waiting for us; let's not disappoint him!"

That rallying cry reminded them of the danger they faced. It snapped them out of their sleepy daze. In under sixty seconds they were in their assigned vehicles and darting through the clear, cool night sky, sirens crying, lights flashing.

From his vantage point in his rear seat in the Engine, Braden could see that the Chief was concerned. The old man was frowning; his eyes were dark.

"What's the job, boss?" Sam asked.

"Get this!" the Chief replied, bringing an image up on a screen on the dashboard. One of the icons of the city skyline appeared, its two tall antennae lit a bright yellow, stuck up like the blades of a giant pitchfork. There were police cruisers circling the building's high, narrow, black structure, painting it with beams of white light. Braden saw thick clouds of smoke coming out of a single window from one of the uppermost floors on the east side, but he couldn't see the distinctive yellow glow of a fire anywhere.

"The Sears Tower," the Chief confirmed. "The fire seems to be seated on the one hundred and third floor; the Skydeck Observatory. Heany and his men will be circling the building, keeping an eye on things while we take care of business. But don't get careless just because they're there. Chances are the Fire Man has planned for them."

Braden agreed, very grateful that Heany's men were backing them up.

The Sears Tower. Braden knew all about it: fourteen hundred fifty-four feet tall, one hundred and ten stories, takes up one hundred twenty-nine thousand square feet on a city block, built with seventy-six thousand tons of steel and sixteen thousand bronze tinted windows. There were two dozen restaurants inside, hundreds of apartment and office spaces, shopping malls, fully stocked grocery stores, clothing stores, shoe stores, every store, in fact, that one could imagine. It was an entire city inside a city. No wonder it took three years to build. It was one of the great building achievements of the last half of the twentieth century. It was called Willis Tower for a while but purists wouldn't let the original name be forgotten. Braden knew all of that yet couldn't remember if the building had ever caught fire before.

It stood like a giant black monolith in the purple night sky and was growing bigger, blacker, with each passing second. The city below it was so far down that the soft yellow lights coming up in between the black buildings actually illuminated no details. It looked like some ethereal, glowing, yellow fog, resembling one of those new electrically-powered oil paintings in the Art Institute.

"Man, are we up there!" Sam shouted, squealing like a dog in heat.

Braden recalled, as they approached the lumbering hulk, that a person could see sixty miles in all directions from the Skydeck Observatory on a clear day.

"We sure are, Sammy Boy!" he shouted back at his partner with a smile.

Braden felt good. He felt confident. Just knowing that this was another trap set him at ease for some reason. All he and Sam had to do was watch each other's backs, put the fire out, then get the hell out of there. Let the police take care of it after that.

The Chief glanced back at Braden. "The Observatory Deck's sprinkler system is dropping down a pretty good curtain in there so it's gonna be wet. You and Sam take the first search and lay down an anchor point. Once you guys contain everything, come out and we'll send Mo and Big George in to mop up."

"Copy that, Chief," Braden said.

Joni swung the Engine around the great black beast, slowly coming up on the east side where the broken window was billowing smoke into the air. Braden and Sam positioned themselves in front of the closed ramp, holding tightly to the ceiling straps, and waited for it to drop. They glanced at each other.

"Two in, two out!" Sam shouted.

"Always!" Braden shouted back. They bumped fists and the ramp hissed as it came down.

Joni had the deck guns aimed right into the smoke coming out of the window, revealing that the entire window was absent. It was as if someone had come up and removed it cleanly. There were no glassy jagged edges around the ten-by-twelve-foot window frame, nothing in fact, to prove that a window had actually ever been installed there. The two thick white streams of water coming from the deck guns pushed the smoke back and did an excellent job at clearing the way for them.

"Okay, Joni," Sam said into his ear mic. "We got enough for penetration. Lose the lube."

"Oh, honey, you say the sweetest things to me." Joni joked. The two streams of water became flaccid then petered out entirely.

Sam turned to Braden. "OOOOEEEE! Joni's primo at what she does. It's a good thing I'm dating a gorgeous news anchor or she might have to put out for me."

"Yeah?" Braden snickered. "The only thing she'd put out is your lights."

"Ow! That hurts, Kid!" Sam said, pretending to be shot in the heart.

"You know what they say, Sam?" Joni interrupted. "The truth hurts."

"But, baby—"

The Chief's voice broke in. "All right, enough of the foreplay, kids. Let's get to that G-Spot before she cools down."

"Aw, copy that, Dad...I mean, Chief," Sam said.

Braden and Sam traded guffaws, attached their SCBA masks, then each of them pulled out two inch hoses from the hose bed. They charged the lines quickly and ran across the ramp with gleaming nozzles in their gloves. Braden broke to the left, Sam to the right. The room was dark; the smoke was still thick but, in some areas, it seemed to be thinning out under the intense bombardment of the ceiling sprinkler system. Yet Braden could feel no ambient heat. The temperature display on his blast shield read a normal eighty two degrees. That couldn't be right.

"That's strange," Braden said aloud.

"What is it, Kid?" Sam asked from somewhere in the smoky darkness of the room.

"It's too cool for there to be so much smoke in here."

There was a moment of silence while Same checked his own display.

"You're right, Kid," Sam said. "There's so much smoke I can barely see a foot in front of me."

Braden's boots made squishy sounds in the wet carpet as he

came to a window. He had an idea: he dropped the hose, lifted his gloved hand, then he smudged his open palm across it in one long swipe, holding his hand in front of him. The beam on his helmet showed that there was no soot on the fingertips of his glove. Judging from all the smoke, if something had been burning in there, there would have been a thick layer of soot residue covering the glass, even with the sprinklers going. He knelt down and inspected the wet carpet. No soot there either. Then what was causing the smoke?

He stood up again and looked around; smoke billowed in great black traveling heaps. It was like being in one of those huge corn mazes. He was cut off physically from Sam, many yards from the window that ventilated the smoke, his only escape route. Suddenly, that confidence he'd felt earlier was gone and the bones in his legs froze. It was a trap all right, and they'd fallen right into it even knowing it was a trap.

"Sam," Braden said. "Something's not right here."

"Whaddaya mean, Kid?"

"This smoke...it's not real—"

"Fake smoke, Kid? Never heard of such a thing."

"I mean it's not from something burning."

"Then where's it comin' from?"

"I don't know, the ventilation system?" Braden's foot kicked something. It sounded like a soda can as it rolled heavily along the wet carpet. Braden leaned over, following the heavy sound. After a few steps he saw it. It was a black cylinder, thick black smoke was coming out of the top. On the side of it, stenciled in white letters, was *U.S. Military.*

"Smoke cans...they're smoke cans, Sam! Military! Get back to the Engine! I'm on my way!"

"Copy that, Kid."

Braden stood up again and turned, but he saw something move out of the corner of his eye. It was to his left and was so sudden that it looked like a separate arm of smoke had disappeared into the main body. It was black but its movement seemed deliberate, almost human. He heard the distinctive sound of rushing footsteps squishing heavily on the wet carpet. The sound was getting closer to him.

The Fire Man is here!

There was another sudden movement, closer this time, on his right side, but again, it was too quick to trace with his eyes.

There's too much damn smoke in too big a room. He could be standing right next to me and I wouldn't know it, Braden thought. *I've got to make it back to the window. It's my only chance.*

"Braden! Your heart rate is off the charts. What's going on?" It was the Chief's voice coming through his ear mic.

Before Braden could answer, an alarm blared from his jacket. It startled him so badly he became dizzy.

Is that my PASS device? he thought. *No! It can't be! I'm still moving and besides, it's a different tone...*

The display on his blast shield flashed and the words "HYDROGEN CYANIDE GAS DETECTED—EXIT AREA IMMEDIATELY" appeared in a long rolling red scroll. It completed two rolls before the realization came to him that he'd better move.

Hydrogen cyanide gas could kill in a matter of seconds; if not for his SCBA mask, he would've been long dead. Braden's mind raced a million miles per hour. *Get out! Get out!* was all that was going through his mind. The smoke had thinned out much more but it was still thick enough to confuse his sense of direction. He saw that frightening shadowy movement out of the corners of his eyes again. In his panic, he'd forgotten he could ask Joni to throw him a GPS map on his blast shield that would lead him to safety. He'd forgotten that he could use the sound dousers to push the smoke away to clear a path. He'd forgotten almost everything that he'd trained almost a year for.

He lifted his arms; they felt like hundred-pound dumbbells, and he put his right hand against the window. He exhaled in relief.

There. If I follow this wall of windows, it will lead me back to the ramp, he thought. *Just keep following it. That's right. It can't be much farther away.*

He could hear everyone trying to talk at once through his ear mic. Someone asked where the cyanide alarm came from; someone else screamed about extrication.

"Kid!" Sam yelled through his ear piece. "You've got to get your ass out of there! I'm coming back in to get you!"

Braden's vocal chords were too frozen with fear to tell Sam not to come in. But he knew Sam would come and get him anyway to pay off that old debt from the warehouse fire gone wrong.

There was another movement on his left; he turned his head and his helmet beam fell upon a tall muscular figure dressed all in black. It was obviously a man; his shoulders were too big to be otherwise. He wore a strange mask with goggles, like a diver wears, but Braden couldn't see the man's eyes through the darkened, alien-like goggles. There was a strap that crossed the man's chest like an "X" which meant he was wearing a backpack of some kind. Braden took all of this in in about a second because the man suddenly reached out, grabbed Braden's helmet, and threw him across the room. He slid across the wet floor, into a part of the room that was relatively clear of smoke.

He lay there a moment then realized his helmet was gone. The hydrogen cyanide alarm shrieked horribly. He reached up, felt for his SCBA mask. It was still there. He sat up and saw large picture windows lining the walls. The long white search beams of the police cruisers crisscrossing outside in what seemed to be confused, random patterns, appeared sharply through the window. Didn't they know he was in here and under attack by a maniac? Hadn't they seen what was going on through his helm cam? The deafening chatter in his ear mic didn't reflect that at all.

He looked at his feet and saw a metallic, fist-sized canister marked with an orange skull and cross bones decal. The screw-top lid was off, lying next to the canister on the wet carpet. Hydrogen cyanide gas! He was less than a foot from certain death.

The mask! The bastard is after my mask!

Braden heard something behind him; he turned his head. The figure in black moved out of the smoke like a panther in the jungle. Every move he made was sleek, graceful, and with a deadly purpose. There was something familiar about those movements, though. He'd seen them before but he couldn't attach a face or identity with it. The black figure came at Braden in a flash. There was a tug on Braden's face and before he knew it, his mask was gone.

Instinctively, Braden had sucked in a wad of fresh oxygen before the mask was ripped away. He held his breath, but he wasn't particularly good at doing that. He probably had a minute plus a few seconds before he'd give in. It depended on how fast his heart was beating, using up all that oxygen. He had to think of something. He did. He had been a thespian in high school, playing the lead in many of the dramas. He began pretending to choke and convulse. He bugged his eyes out as far as they would go. The dark figure stood by the window, staring at him with those emotionless black eyes.

Then Braden lay his head down and stopped convulsing. The whole time, voices were streaming frantically into his ear mic like a studio audience in an earthquake. He closed his eyes and lay still. After a few moments Braden heard footsteps getting closer. Then he felt hands grabbing his jacket and pulling at it violently. The Fire Man was going through his pockets. What was he looking for?

Finally, the pulling, the violence stopped, and Braden heard the footsteps going away again. Good thing, too, he was running out of breath. A few more seconds and the jig was up. He opened his eyes and watched the black figure cutting a large hole in a window with Braden's laser blade, all the way to the floor.

What the hell is he doing?

The man finished his circuit, threw the laser blade away, and kicked the window out. The glass fell forward, toppling over as it dropped away. The long blades of white light coming from the police cruisers still didn't seem to be alerted to what was going on in there.

The pack on the Fire Man's back was too large to be just a backpack. A parachute! It was a parachute! The man looked back, making sure Braden still lay dead, then he jumped through the hole he'd made in the window.

Braden, unable to hold his breath any longer, exhaled loudly and scrambled to the window. What was that odor...almonds? Bitter almonds? He took one desperate breath and held it as he made for the window. Already, he felt his throat constricting. There was a terrible burning in his eyes. It was only a few feet to the window but it seemed like a mile. Braden's elbows and knees felt like they were going to explode, the muscles in his entire body were frying in pain. He forced himself to that window and its gloriously fresh, life-giving air. He saw his baby girl's innocent, new face looking up at him, smiling. He saw Amy's face looking up at him alongside Evie. They were both smiling at him and he wanted them to stay that happy forever. Now they were fading, as if someone twisted the dimming switch on the wall. Fading, darkening.

Something cool and breezy splashed into his face. He

opened his eyes. He was looking face down over the city; his head had made it out through the hole in the window. He saw a black, rectangular object slowly falling away from him, towards the foggy yellow valleys of the city. The parachute. It shrank as it fell towards the glowing yellow streetlights of the city below. It caught a gust of wind, veered to the south, then gracefully disappeared into the shadows of the buildings.

Finally, the police cruiser lights found Braden. They all met at his body at once. There was more frantic shouting in his ear mic but he didn't care about that anymore. His entire body burned yet he knew there was no fire. The fire was inside, in his lungs, in his blood stream.

Despite the bright lights and all the noise in his ear, everything faded away. That dimming switch was slowly going all the way down to black.

Twenty One

The man had to free fall a little longer than he'd planned but it worked. He didn't open the parachute until he was well underneath the mass of circling police cruisers and their searching beams of light. He couldn't believe they didn't see him. He had either been extremely lucky, or they were inept clods.

A sudden updraft of wind coming up from the streets of the city pushed the man's parachute west as he descended. He wanted to go east. His mark was the empty baseball fields in Grant Park. *The farther from the Sears Tower, the better,* he thought. *But don't panic. Panicking will kill you. Control the situation. That's how you were trained.*

Already, he'd glided past Van Buren Street and was coming perilously close to crashing into the roof of an office building. He had to raise his feet as he skimmed over the building but he cleared it, barely. He was thankful there were no chimney pipes or clothes lines. The south arm of the Chicago River appeared below him; it ran like a long river of black ink in a dotted landscape of white light below. It stretched away from him as far as he could see. He passed high over the Eisenhower Expressway and saw it painted with the headlights of ground cars. Above him he saw the Skyway, glittering with flashing safety lights. The beauty of the city at night stunned him, taking his breath away. It was like looking at an unimaginably large Christmas tree on the Fourth of July. All the miracles of modern human technology were displayed around him and the man knew that if an alien ship came down from space, seeing what he saw, the aliens would feel the same way about it as he did. Yes, it was beautiful, but the man had a task to finish. He threw this silly penchant for sightseeing from his mind. He had to stay focused.

He still hadn't been seen and with every police cruiser in the city circling the Sears Tower, all he had to do was fight the swirling current, head east, and make a safe landing at his mark. After that it would be like water running over a pebble. Especially with Rathman finally out of the way.

Oh, it was the sweetest thing he'd ever seen, watching that punk squirming and heaving there on the floor, dying that horribly painful death. God bless whoever invented cyanide gas. And his eyes! The way they bulged out of Rathman's sockets and the limitless fear the man saw in them, it made him boldly laugh out. Revenge was the sweetest thing in the world. When Rathman finally gave up the ghost and lay there, still and limp, his skin pale and lifeless like a wax figure, the man felt born again, into a free and beautiful world. The man, his bloodstream still charged with adrenaline, shrieked out in joy. His plan had gone perfectly; now the rest was up to him.

Ahead, Roosevelt Road appeared, lit brightly with ground traffic. He knew that if he crossed over that he was too far south and would have to double back, against the wind. He didn't relish the thought of fighting the crosscurrents coming off Lake Michigan if he should have to head northeast. It would tear him and the parachute to pieces.

The man pulled long and hard on the left drawstring. The parachute fought him but it finally began to respond; he felt his legs get heavy as he turned in the air. After a minute or so, he was finally heading east. The flat darkness of Grant Park waited just beyond the hotels and stores on Michigan Avenue. The immense black body of Lake Michigan lay like the end of the world beyond the park. In that black endlessness he saw the unmistakable, brightly illuminated outline of the White Cap. Maybe when this was all over, he'd go there to celebrate. He figured he'd earned an expensive steak and a glass of wine.

Suddenly his body was buffeted by a stern wind. It was like running into a brick wall. He kept his hands tightly on the drawstring grips and recovered, keeping his bearing east. Things calmed down after a few seconds but the breeze coming up from the city smelled like burgers being cooked over an open flame; it made his stomach rumble. That delicious aroma was probably coming from Joe's Jazz Joint, a restaurant on Navy Pier. He'd been there many times because they played live jazz and he loved jazz. Not the crappy, shallow, computer created, button-number-three bilge that was on the radio nowadays. But real jazz, with saxophones and percussion and a voice that bleeds with raw emotion. The man's eyes fell upon the pier; it sparkled like a wall of different colored diamonds. The giant ferris wheel, the largest part of that sparkling wall of diamonds, turned in slow motion.

Then he noticed that his speed was slowing; he was losing altitude. He was a few hundred feet above the city now as he fell towards State Street, well short of his mark. He'd need a boost of some kind and he knew where to get it. He headed towards State Street, the buildings rose up towards him like giants awaking from slumber. The man was too low to avoid them so he steered himself between the buildings, gliding east over Harrison Street. It was a straight shot to Grant Park from Harrison; he saw how the city opened up at the end. Freedom!

Below, the man saw cars speeding along, stoplights changing colors; he heard the squeals of their brakes, the honking of their horns, the rising crescendo of their engines as they accelerated. Amazingly, when he looked up he saw that he was low enough to be under the second tier of air-cars that came off the Skyway and moved in slow, organized lanes between the buildings. Many of the windows in the buildings he passed by were lit; he saw people in them. Could they see him?

Up ahead, State Street and Harrison Street met. When he hit the junction, he was only a hundred or so feet high. But a swirling current of cool air suddenly filled the parachute and swept him up, bringing him two hundred feet in the air again. The man's momentum carried him past State Street as he gained altitude and when he passed Michigan Avenue, the man knew he'd made it. The metallic and glass walls of the city fell away suddenly; he was gliding high over trees and grass. The busy sounds and smells of the city also fell away, becoming strangely silent.

He could hardly contain his excitement. No one had seen him and if they had, he'd be long gone before the authorities arrived.

He rose a little higher into the air. In the darkness he saw the ghostly forms of four dirt baseball diamonds arranged in a huge square. They were facing each other from long expanses of low-cut, dark, grassy fields.

His mark!

The man pulled back on the grips, bringing the angle of the parachute up into the air where it caught a mouthful of wind and slowed. He slowly descended, aiming for the northwest diamond. The ground came up to get him; he readied himself for landing. He arched down over third base. His feet hit the ground in a long skid; he pumped his legs as fast as he could so that the momentum of the parachute didn't throw him onto his face. Pulling back as hard as he could on the grips, making the parachute almost vertical, he stopped with such a violent jerk it pulled him backwards. The man fell onto his back and lay there as the nylon parachute coughed itself free of wind resistance, finally falling on top of him like a bed sheet.

The man waited a few more seconds, listening for raised voices or sirens but heard nothing. Then he threw the parachute off and quickly stood up. He unsnapped the shoulder buckles that held the parachute to his chest straps. After that he shed the chest straps, letting them fall to the ground. He leaned over and began sweeping the parachute up into a tight ball. When he picked the chest straps up he noticed that he was standing on the pitcher's mound. He began laughing. During the long, involved planning of this event, he'd jokingly put an "X" on the map exactly where he was standing. He couldn't believe it. Everything *had* worked out perfectly after all.

He ran off the mound and to the bench on the west side of the diamond. There was a big covered, city garbage can there. It was painted yellow and seemed to glow in the dark. He lifted the lid and placed it on the ground, then he threw the entire pack into the plastic lining of the can. He stopped and listened again before he continued. Nothing. Still safe. He slipped his sneakers off, unzipped his military-issue skysuit and slipped out of it just as if he were wearing a diving suit. He threw the skysuit into the can and covered the can with the lid. He wore a T-shirt and skin-tight nylon breeches, just what joggers were wearing at night nowadays. The light breeze in the park refreshed him as he slipped his sneakers back on.

Time for the final leg of the plan.

The man began jogging south, across the grassy outfields, making it to Balbo Avenue in just over five minutes, according to his military issue watch. He stopped on the sidewalk and looked for a cab. Because Balbo Avenue connected Lakeshore Drive with Michigan Avenue, he thought for sure there'd be a line of ground cabs going back and forth, but there wasn't. Which was fine with him. It gave him a chance to catch his breath so that he'd be breathing normally by the time he did find a cab. The last thing he needed was for an idiot cabby to become suspicious, connect the dots, and turn him in. So the man began walking west towards Michigan Avenue. Even from where he was, the man saw twenty or thirty cabs rolling along Michigan Avenue. Easy pickings.

Once he made it to the corner, Michigan Avenue ran in front of him like a metallic river. His blood pressure was returning to normal, and the charge of adrenaline he'd been living on for the past half hour had faded. He waved a cab down and got in. The air inside the cab smelled like sour grapes; the driver was a skinny black man who had an African accent of some kind. Strange drumming music played loudly on the radio.

The man gave him the destination and he gave the cab driver a twenty-dollar tip when he got home. The fare was just under fifteen.

Twenty Two

Braden sat up in the bed in the Station 85 hospital recovery ward. The entire crew stood around him in the room, even the Chief's son, Roger, had been worried enough about him to come in. Braden was glad that they were all there, it made him feel better physically and mentally. He'd learned from Danny during his quick ride in the ambulance that Sam had rushed in and pulled him out of the Tower. He hadn't needed to be told who did it. He already knew.

The nurse came in, took his vitals, and quickly left the loud, crowded room. Dr. Payne was somewhere down the hall in a darkened room checking Braden's ultrasound for the progress made by the nanobots in cleaning his bloodstream. Earlier he'd said everything looked better than usual and that Braden was healing much faster than expected. He was impressed with Braden's strong constitution and had told him it would go a long way in getting him back on his feet. That seemed to tip the balance. The hydrogen cyanide molecules were almost completely cleaned from his bloodstream, which explained why Braden had to urinate so often.

They were all elated when Dr. Payne came back in.

"There'll be an extra few cents in your check this week, Doc," Sam joked and slapped the doctor on the back.

"Don't give it to me, Sam," Dr. Payne said. "Give it to Debbie and Danny. They got to Braden in time with the nanobots. They're the heroes here."

Everyone cheered and slapped the designated heroes backs as the doctor quickly made his way out of the room, relieved to be out of back-slapping range.

"Well, Kid," the Chief began. "How does it feel to finally break in your hospital bed?"

Each of the firefighters had a bed of their own in the recovery ward; Braden's had been the only one still wrapped in a protective sheet of plastic. He'd often wondered how long it would take him to "break it in." There had been an unofficial wager going on with all of them; even Braden had joined in. Someone gave Sam twenty dollars, picked a date, and the closest one to that date would win. Everyone with the exception of Braden had picked an earlier date so Braden was now a hundred and twenty dollars richer. He'd secretly spend the money on Amy's Christmas present. No need for her to find out where he got that much money; it would only upset her. She wouldn't understand that making light of their mortality was how some firefighters dealt with the dangers of their job.

"How do I feel?" Braden repeated and ruminated a moment. "I guess I feel that now I really am one of you guys. You've all paid your dues. This was just my turn at the register."

"Well said!" Sam shouted and they all excitedly agreed with him.

"Sam!" Braden shouted over their voices.

"Wassup?"

"We're even. Thanks."

"My pleasure, partner," Sam winked at him.

There was a deep voice coming from somewhere outside the room, Chief of Police Heany's huge form appeared in the doorway. He had to lower his head to get through the door and when he came in everyone quieted down. They knew Heany never appeared in person unless it was serious.

"Sorry to interrupt," he said in a voice that sounded like a lawn mower starting. "I've got some official police business to conduct." He turned his attention to Braden. "Glad to see you're feeling better, son."

"Thank you, sir," Braden said. "That was a close one."

"Too close. In the ambulance you mentioned a tall man in black wearing a parachute."

"That's right, sir," Braden said. "He looked like Special Forces. After he thought I was dead, he used my laser blade to cut a hole in the window, then he jumped through it. I don't know how, but your people missed him entirely. I watched his parachute glide down to the ground for at least a minute before I blacked out."

"Yes," Heany mumbled, a little embarrassed. "You said that quite emphatically in your statement. I'm still trying to figure that out myself. Anything else come to you recently that you may have forgotten to tell my investigators?"

Braden lowered his eyes and sighed.

"You holding something back, son?"

Braden lifted his head and his eyes fell upon Roger who was standing next to the Chief. It was time to show his hand.

"Roger," Braden said. "Where's Stan?"

Roger shrugged his shoulders. "I don't know," he replied. "I haven't seen or talked to him for a week or so. It's strange now that I think about it. He usually calls me two or three times a week."

"Stan?" Heany echoed. "Stan who?"

Braden nodded. "The man I think is responsible for all of this is named Stan Winslow—"

"Stan Winslow...you can't be serious, Kid?" the Chief said. His whole body stiffened at this revelation. "He and Roger were friends when they were children. I've watched him grow up. He was like another son to me. He can't be the Fire Man!"

"Look at the facts, Chief," Braden said. "He's ex-military, a paratrooper. Who else would have the balls to jump out of the hundred and third floor of the Sears Tower and still be invisible to over a dozen police cruisers? Also, there were U.S. Military smoke cans up there, who else has access to that kind of equipment? And don't forget the military grade C-4 on the boat."

"And you know what?" Roger interrupted, his voice excited. "He was dishonorably discharged."

"What was the charge?" Heany asked.

"Insubordination to a commanding officer. There was some kind of difference of opinion during a secret ops mission. He punched the CO right in the face."

"But what would be his motive for attacking you?" Heany asked Braden. Chief Kelly looked on in disbelief and listened.

"Jealousy," Braden answered. "I didn't know he was dishonorably discharged. It makes perfect sense now. I'd beat him out of the only job opening in the city he's qualified for. I was right all along...I *was* the target. He was the one who was responsible for the debris pile in the obstacle course; he was the one who put the weights on Victor's ankles. I mean, look at it this way: here's a man who's been trained to jump out of moving planes, to kill people with a blade of grass and a stare, then he gets kicked out of the military for insubordination. He comes back to Chicago, a ticking time bomb, strikes up his old friendship with Roger once Roger has completed his own military service, and suddenly, a position opens in Station 85. All he's got to contend with is Roger until this young punk from Nowheresville shows up and beats them both out. He's angry, Chief. Angry at me, and angry at you for choosing me."

"Why didn't you tell us your suspicions before, Kid?" the Chief asked.

"I can't just go around making accusations without any proof, Chief. I wanted to wait until I was sure."

The others stood stoically, their mouths open in shock. Braden's assessment made sense and that meant it could be true.

"I'll get a cruiser to Winslow's place immediately," Heany said and turned to leave but Braden stopped him.

"There's more, Heany," he said. "But I have to talk to you alone about it."

Heany nodded and told everyone to exit the room. Begrudgingly, they did. Heany closed the door behind him, then stood at Braden's bedside, waiting. Braden started talking finally, relieved to let it out.

"In order for Stan to do all of this, he had to know details about me and the station. Details like whose turn it was to perform the primary search of a certain job; when and where to set a job so that Station 85 would show up; what tools we would use during a job; and be able to gain access to Victor, the Victim..."

"You're talking like he had help, Kid. Like he had an inside man in the station," Heany said, scowling.

"What else explains all of what I laid out, sir? Stan knew stuff no one else but a firefighter in Station 85 should know. He had to have had an inside contact. People just can't walk in off the street and go up onto the roof of a station house where all the apparatus is. There's too much security."

Braden could see the gears turning behind Heany's dark

eyes. He knew Heany was having a hard time digesting what he'd been eating and Heany wasn't happy at all about it.

"I'll look into it, Rathman. In the meantime, get yourself out of here and back on the job ASAP," Heany said as he turned towards the door.

"Any reason why?" Braden asked suspiciously.

"My daddy, who was a detective in this town a long time ago, always said that the best way to catch a thief was to leave your jewelry out," Heany answered.

"I get it," Braden said. "You want to flush Stan out and I'm the bait."

"You know," Heany said, "the Chief was right, you're pretty bright, Kid," and with that Heany was through the door.

The others didn't come back in after Heany left. They had gone, too. Dr. Payne probably kicked them out so that he could get some rest. The peace and quiet was a welcome diversion from all the earlier noise. He thought of Amy and Evie and was glad to be alive to fight again. He saw the cap of a police officer through the small square window in the door and realized Heany had stationed a guard there. He felt safe and secure in this small, antiseptic, white room. His eyelids grew heavy. Soon, he was asleep.

Braden dreamt of weird, nonsensical things. Big black firefighter boots walking past him on a marble sidewalk without legs or feet in them. A rocket ship from the twentieth century rising into a light blue sky, a long, thick stream of white water coming out of the bottom instead of flame, pushing it spaceward. The city of Chicago in what appeared to be the future…there were impossibly high skyscrapers with swirling domes and a landscape of graceful bridges that spun around buildings like twine, connecting every building in the city with another. Everything was shining, white, clean, and perfect as if the city had just been built yesterday. Soon, night fell and the new city became a dark, jagged shadow in the moonlight.

This city was full of secrets and danger; he was afraid of it. It was a city he didn't recognize anymore or want to live in. With that realization the entire silhouette of the city began shaking but the ground was still, unmoving. Those long graceful bridges, those impossibly high skyscrapers, fell over like wooden blocks stacked on top of each other. When the landscape was nothing more than wreck and ruin, the ground started shaking. Giant fissures opened up and swallowed the remains of the city like a million hungry mouths. Braden felt a sense of doom and now his body was shaking, exploding apart like a statue made of hollowed plaster.

When he awoke he saw Amy standing at the foot of his bed; her hand was on his right shin. She was shaking it gently, trying to rouse him. Her long blond, curly hair looked almost white, her soft porcelain face looked radiant under the cool glare of the ceiling lights. He expected her to have a worried, horrified grimace on her face, or anger, but it wasn't there. She stared at him quietly; love and respect glazed over her eyes. Or was that tears?

"Hey, firefighter," she said, smiling. "You look scared out of your mind."

He nodded, relieved to be awake and away from that horrible nightmare. He realized he was sweating and wiped it off his forehead with the back of his hand.

"Bad dream, babe," he said.

"Dr. Payne told me that you might have them for a while still," she said. "Something about the reaction of your brain chemistry to the nanobots."

"If that's the case, I'm never going to sleep again," he said.

He waved at her to come sit by him on the bed. He saw that she wanted to talk. She made her way around the bed and sat down, taking his hand in hers.

"I hear they're letting you out of here tomorrow," she said.

"Yeah. I'm feeling much better. It wasn't as bad as you think," he countered, bringing her hand to his mouth and kissing it. "How's Evie?"

"She's fine. I dropped her off at my parent's house. Your parents are on their way."

Braden nodded.

"I've been watching the news, Brad," Amy said. "And the Chief filled me in on everything that's been going on."

"Everything?" he asked.

She nodded and looked down at their hands entwined tightly together. Braden tried to say something but she put her fingertip on his lips.

"No. Don't say anything," she said. "You don't have to,

darling. I've been thinking about us lately, a lot, and I've come to understand a few things. I want to tell them to you."

Braden stared into her beautiful blue eyes and listened. He was afraid of what she would say next.

"I've come to understand that you love this job. That it's what you are and it's part of what made me fall in love with you in the first place. You've shown me that it's better to live life right in the face like you do, helping other people, than to cower in the shadows behind a desk, everyday waiting for your arteries to harden and for death to come get you. I've come to the realization that you would be unhappy doing anything else and if you were unhappy, I would be unhappy too. There wouldn't be a future for us in a marriage like that and I don't want anyone else. So I want you to understand that, no matter what happens, we're in this together...to the end. Sure, I'll get upset sometimes and it may seem that I'm at the end of my rope, but I want you to know that I understand. I don't want you to change or quit what you've always dreamed of doing. I want you to understand that I support you, I'm proud of you and I love you. I always will."

Braden's eyes burned with tears but he held them back. Instead, he pulled his wife closer, kissed her, and held her so close that their hearts were touching. He wanted to make love to her but he knew there wasn't enough time; his parents would be here soon. Besides, there was a security camera in the ceiling. If that got out on the Internet, she'd never forgive him. Maybe tomorrow night as they lay together in bed in the dark of their own room. He suspected he was lucky to have a wonderful woman like Amy fall in love with him, but now he realized it fully. Unselfish, caring, supportive, and she could cook. He didn't want anyone else, either. There wasn't a better woman in the world.

She sat up, still holding his hand tightly; her eyes were red and moist.

"Now, there's a maniac out there setting fires...you have to help them catch him, Brad, before an innocent person dies."

"Yes, boss," he said and they laughed quietly.

Twenty Three

Two days later Braden was cleared by Dr. Payne to go back to work. He was excited about returning.

Amy made him stay in bed the entire day before and she took care of his every need. He and Evie watched his judge shows on WFLD on the bedroom holo, but being only four months old she really didn't quite get into the spirit of things. Braden napped later in the day when the local news began on ABC; Kathryn Gold was doing yet another special report on the Chicago Fire Man. It was nothing but rehashed news and irresponsible supposition but what else did a person expect from the press nowadays? Any sign of journalistic integrity was thrown out the window during the presidential elections of 2008. He remembered the teacher talking about it in Social Studies class in high school.

It was best to just fall asleep and forget about the Chicago Fire Man for a while. Let his body get strong again. This time, though, he didn't dream. He awoke to the smell of his favorite meal wafting through the air...Amy's patented meat loaf. Braden always told her she should go to cooking school and was glad that she was seriously considering it. The extra income would be extremely helpful. He would support her whole-heartedly in it just as she supported him.

After they put Evie to bed for the night, they made love for the first time since the birth then fell off to sleep in each other's arms, spent and satisfied.

But since that boat fire, Braden hadn't been sleeping well. He brought a large, industrial strength flashlight to bed every night, waking Amy every other hour. Any noise in the apartment would startle him, he'd click on the flashlight and the dark room would be instantly illuminated by a long, searching beam of white light. After a few minutes of silent investigation, the flashlight clicked again and the room fell dark. This went on three or four times a night and finally, Amy said something to him.

They were lying in bed and he had the flashlight in his hand.

"Braden," she said, staring at the flashlight. "I'm getting a little worried about you. I've been putting off talking to you about it for fear of making things worse."

"The flashlight?" he asked.

She nodded.

"I'm all right, babe. Just making sure everyone is safe, that's all."

"You don't think it's strange—"

He cut her off. "That I want to keep my family safe? Not at all."

"I think it's more than that, Brad," she said. "I think it has to do with all the stress you've been under from the job. You were nearly killed. Maybe seeing a counselor would help."

"Really, I'm fine, babe. There's nothing to worry about."

And that was that. Braden could be very stubborn. Amy slept with the covers over her head after that.

It was almost 9:00 p.m. when Braden landed his Camaro in his spot next to the station apparatus. The sky was neon orange sherbet as the setting sun fell under the horizon. Sam was already there. Every time he saw Sam's white '68 Cadillac and that huge trunk, it reminded him of the night they'd locked him in there and pretended to be running from the police. He wondered what Sam's firefighter initiation was like. He'd probably planned it himself.

The dome above closed as Braden got out of his air-car. He was excited to be back, even though he'd only been gone a few days. When he was here at the station he felt as if he had some element of control in his life, that he could actually do something about Stan Winslow and his insanity. He was in his natural element here, like a bird in the sky.

Noise was coming out of the game room. It sounded like a boxing match was going on in there; voices were excited and cheering. He started in that direction but the door to the Chief's office opened and Roger came out with his father. They shook hands.

"How're you feeling, Braden?" Roger asked.

"Eager to get back on the job, Roger. Thanks."

"Great. Well, I've got some errands to run for my father so I'll talk to you later. Good luck," Roger said, shook his hand again, and headed for the elevator.

Braden liked Roger. He was a lot like his father, the Chief, in so many ways. Braden hoped that if there should be another opening, Roger would try again. He'd make a great addition to the crew. Braden never asked anyone whose place he himself had filled. He was afraid the answer would be a sad one and he didn't want to feel like a ghoul, feeding on the dead. None of them ever brought the subject up so he just let it alone. It would inevitably come out someday.

There was another crescendo of cheers coming from the game room but the Chief waved him inside the office. Sam was already inside and sitting. Braden went in and sat down in the chair in front of the Chief's desk.

"Welcome back, Kid," the Chief said, leaning forward, his elbows on the desk. The big window behind him showed the darkening city skyline below. It reminded Braden of that terrible nightmare he'd had in the recovery room downstairs.

"Thanks, Chief," Braden said. "It's great to be back. I feel normal again."

"Good. I'm glad that you're here a little early. I wanted to bring you guys up to date on the investigation concerning the Chicago Fire Man."

Sam and Braden stared at the Chief intensely.

"Heany's people haven't been able to locate Stan Winslow so an APB has been sent out to every police station in the city. Heany also had an FBI profiler look at this case and it looks like you were right, Braden. Stan seems to fit the profile of an arsonist. His single-minded, angry obsessiveness with you is the only reason other people haven't been killed yet. He's been focused primarily on killing you. We've got to get him before that changes."

"Right, Chief," Braden said, trying to hide the fact that he was uncomfortable being the target of a murderer. He jiggled his legs nervously.

"To that end, Heany says the profiler told him we should be getting another anonymous call in the next couple of days so I need you guys ready and willing. I need everyone to be working together as a team."

Sam and Braden nodded.

"If it were up to me, Braden, I'd be sitting you down until this is all over, but Heany, the Mayor, and his aides think this can't be resolved without you."

"I think *bait* is the word you're looking for, Chief," Braden said.

"So we all understand each other?"

"Affirmative, Chief."

"I don't like it," the Chief said, his voice rising and hot with anger. He focused his tired eyes on Braden. "I don't like it at all. It goes against everything I believe but maybe they're right, I don't know. I just put out fires. All I know is that you're the best asset this station has had in years and I'd hate to lose you. It would be a great loss for the city. Do you understand that, too?"

Braden smiled respectfully, taking what the Chief said as the compliment it was.

"Good," the Chief said, lowering his eyes. He sighed and sat back in his chair, glancing at Sam. "You need to watch his back, Sam. No BS. No idiotic rushes into a burning building. Again, we do this as a team. This is life and death. You have to be smart and not put Braden in a position where he needs to save your ass."

"Copy that, Chief," Sam said, stirring uneasily in his seat.

A small grin flashed at the left corner of the Chief's thin mouth. "A lot is riding on how we tackle the next Fire Man trap," the Chief said. "I'm gambling we come out winners. Of course, I haven't won a bet at Arlington Racetrack in ten years. I have a penchant for picking only long shots. The rewards are a lot better when they come in."

"I'll take a piece of that action anyway, Chief," Sam said.

"Me too," Braden said.

"That's all for now, guys," the Chief said and motioned with his hand that they were free to go.

As Sam and Braden stood up, the old, weathered, black

phone on the Chief's desk trilled. They froze. The Chief's face went from grim satisfaction to dark worry. The creases in his forehead deepened as he stared at the phone. They knew this particular trill came from Stacey. It was like the Bat Phone when the Commissioner called—and only bad news would come from the other side.

Instead of picking up the receiver, the Chief answered on speaker, allowing Braden and Sam to listen in.

"Whatcha got, Stace?"

"Chief, I'm gonna put a call through that you have to take."

Sam and Braden exchanged concerned glances.

"Do it, Stacey," the Chief ordered. There was a click followed by heavy breathing. It sounded like the person on the other end was crying.

"This is the Fire Chief Kelly of Chicago Engine Station 85, go ahead."

"I-I'm going to kill myself, Chief," the voice said. It sounded low and emotional and Braden couldn't recognize it. The man was trying to disguise his voice.

"Stan? Is this you?" the Chief asked, rubbing his eyes with his fingertips.

"I've done everything I can to kill Rathman...but he's like a cockroach, he can't be killed!" the voice rumbled angrily. Sam and the Chief looked at Braden. "I've lost. He's beaten me. But...but I'll still have the last word. Others will follow me into death...can you save them?" the connection clicked and there was silence.

"Stan! Stan!" the Chief yelled into the phone; his face was red and contorted with fear. But the dial tone was only thing that answered him. He reached forward, picked the phone assembly up, and threw it at the wall. It shattered like black glass, falling to the floor in a hundred pieces. Sam and Braden jumped back out of their chairs at the Chief's sudden outburst, standing against the wall. The Chief dropped his head down and leaned against his desk on his knuckles. Braden understood his frustration.

They stood like statues in deep silence for a few moments. None of them looked at each other. Then there was a low, echoing thud outside, like a bomb had just gone off. They looked through the window in the direction of the sound. In the distance, a towering column of smoke rose into the air and swirled in the evening breeze.

There was just enough light left to see its flowing, cobra-like outline. A flicker of something bright appeared at the bottom of that column of smoke; it became brighter, larger, with each passing second.

"Fire!" Sam exclaimed.

Alarms exploded through the thick silence of the Chief's office; this brought them all back to life. The Chief hurried around his desk and followed Sam through the door. But Braden remained there, staring at the blazing deathtrap in the distance. It was like that fire in his friend's Nick's house when he was a kid. This fire was in that same neighborhood...on that same block.

Braden knew what was coming; he knew the final card the Fire Man was playing, and he didn't want to deal with it. But he heard all of them gearing up outside, calling him to action. All of this was because of him; he couldn't let them down. He couldn't let the city down. He had to see this through.

He was a firefighter.

Twenty Four

The Chief called Heany on the way to the job but Heany and his people were already at the scene. Apparently, the FBI profiler had predicted the Fire Man's next target and Heany had had two of his people staking out the house when it blew to high hell. If not for the fact that they were hidden in a reinforced unmarked ground car across the street, their families would've been getting insurance checks tomorrow.

Heany told the Chief that there was no warning. As soon as the people that lived in Braden's old house turned out the lights for the night, the house blew. His people didn't see anyone go in or come out since before dusk.

"Could it have been a natural gas explosion?" the Chief asked.

"Could be, but that would make it one hell of a coincidence, wouldn't it?"

"Yeah," the Chief said uneasily and put his cell phone away.

"Incident Commander on the radio, Chief," Joni said and switched Chief Roy Clifford's voice to the cockpit's external speakers.

"Kelly here, Roy," the Chief said. "What do you want us to do?"

"Great to have you with us," Clifford said. "We're all busy up here trying to control the fires that are blazing on these houses. I need you to concentrate on the blast origin. That crater is all that's left of it. Maybe your people can find something in the rubble that'll tell us what happened here."

"Copy that, Roy. We're on it. I'll stay in touch."

Braden was so horrified he couldn't swallow as they came down out of the night sky and approached the smoking crater where his house used to be. It was nothing but flashing red and blue lights and fire below them. It made the sky above glow eerily pink.

"Christ almighty," the Chief whispered. "It looks like an atomic bomb went off."

The Engine landed in the street. When they went down the ramp, they saw that the destruction was even more fearsome up close. Braden stood in the street, his legs frozen. He recognized the neighborhood: old two and three story houses, perfectly manicured lawns. Across the street was Nick's old house, run-down, boarded-up, a For Sale sign hovering in the front yard. To his left and covered in flames was the Williams' house, to his right was the Brokke's house, also in flames, in between, where his old house should have been was a deep, smoking, square crater. He saw pipes sticking up, mangled and twisted from the force of the blast. Some were spewing water and he could barely make out the old stone foundation his house once rested on. He was eternally glad his parents had moved to a downtown condo when he left the house for college a few years ago. There was flaming debris strewn in every direction and the hints of fire on the roofs of houses a few blocks away.

The sky above was heavy with an attack force of fire engines, ambulances, and foam tenders from other stations. Braden counted three stations, not including them. They were throwing everything they had at the sizzling fires on his old neighbors' houses; their deck guns were trained down at forty-five degree angles, blasting intensely in a desperate direct attack technique. Some were alternating their spray with fog nozzles in an effort to cool the air over the fire.

The house that lay directly behind the crater, the Long's house, was burning out of control. The steep, pointed gables of the roof funneled flames into the air like a flame-thrower. A red engine from Station 76 hovered just above the ground in the yard, its white ladder extended and attached to the third floor window frame. The fire must have been too hot to bring the engine closer. A firefighter was inside the house helping kids through the uppermost window and onto the ladder where another firefighter was taking them and easing them down the rungs. It looked like the Longs would be rescued; Braden was grateful for that. Then he thought about the family living in his old house when it blew.

His legs became animated. He found himself running through the maze of police and firefighters to get to the Chief. He found the Chief standing with Heany just inside the tape the police used to cordon off the area.

"Chief," he said. "That's my old house!"

"I know it, Kid," the Chief said. "I recognize the neighborhood." Heany stared at Braden sadly.

"But...the people living in—?"

"I'm afraid so, Braden," Heany interrupted. "A family of six. The Murkey family. My people are finding their remains all over the neighborhood."

Braden was stunned to silence. He couldn't understand the anger, the blind fury a person had to feel in order to commit such a terrible act. It was true evil. He hoped Winslow was true to his word and was in there with them when it blew.

But Heany wasn't finished: "...and anyone in the neighboring houses sleeping in the rooms that faced the blast are probably dead also. Clifford's men are trying to find out."

Braden looked at the Williams' house, then at the Brokke's house. The flames had hid the true depth of the effect of the blast. Half of their frames were gone, imploded inward like a pile of matchsticks. He saw wooden studs sticking up, and melting roof tiles falling into the glowing heat. Heany was right...anything caught in there was gone.

"My God," Braden murmured, his body trembling.

Big George came running from the smoking remnant of the crater. He held the chemical tester in his hand; it was beeping wildly. He stopped in front of the Chief.

"We got an affirmative in the blast origin, Chief," he said breathlessly. "Off the chart readings on C-4. Pretty pure, looks military grade. The bastard must have used a truckload of the stuff."

"That would take time. How did he get it into the house without anyone knowing?" Braden asked.

No one could answer that.

The engines were making slow turns above the neighboring

houses, ejaculating their contents down onto the burning chaos. When one emptied itself dry; it went off to refill while another engine took its place. Other engines were laying down a protective wall of water on the rest of the houses in the immediate area. One of them had a hose attached to the plug of a hydrant a few houses down and was keeping a steady stream of high pressure water spearing into the fire. It wasn't enough.

There was a loud rumble, like a horde of horses stampeding through a field, and the sky suddenly became brighter. Braden put his arm up to shield his eyes from the light as the Brokke's house became completely engulfed in a tower of whirling yellow flame.

"Stay back everyone! We've got us a Dancing Lady!" Chief Clifford shouted through Braden's ear mic.

Braden had never seen one before but he'd read about them in his firefighter manual. He watched in a kind of hypnotized trance as the towering column of flame twisted and turned like a neon tornado, dancing to a song only it could hear. Its rolling body fluttered to the left and to the right while little arms of flames waved in the air like some satanic ballet dancer in Hell. It was unbelievably beautiful until he felt the heat from it on his face.

"This is out of control, people!" Chief Clifford shouted angrily through Braden's ear mic. "Get a handle on it now!"

A series of affirmatives snapped off in reply and the engines above circled the dancing column of fire, attacking it with thick streams of water from their deck guns. They were opened full blast and the surrounding structure sizzled when any amount of errant spray hit it. The heavy scent of burnt wood filled the air.

"We better hurry this along! Big George!" the Chief shouted. "Take Mo and go back and see what else you can find."

Big George nodded, pocketed the chemical tester, and ran back into the smoking crater. Braden felt helpless to do anything. He asked the Chief what his orders were.

"Stand down for now, Kid," he replied. "At least until we get this under control."

"Stand down? But, Chief—"

"I said stand down, Rathman!"

Braden threw his hands down angrily and turned his attention back to the action. He saw Sam standing near the edge of the smoking foundation of his house. He was holding a two and a half inch hose he'd pulled from the Engine and was fogging water down into it, keeping it cool so that it wouldn't flare up again. Big George and Mo were in there digging around for evidence. Debbie and Danny were parked in the Long's backyard, tending to the rescued family members that were coming down the ladder. The Foam Tender was parked in the Williams' front yard, spraying its magical wet water onto the flames from its deck guns. It looked to Braden like it was too little, too late.

Braden heard an excited howl. He watched as Big George's huge body climbed out of the foundation and ran towards them. There was something big and heavy in his raised right hand.

"Whatcha got, BG?" the Chief asked.

Big George stopped, out of breath again, and gave what looked like a giant charred spider to Heany. Heany's eyes grew large; after inspecting it closely, he gave it to the Chief.

"It's a receiver for a remote detonator," the Chief said excitedly. "Good work, BG."

Braden looked at Heany, whose eyes grew even larger. Both of them realized it at the same time.

"What would a person who threatened to kill himself in the blast want with a remote detonator?" Heany asked.

"My thoughts exactly, sir," Braden said.

The Chief looked at Braden with narrowed eyes. "Are you telling me he wasn't in that blast?"

"That's what it looks like, Chief," Heany interrupted. "I'll let my people know. They'll pick this perimeter clean like fire ants." Heany turned and went back to his cruiser.

"Christ!" the Chief muttered to himself. "Will this nightmare ever end?"

Braden was tired of it, also. He had been depending on the instability of Stan's mind to put an end to all of this but it appeared that there were still a few surprises left. He turned and went back to the Engine. The air smelled like everything that could possibly burn was burning and it made his stomach queasy. On his way to the Engine he saw Nick's old house sitting there, peaceful and dark, untouched by anything resembling a flame. But the roofs of the houses all around it were smoldering with fire that the engines had put out. Why was Nick's house so lucky?

He leaned against the rear of the Engine, staring at the empty house. The windows were boarded up, the white clapboard siding needed painting, some needed to be replaced, the gutters were hanging off the roof like icicles, and the lawn needed mowing. It looked as if it had been abandoned for years. No one was going to buy that house in its present condition. But if the house had been abandoned for years, why was the front door open?

The screened door was closed but he could see the unmistakable shadow of the inner door opened about a foot. It struck him as an invitation to come in.

"Chief!" Braden called and waved him over.

The Chief came, stopped next to him, and looked where Braden was pointing.

"Does it seem strange to you that that door is open?"

The Chief leaned forward and squinted. As a deep frown cut into his face, he called Heany over and showed him. Immediately, Heany called for a squad of five back-up officers. Once the officers arrived, Heany led the Chief and Braden across the street. They went up the porch cautiously. Heany had his city-issued Baretta 9000 in his hand, the other officers' weapons were cocked and ready.

"My people will go in first, check things out, then we'll call you two in," Heany whispered. The Chief agreed.

Quietly, Heany used his free hand to open the screened door, then he used his gun hand to push open the inner door. It squealed like a mouse in a trap; Heany shook his head angrily. Any element of surprise they had was now gone. He stepped in anyway, followed by his five back-up officers. The Chief and Braden stood with their backs against the siding on either side of the doorway. Braden stared across the street; it seemed so strange not seeing his old house there. He'd looked at it a thousand times from this same vantage point when he was a kid and it had always been there, would always be there, unchanged forever. Now it was a flattened, flaming crater of rubble.

"You all right, Kid?" the Chief whispered.

"Yeah, Chief," Braden answered. "I'm just thinking about how some things you think will last forever don't."

"Yeah. I'm sorry about your house, Kid. You must have a

million memories associated with it."

"Affirmative," Braden whispered. "And they were all good."

"Learn through pain, Kid," the Chief said. "Sometimes it's the only way."

Braden nodded silently. Then he wondered if this conflagration had made the news yet. He looked up into the sky but didn't see any news vans yet. Kathryn Gold was usually the first on the scene. They were probably on their way. Ah, yes, a brightly lit caravan was coming from the south, the giant numbers of their respective channels embossed on their sides. It reminded him of a shark-feeding frenzy. The vans split up and took up stable positions just outside the safety perimeter the police cruisers had set. They were taking stock video footage to use as filler when they filed their reports.

"Leeches," the Chief muttered.

Maybe so, Braden thought. *But they're only doing their job and don't seem to be interfering with the operation.* Braden preferred to make them his friends: that way they would help instead of hinder.

Braden and the Chief heard small voices and strange noises coming from inside Nick's house. Then they smelled a horribly familiar odor, sweet and putrid. Braden gagged.

"The smell of death, Kid," the Chief said as he covered his nose with his gloved hand.

"There's one thing that never changes," Braden quipped.

They waited out there and for a long time they heard nothing coming from inside. The firefighting across the street went on and on, never letting up for a moment. It looked, though, as if the swirling inferno was finally being knocked down. The Dancing Lady made her final move once an engine swung over and buried it under water.

Braden was getting concerned about what was going inside Nick's house. They'd been up there and quiet for too long. Maybe something was wrong.

"Should we go in, Chief?"

Just as the Chief was about to answer, heavy footsteps thudded from inside the house. The door squealed again and Heany appeared. His face was screwed up tightly and his mouth was just a slit.

"You guys better get in here and see this," he said.

Quickly, Braden and the Chief went into the house, following Heany up the steep line of stairs that lay on the right. They went all the way up to the top floor, turned down a short hallway, and approached a room in the front of the house. Braden remembered it as Nick's old bedroom. The two of them had played up there for many countless hours when they were kids. Through the doorway Braden saw police officers walking around as the room lit up with white flashes from a digital camera.

The stench grew more powerful; Braden had to breathe through his mouth to stop from gagging. They followed Heany's huge body into the room. He pointed at the floor in front of the only window. Stan Winslow lay on his back; his eyes were unfocused and staring up at the ceiling in one of those blank, unfocused stares only a dead man had. His arms and legs were bent at the joints, rigor mortis, and he had a gun hanging off the index finger of his right hand. There was a bloody bullet hole in his right temple and no exit wound that Braden could see. A clear case of suicide. Next to Stan's contorted body was a small black box. It had a flashing light and a switch on top.

"The remote detonator," Heany said as he knelt down over it. "It's been activated."

"Well, now we know why he used a remote detonator," the Chief said. "He didn't have the courage to blow himself up. He must have had a chance to think about it and changed his mind. So he took the easy way out...a bullet through the brain. Quick and painless."

"Yeah," Heany said and frowned. "Most arsonists are cowards. That's why they choose that form of crime."

But nothing Braden saw in front of him looked right. It seemed staged in some way: the opened door that invited them in, the convenience of finding Stan's dead body lying in front of a window that overlooked the blast sight, the fact that the house was untouched by the blast at all, and the strangest thing of all was that rigor had already set in. Braden had learned from Dr. Payne during his First Aid classes that rigor sets in an hour or two after death. To Braden's estimation, it looked as if Stan had been dead two hours, maybe more, but the fire had started less than twenty minutes before. And there was something about the actual means of death, the gun and the bullet hole, that seemed strange but he couldn't put his finger on it. Did Heany suspect anything like he did? Braden knew Heany had been on the force forever and had seen his share of suicides. A person, after a certain amount of time and experience on the job, develops an intuition about things. Heany had that time and experience under his belt. He was the expert and Braden didn't have the courage or experience to step on his toes.

Braden stared at Stan Winslow and was uneasy about the whole thing. Something wasn't right. He felt as if he was being watched. He wanted to get out of there.

"At least it's finally over," the Chief said, smiling at Braden. "What's the matter, Kid?"

He wanted to tell them about his suspicions. He wanted to, but then something came to his mind.

"Did you ever tell Stan about the fire here in Nick's house all those years ago?"

The Chief looked up at the ceiling and thought about it.

"No," he replied. "I never did. No reason to."

Braden pointed down at Stan.

"If Stan never knew where I lived and he never knew where Nick lived, what the hell is he doing here?"

Heany stood up; he screwed his face down into a tight ball of frustration.

"He was obsessed about you, Rathman," Heany said. "He found out."

"How?"

The Chief and Heany traded worried glances.

Braden looked down at Stan again and saw the gun hanging there in his right hand. Then it hit him why the gun and the bullet wound seemed strange to him. He remembered the injury Stan received during his obstacle course test, how he couldn't use his right arm for a while after that. He remembered shaking Stan's hand at the Hot Zone afterwards when they congratulated him and he remembered what Stan had told him.

"Christ, Chief," he said. "Stan was left handed!"

Twenty Five

That little detail changed everything. Braden felt compelled to tell them all about his suspicions. Heany and the Chief listened patiently to everything Braden had to say. They took him seriously. After Braden finished, the inevitable question came up.

"If the Fire Man isn't Stan Winslow, then who is he?" Heany asked.

Braden looked down at Stan again; it looked like the rigor was finally relaxing as his hands were lower on his abdomen and his legs were straightening out.

"Obviously, someone who knew Stan, knows me, and has military experience. There's a common link between all of that," he answered.

"Well, that could be anyone, Kid," the Chief said.

"You're right, Chief," Braden answered. "But it was also someone who had intimate access to the station house or someone who had a contact on the inside."

"What are you saying, Kid? I'm fresh out of kindergarten. Spell it out for me," the Chief muttered, trying to control his frustration.

Braden had a suspicion of who it was but again, he didn't have the evidence to make the accusation, so he still played that card close to his chest.

"I don't know, Chief," Braden said. "All I know is that Stan was just a patsy; someone made it look like he killed himself here to throw us off. The Fire Man is still out there."

Heany glanced at the Chief. "I think the kid is right, Chief. It all makes sense once you think it through," he said tiredly. "So we're back at square one."

"And we probably haven't heard the last of the Fire Man," Braden murmured.

The Chief put his hands on his hips and shook his head.

"You guys better finish the mop up out there," Heany said. "We'll squeeze whatever evidence we can out of here and clean this mess."

The Chief nodded and Braden followed him out through the house. The air was heavy with ash but it smelled only of burning wood again.

Braden didn't like the Chief's silence.

"You all right, Chief?" he asked.

"I don't know, Kid," the Chief answered as they crossed the street. Up and down the block, there were people in robes and nightgowns standing in their front yards watching the firemen do their job. They stood quietly, staring at the destruction as if they were hypnotized. "I feel like I'm living in an old James Patterson novel, only this book seems to have no ending. It just goes on and on."

Braden agreed with him. He was physically and mentally exhausted. He didn't know how much longer he could go on. Sam stood in the front yard of Braden's old house as they crossed the street and when he saw them, he ran up to them.

"Hey! Where have you guys been? I was worried something happened," he said, sounding relieved.

"We found Stan Winslow's body back there in that house," the Chief said.

"His body? So he killed himself after all?"

"No," the Chief replied. "It was only made to look that way. He was murdered. Stan wasn't the Fire Man. We still have a problem."

Sam frowned. "Who the hell could it be, then?"

No one answered him.

"Well, we're almost finished here," Sam said. "Chief Clifford's men were going to check and see if there was anything to salvage but there really isn't. The destruction was complete. Clifford said he's never seen anything like this."

Braden looked around; the job did indeed seem to be well in-hand. The fires on the neighboring houses had been quelled and the sky was clear of hovering apparatus, all of which were grounded now. Everyone was in the process of making sure all fires in the area were truly out. The large spotlights from the Station 85 Engine illuminated the entire scene and Braden saw that the Brokke's and Williams' houses had been completely lost. All that was left of them was a smoldering heap of charred debris on each side of the crater.

"Do you have a K count?" the Chief asked Sam through an exhausted sigh.

"We have a solid number of fourteen. All of the people in these three houses are confirmed dead, even the children and pets. We found somebody's crispy critter on a roof three houses down. We're still trying to determine whose it was. Everyone else in the neighborhood is accounted for. Heany's people are going through the rubble now, looking for more evidence. The Fire Man did a pretty good job at hiding his tracks."

Braden couldn't believe it. The Williamses and the Brokkes were all dead. He'd had countless glasses of Mrs. Williams' sun tea when he was a kid. He'd played baseball with Steve, the oldest Brokke kid, in the park down the street. Now they were all gone. The Chief stared at the carnage, his old, battered eyes welled up with tears.

"God, I hope you're wrong, Kid," the Chief mumbled, trying to control the emotion in his voice. His wet old eyes fell upon Braden. "I hope the Fire Man was Stan Winslow and that this nightmare has ended."

"I...I hope so, too, Chief," Braden said, but he was sure. The Fire Man was still alive.

It took them another hour to mop up to the point where a fire couldn't flare up again, then they left Heany and his men to the rest of it.

"I don't know what we'll find now that the entire area has been deluged with fire and water," Heany said to the Chief. There was surrender in his voice.

"I know, Heany," the Chief began. "You often tell me that firefighters are evidence destroyers but do the best you can anyway. Maybe you'll find something we missed."

Heany let out a long, low mumble and turned back towards the debris field, barking commands into the police band radio hanging on his chest.

Station 85 was the last station to leave the scene. Chief Clifford transferred command to Chief Kelly once the fires were put out. All of them were exhausted. Nothing was said in the Engine as Joni flew them back to the station. Braden surmised that it was the same in the Foam Tender. Sam belted himself into his seat and caught a quick nap while the Chief sat up front, alone with his thoughts. There didn't seem to be a good enough reason for any of it. Jealousy, anger, rage, revenge...none of it was a good enough reason.

Braden couldn't help feeling guilty about the events of the past few months. He'd promised Amy that he'd help capture the Fire Man before any innocents were lost; he'd failed at that. He had done everything he could, but it wasn't good enough. Both the Brokkes and the Williamses had small children and he'd let them down. He wasn't the hero of the Mayor's residential fire anymore...he was just Braden Joshua Rathman, firefighter, husband, father, son...human being. Failure. But it was a realization he welcomed. He'd begun to believe all that hero talk, how he could do no wrong, that he could protect the entire city by himself.

He'd wrongly guessed who the Fire Man was. He should have known where the next incident was going to be. He should have seen everything but he wasn't as smart as he thought he was. Yet, now that he'd failed so miserably to stop the Fire Man from killing innocents, he felt liberated. He felt like the chalkboard had been swept clean and he could begin all over again. It gave him a renewed spark of energy. Once they got back to the station, he'd sit down somewhere alone and try to figure it all out. He knew he had all the pieces he needed to accomplish that. It was just a matter of throwing some objective brainpower at it.

The Engine flew over the sleeping city and when it landed Braden was still silently ruminating. He didn't feel the gentle lurch when the Engine stopped; he didn't hear the ramp as its hydraulic fittings hissed, sending the ramp down. Joni, Sam, and the Chief went by him and down the ramp. The Chief looked back at Braden still sitting there, and went back into the Engine. He gave Braden a gentle pat on the shoulder, waking him up.

"Come on out, Kid," the Chief said. "There's nothing else we can do."

Braden got up, followed the Chief down the ramp and onto the surface of the roof. The large white dome slowly came together above them, its motors humming like a bee's wings, closing them off from the dangers of the outside world.

All of them, Mo, Thom, Big George, Paul, Debbie, Danny, the Chief, Sam, Joni and Braden met in a circle outside the kitchen entrance. Braden stood there, his head down, his posture stiff.

"Cheer up, hero," Sam said. "You told me once that you can't save them all. Well, you're right. Take your own advice."

Braden nodded. That helped. Sam was a good friend.

"They'll get this maniac, Braden," Joni began. "An arsonist always makes one fatal mistake that leads right back to him. You'll see."

All of them were enthusiastically agreeing with what Joni had said when the cell phone in the Chief's pocket rang. Everyone fell silent and listened as the Chief brought it up to his ear. A call on his cell phone was for an emergency only. He put it on speaker.

"Chief Kelly here," he said. "Hi, Stace, what's up?"

"Chief, are you alone?"

"No, I'm with the whole group. Why?"

"Chief, get everyone out of there! The last call from the Fire Man came from here, inside the station!"

Everyone glanced sharply at each other. To Braden, they all seemed genuinely shocked.

"Inside...our station?"

"Yes, Chief."

"Are you sure, Stace?"

"Without a doubt. I ran through the triangulation three times because I didn't believe it myself."

"All right," the Chief said. His voice suddenly became strong and commanding. "I'll get everyone out. Tell Heany about it and get him over here so he can talk to you. Good job, Stace."

Stacey hung up without a reply.

"What does that mean exactly, Chief?" Joni asked.

"It means I made the call from the Hot Zone," a voice echoed from the distance.

Out through the door of the Chief's office came a tall figure dressed all in black. Braden recognized the suit from the Sears Tower fiasco and his heart stopped. None of them had their SCBA masks on; if the maniac opened another cylinder of hydrogen cyanide, they'd all be dead. But the man wasn't wearing a mask with those alien goggles this time. No, his face was there for them to see clearly. Braden and the rest of them recognized the man at once and a collective gasp filled the air of the dome.

As the man came closer they saw that he had a belt strapped around his chest and on the belt were long, thin rods of gray clay-like material. There were so many that there was no space between them. He had his hands out in front of him; they were balled up in fists so tightly that his knuckles were white. His forehead glistened with sweat; his eyes were wide and filled with crazed defiance.

"Roger!" the Chief exclaimed. "What the hell is this all about?"

Roger took a few more slow, careful steps. He stopped in front of the Engine, about twenty feet from them. He smiled and cocked his head to the side. Braden had seen that same smile on a man in an old documentary; the man's name was Charles Manson.

"Haven't you figured it all out by now, Father?" he asked through that evil smirk. He glanced at Braden. "You already have, haven't you, Rathman?"

Braden nodded stoically, trying not to move too quickly and startle him. He knew that it was military grade C-4 strapped to Roger's chest and that he held the detonator in one of his hands. But what was in the other fist?

"Y-you're the Fire Man?" the Chief asked, his voice betraying pure, honest disbelief.

"I'm afraid so, Father."

"But why?"

"Oh. come on, Father! You've raised me alone all these years, you brought me up to believe that I could be like you, the thing I wanted to be most in the world. My whole life was spent trying to please you. I joined the military because that's what you did; I wanted to be a firefighter because that's what you did. I'm your son and you gave the job that was meant for me to this little punk hero, Rathman. I did my best to screw him over during the obstacle course test, but the pile of debris and the weights on Victor, the Victim's ankles didn't even faze him. So I lost to him…something that should have been my birthright. But you still should have chosen me, Father. I was your son, not him! Not Rathman!"

Braden didn't like that Roger was using past tense to describe his relationship with the Chief. The others were frozen in fear, even Sam. Braden had to figure out a way to stall for time. Heany would know how to handle this once he got here.

"Son," the Chief said and slowly put his palms up. His hands were shaking. "You know I love you. But what else could I do? Braden beat you out fair and square; how would it have looked if I ignored what he did on that obstacle course and made you a firefighter instead? He broke the citywide record for God sakes! Those results go directly into the city's main computer. Somebody would have seen it and I would've been accused of nepotism and lost my job. As a Fire Chief, Son, I have to make all my decisions in the interests of the people of this city. It's never personal. It can't be. You have to understand that."

"The Mayor does it and no one bitches about it!"

"I-I'm not the Mayor, Son."

"No, you're not," Roger echoed and his smirk disappeared. "That's why I started all of this with the Mayor's residence. Being trained as an electrician in the military, it was so easy to get into that house and tell the Mayor he needed to upgrade his box. He knew I was your son so I had full run of the place. Setting that fire was like playing in a sandbox, dirty and fun. But the Mayor has a sudden scheduling change that night and then Rathman here manages to save his precious daughter and himself anyway. I knew then that I had to get Rathman out of the way permanently, but I had to make it look like someone else did it. Fortunately, Stan was a ready-made pawn, perfect to take the fall and keep the police off my trail. He thought we were close friends even until the end when I put a bullet through that thick skull of his. Poor bastard! He wanted to buy a house and I knew that that house across from Braden's old place had been for sale for years. It was perfect! So I asked him to meet me there under the pretense that I knew the real estate agent and I could give him a tour. Once we got up to that bedroom I capped him. It was too easy. I made everything, the boat fire, the warehouse fire, the Sears Tower debacle, look like Stan was the Fire Man, and I knew that Rathman suspected him. All Rathman had to do was die and then the police find Stan's body and I come in and take Rathman's place here in the station. But Rathman didn't die! Fooling me by pretending to be dead in the Sears Tower was the last straw. If Rathman wasn't going to die, then other people would. And they did. But I'm still not finished yet. All of you are next!"

Braden swallowed hard. He had heard the tension in Roger's voice elevating.

"Why did you blow my old house up, and how did you find out where I lived?" Braden asked.

"My father, of course," Roger answered with a sick grin. He was sweating more profusely now. "My unwitting but useful contact inside the station house. He never had any idea I was using him to gain access to the station house, to learn your work schedules, to plan the jobs I sent you to. I've heard the story a hundred times about how the two of you first met, Rathman, and it made me sick. All I had to do was feign interest in the story and ask him where exactly you used to live and the answer came out like water out of a hose. I used the friendlies I still had in the military to secure all the C-4 I'd need and my experience as an electrician to gain entry to the house. Those poor people thought I was rewiring the electric in their basement. It was, again, way too easy. As for why, well, blowing your old house up was a two-pronged victory for me. It was a sign to you that I could get to you no matter where you hid and then it served as a distraction while I lined the roof of this fire station with C-4. I knew it would take hours to knock that fire down and I knew finding Stan's body would keep you there even longer. Now it looks as if this final plan will be the successful one."

"Roger! Did you say the roof is rigged to blow?" the Chief asked incredulously. Braden could tell he was starting to lose it. The Chief's face was white; his age lines were deeper than they'd ever been.

"Yes, Father," Roger answered. His voice was calm and defiant, like a man sitting in the electric chair wanting to die. "Haven't you noticed that I'm holding two detonators? If I release the pressure in my left hand, the entire roof will blow. If I release the pressure in my right hand, I blow the belt around my chest and finish all of you."

"Haven't you killed enough people, Roger?" Braden asked and stepped forward, his hands low and out in front of his body. "What did those people living in my old house have to do with this? Or anyone else here? It's me you want...let everyone else go."

"Always the hero, aren't you? No can do, Rathman," Roger said. "We're all gonna go together. It's the only way."

"Roger," the Chief pleaded. "In the name of all that's good, please stop and think about what you're doing!"

"I have, Father. For almost a year, thinking is all I've been doing. Thinking and planning. You should have thought about how much I loved you and how it made me feel to fail you. It was then that I realized that your job was more important to you than I was. Well, I won't fail you anymore."

"Son, you're wrong. You've got to believe me...I've done everything I could to love you and bring you up right—"

"Save it, Father. It's too late."

It all happened so quickly. Braden saw Roger open his left hand and something snapped in his palm. Roaring bursts of cloud and brick filled the enclosed air of the dome, starting from the elevator, going over the store room, past the bunkrooms and the kitchen. The ground beneath their feet shook like a Northern California tremor, toppling some of them to the floor. Braden kept his balance as the series of blasts continued from the southeast corner of the station then headed along the rim northwards towards the apparatus. Roger stood there in a dazed state of nirvana: his eyes danced with pleasure, his grin became a toothy, insane laugh. The floor shook more violently. Braden saw cracks spreading across the cement surface. Sections of the floor were snapping up like popcorn. The whole place was coming down but Roger just stood there, laughing. The dome above them rattled visibly and began tearing itself apart down the seam where a row of hydraulic locks held it together. The loss of its foundation put too much stress on it and it began imploding. It shuddered, twisted itself apart with a sickening moan, stars appeared through the widening seam.

Their eyes met. Roger looked at him with a hatred Braden could never understand. Roger knew he had won. It truly was over.

Finally. Braden's eyes fell upon Roger's right hand and he saw the fist open; he saw a dark blur come between them. There was a flash, a thunderous whoosh of hot air, a sense of flying, then there was nothing.

Twenty Six

It was an all-consuming darkness, a darkness deeper than the universe is large; it was a darkness only the dead can see. Then there were things in it, short-lived ghostly visions that appeared out of the nothingness and were swallowed back into the nothingness. He saw shimmering faces; thought he recognized some of them. He saw a dog running at him, its angry drooling teeth bared; there was a dead squirrel in someone's hands, its long furry tail and body was frozen, yet the sun was shining and warm; there was a small boy, his boots were stuck in the mud of a large grassy field and he was crying for his mommy.

As the images went on, one after the other, they became clearer...a bicycle wheel running over a large spider and a million little copies of her pouring out of her squashed body; a rusted, hollow, hand grenade found in the woods and a woman frantically yelling at him to put it down; somebody stepping on a nail and wailing loudly.

What were these? The future? The present? No. They were memories. Yes! They were memories. His memories. He recognized them now. The time he had appendicitis and was throwing up into a large white plastic salad bowl in his bedroom, standing in the back of his father's truck with the rest of his baseball teammates in the annual Fourth of July parade, the lights and sounds of fire trucks filling the sky in front of them, seeing Amy for the first time at school...she'd been dating Nick and they were holding hands and Braden was envious.

But why was he seeing all of this? Was this what death was...

an endless stream of memories strung out forever on a black canvas of consciousness? He heard strange, alien sounds...low moans like metal girders twisting in the wind, the rumbling exhalation of what could have been a giant snoring nearby, heavy thumps and prickly streams like a waterfall of gravel hitting the ground. These sounds didn't match what he was seeing.

Strange.

He smelled things, too. Something was burning but there was more than wood and rubber in it...there was a scent of spice, a scent he'd never smelled before. It made him nauseous and it was making the images running past him disappear. Even that deep, endless darkness was fading, turning to gray then white. The movie was over; the lights were coming up.

Braden opened his eyes and saw the whole of the night sky hanging over him like an umbrella. There were tiny sparkles of light flashing way up there in the dark distance. He'd seen them before, when the dome was splitting apart above him like a pair of undersized pants. They were stars in the night sky. He was alive!

He tasted iron in the saliva of his mouth: blood. He mustered the strength to sit up quickly and found that his whole body ached with terrible pain, especially his chest. It felt like he'd broken some ribs; this made it difficult to breathe. He looked down and saw that his jacket took the brunt of the explosion; it was shredded and covered with blood. But it wasn't his blood. He remembered a shadow appearing between him and Roger just before the blast occurred. Someone had jumped between them to protect the rest of the station crew. But who?

His helmet lay heavy on his head; the blast shield was down, riddled so badly with cracks that he could barely see through it, evidence of the strength of the blast. That bit of luck saved his life. He reached up, unstrapped the helmet, dropped it to the rubble. When he gained the strength and courage, he leaned forward and managed to stand up, despite the crippling pain in his sternum.

Then he took in the devastation.

The brick walls of the roof that were the foundation for the giant white dome were gone; all that was left was flaming, smoking rubble. Beyond that the twinkling lights of the city sparkled. A brisk cool wind swirled up dust and debris, making it seem as if he stood in a fog. One half of the dome was missing, probably laying on the streets below, but the other half had collapsed to the roof and was nothing more than a burned, half-bowl-shaped skeleton. The kitchen, bunkroom, game room, the Chief's office, even the elevator, all were flattened into an unrecognizable landscape of brick and mortar. He'd seen films of Berlin at the end of World War II that looked just like this. In the distance, near the edge of the roof, a line of twisted metal pipes stuck straight up, spewing water down from showerheads that apparently survived the blast. Strange that the drywall was blown away yet the metal pipes inside still stood as if nothing had happened. The water fell in long, heavy streams and it was the only place where there was no smattering of fire or smoke.

Braden turned and saw the crater in the floor where Roger had blown himself up. A wide, jagged, gaping hole had been blown through. He could see the white walls and tile of the hospital below. Sandy, one of the nurses lay under a steel beam on the floor, her body crushed into two gory halves; blood pooled in her open mouth. She'd been the one who helped Dr. Payne with Evie's birth.

He had to turn away from her and saw that the front of the Engine lay half in the hole, the entire front end gone, all the way back to the crew cabin where his and Sam's seats clung to the bulkhead. It looked as if God had come down and sheared it away with a knife. The rear superconductors held it firmly to what was left of the surface of the roof. But for how long? The ambulance and the Foam Tender had been thrown backwards. They also sustained terrible damage to their front ends. The ambulance's rear end hung over the edge of the roof and looked perilously close to taking the fall. All of them were beyond the skills of Michael Perry and his team. They would have to be replaced, at great cost to the city.

It was destruction on a scale he'd never personally witnessed before and it made him realize how lucky he'd been to survive, again. The Kevlar in his gear probably had much to do with it. He started to cry but still controlled his emotions. It would have been so easy to just fall apart; everyone would have understood. He wanted to. But he fought back the tears, the urge to faint, as he began searching for survivors.

Surely he wasn't the only one. He couldn't be.

Braden stumbled over a wide crack in the floor. He righted

himself then carefully climbed up a rise of smoking brick and cement debris. The dusty air swirled again. He avoided sucking it in by taking in short breaths. He wondered where the hell Heany was. And where were the other stations to help them? He wondered how long he'd been unconscious. It couldn't have been too long if no one had arrived yet. But there weren't even sirens in the distance. *Does anyone anywhere even know what happened? Had Stacey managed to contact Heany before the blast?*

Braden made it over the debris to more level ground. The steel beams under the floor moaned in protest; in places it seemed like he was walking on a trampoline. He had to be very careful how he stepped and distributed his weight. It wouldn't take much for the entire roof to fall in.

Braden stopped and called out, but no one answered back. His voice was scratchy and rattled with pain. It was a miracle he could say anything at all. He called out again; this time he heard a cough to his right. He heard the cough again; his legs moved faster, towards the sound. Finally, he saw the dark outline of a firefighter's jacket and breeches partly buried under rubble. An arm stuck out, bent ninety degrees between the elbow and the wrist. Broken. He saw a white helmet: it was the Chief, lying face down. Braden hurried as fast as his aching body would let him and knelt down next to the Chief. He quickly threw off the smoking debris, turned him around so that he lay on his back. He took the Chief's helmet off and slapped him gently on the cheek. The old man's eyes opened.

"Rathman," the Chief whispered, his voice weak yet resonant. "Anyone...else...survive?"

"I-I don't know yet, Chief," Braden replied. "I'm still looking."

The Chief shook his head slowly, left and right, but Braden didn't see any sign of pain on his face. Just a deep, intense sadness, as if the entire weight of the universe had fallen in on him.

"Find them," the Chief whispered.

"I'll try, Chief," Braden said. "But first, I'm gonna need your cooperation to get you to the showers. You'll be safe from the smoke and fires there. Can you walk?"

"I-I think so."

Braden told him to hold onto his broken arm, then carefully

helped him to his feet. He led the Chief over the dangerous, debris-laden floor; it took a long time. He laid him down in a clear, wet area by the showers, just inside of the spray's path. The spray fell on the Chief's face and began washing the dust and soot away. He opened his mouth and allowed the spray in, swallowing when his mouth was full.

"You'll be okay here until they arrive," Braden said. The Chief coughed and let Braden go to work.

"Hey! Kid!" a voice called out. It was Sam's. Braden's heart warmed with hope at hearing him. If Sam was alive, there was a good chance the rest of them were, too.

Braden followed Sam's voice, finding his partner trapped on his back under the steel frame of the dome. Sam saw him and waved.

"Are you all right, Sam?" Braden asked in relief.

"It's gonna take a lot more than an insane suicide bomber strapped with a ton of C-4 and a ten-ton dome to do me in, Kid," he replied. "Get this damn thing off of me!"

This gave Braden new strength. He leapt forward and began prying the steel frame off Sam with a twisted piece of metal he found in the rubble. With Sam's help, the frame lifted just enough so that Sam could pull his legs out. Braden helped him to his feet and they embraced. The only injury Sam appeared to have was a cut on his chin and a bloody nose.

"Glad you made it, Sam," Braden said.

"Me too, Kid," Sam said. "Have you found anyone else?"

"Just the Chief. He's pretty shook up. His right arm is broken. I put him by the showers."

"Good," Sam said. "Let's split up and see who else we can find before help arrives and clutters the place up."

"If it arrives," Braden countered.

Sam took the east side of the roof while Braden took the west. There didn't seem to be any pattern to the destruction. It was just senseless, random chaos but they tried to make sense of it anyway. There were shattered toilet bowls half buried under piles of brick; a line of lockers lay against the north wall, facing outward, nearly bent in half. The kitchen table lay upside down, only three of its legs were sticking up, the fourth was lost to history. The vending machine stood stoically near where the elevator doors were; its

Plexiglas front was cracked but the bags of chips and pretzels inside were undamaged in any way.

They dug through the debris if they found something promising that resembled a body part; fortunately, they'd come up empty. A few minutes later, Sam shouted out and when Braden reached him, he saw that Sam had found Paul Rose, the Foam Tender Leader. Sam was kneeling over him, taking his pulse with his fingers pressed to Paul's jugular.

"He's alive, but barely," Sam said.

"Should we move him?" Braden asked.

"No. We better leave them where they are until help arrives, that way we don't harm them any further," Sam answered, took his helmet off, and lay it on top of a pile of nearby rubble. "It marks where he is."

Braden found his helmet and did the same thing for Joni when he found her, though she had died instantly in the blast. Most of her face was missing. He had to identify her by reading the passport that hung off her damaged jacket.

Finally, they heard the screaming sound of sirens in the distance; when they looked into the black sky, they saw flashing lights coming at them from every direction.

"It's about damn time," Sam muttered.

"What do you think took them so long?"

"No one probably believed the call when they heard it. They had to confirm it for themselves. Make sure it wasn't a crank call."

"Yeah...I still don't believe it and I was in it," Braden murmured.

They continued their search. In the rubble in back of the Engine, Braden found the waist and legs of someone who wore firefighter breeches. The boots were bloody and pointed in different directions. He called Sam over and Sam had to stop himself from vomiting.

"Who do you think it is?" Braden asked.

Sam took a minute to compose himself then he answered. "Thom."

"Thom? Why do you think it's Thom?"

"Didn't you see him jump between you and Roger just as the belt blew?"

"I...I saw a shadow, a blur, but I didn't see who it was."

"Well, I saw it," Sam said. "Bravest thing I've ever seen anyone do."

Braden looked down at what was left of Thom Brandt; he couldn't believe it. This was the man who froze like a corpse in the Mayor's residence and left Braden on his own to die in the fire.

"Why...why would he do that?" Braden asked; he was beginning to feel dizzy.

"He may have had some problems, Kid," Sam began. "But he was a good man and he was a firefighter. The Chief knew he'd come through someday; that's why he kept him on. Everyone who survived this thing owes Thom their lives."

"What about his family?"

"Full bennies, Kid. He died on the job."

Braden harbored a new respect for Thom and forgave him for what had happened in the Mayor's residence. Thom was more than a good man. He was a hero.

Sam shook his head in disgust. "We probably won't find anything left of Roger. He was ground zero. Nothing but fricking molecules left."

Braden wanted to sit down. He didn't know if it was all the gore, the stress, an internal injury he wasn't aware of, that was making him feel this way. All he knew was that he wanted to black out again. He found a pile of rubble and sat down. The sirens were closer now. The sky was flashing brilliantly with artificial light. It looked like a thunderstorm was coming but Braden knew better. It had already come.

"Are you okay, Kid?" Sam asked. "You're looking kind of pale."

"I don't...know," he said and everything went black again.

Twenty Seven

The elevator doors slid apart and Braden stepped out onto the new roof of the station house. It was a cool, sunny September morning. A brisk autumn breeze was coming in off Lake Michigan, carrying with it the odor of burnt wood and fresh paint. He wore a black leather jacket and jeans with sneakers. Very comfortable, even though his broken ribs were still wrapped and sore.

The construction workers had taken the weekend off from rebuilding the station because the cement in the double-wide foundation walls that was to hold the new dome hadn't set yet. It would take almost two weeks to set; that was fine with Braden. He was glad to be alone up here to face this demon.

He saw where the unfinished kitchen, bunkrooms, showers, the Chief's office, and the game room were. Like the foundation walls, they were built with reinforced concrete, dull and gray and featureless. The structures looked like ancient adobe houses plastered over. No more brick. Cement would stand up better if someone should ever again detonate himself with a belt of C-4 up there.

The memory of that horrible night gave Braden chills and he'd still been having nightmares about it. Hence the demons he had to exorcise. Amy had been so worried that she'd taken it upon herself to get him counseling. He liked the therapist, Dr. Rhinan. He had a quiet, secluded office in a building downtown near the Loop. He listened eagerly, patiently, and made no judgments. That's all Braden needed. So when Dr. Rhinan suggested that he go back up to the roof where so much tragedy had occurred, Braden thought it was a good idea.

He was told that the new roof was also specially reinforced with a mix of titanium and Kevlar. He couldn't wait to see it when it was all finished and painted. He especially missed the station's giant crest that always welcomed him when he came out of the elevator. It helped that the Mayor had made a special allotment through City Hall: the city of Chicago was paying for everything, even the new apparatus. Numbers like four million and ten million dollars were rumored in the news but everyone knew that the city could afford it, whatever the cost ended up being. Having the Mayor's hand in things also made the process move along much faster concerning unions. That was always a good thing.

White clouds moved slowly in the blue sky above. A flock of gulls spiraled in and out of the clouds' cottony whiteness. Their hungry caws echoed loudly overhead. It seemed to him that gulls were always hungry.

Braden went to where the new Engine would be parked and stood there looking down at the smooth, raw floor. They were going to cover the entire floor with a generic white tile that was scratch- and stain-resistant. Sounded like a lot less work for the two new probies that were to take Joni's and Thom's place in the crew.

He remembered the solemn ceremony the city had held for them at Forest Green Cemetery a week after the disaster. He remembered how sad everyone was...and how proud. Especially Thom's lovely wife, Amber. She had been the model of grace and dignity with her five children, who didn't shed a single tear during the whole thing. They were as brave as their father was.

Joni didn't have a husband or boyfriend but her mother and father had been there and Braden remembered how tightly Joni's father was holding her mother. The rest of the crew had been there too, despite their injuries. Paul Rose's was the worst injury, a piece of wall had fallen on his head but his helmet turned what could have been instant death into a concussion. Debbie's leg had been broken in two spots; she wore a weight-bearing cast that sent vibrations into the leg, causing the bone to heal quicker. She stood, leaning against her husband; he seemed attentive and loving. Braden hoped they worked through their problems. Maybe this tragedy would make them closer.

The Mayor and his wife had been there but they'd stayed in

the background, not wanting to bring attention to themselves on a day as sad as this one was.

Heany arrived with what looked like the entire Chicago police force. They lined up at the heads of the caskets and stood like statues. There was so much brass and gun power there it almost resembled a military funeral. The only thing Braden couldn't remember were the exact words the Chief said over their graves. His broken arm was in a slingcast as he read from a small piece of wrinkled paper in his good hand. Words like courage and sacrifice stuck out in Braden's mind but it had been too painful for him to listen to the Chief's entire eulogy. He would have broken down.

He did break down when their coffins, each topped with their respective damaged helmets, went down into the holes while a lovely woman who worked for the cemetery sang a sad, mournful song.

Terrible, terrible day.

Braden tried to look down through the cement floor and imagine the new, updated state of the hospital below. It had been completely rebuilt already and was functioning. Dr. Payne had been downstairs on the second floor in Billing when the bomb went off, so he had been safe. Steel beams had broken through to the exercise room on the fifth floor and everything under that had miraculously avoided damage. They said the station would be completely operational by earlier, becoming a cadet, the event that had set all this horror in motion. It had been the busiest and fastest year he'd ever lived through. He hoped everything settled down now, that he could just do his job, go home to his family, live a normal life.

Braden heard the elevator ping and turned to see the Chief walking through the doors. He wore a long tan overcoat with the right sleeve empty. His arm was still slung in a cast underneath. The Chief's shortly cropped hair had turned a sharper, brighter shade of silver since the last time Braden had seen him. He looked much older than his fifty-three years. He even walked like an old man; his steps were slow, cautious, and deliberate as he approached Braden.

"I knew I'd find you here, Rathman," he said and stopped in front of Braden. They shook with his good hand.

"Counselor's orders, Chief. I also wanted to see how far along they are," Braden said. "I'm anxious to get back on the job."

"I know what you mean, Kid. I never liked staying home and taking the city's money either when I was younger and got injured. Now, it's a different story."

They glanced at each other and fell into an uneasy silence.

"Chief," Braden said. "I know we haven't talked about it since it happened but I want you to know that I'm sorry about Roger. If I'd known where it was going to lead I would've stepped out of the way."

The Chief's eyes looked directly into his. "Look, Kid. You've got nothing to be sorry about. You did what you had to do within the rules and came out on top. That's what being an American is all about. Don't ever be sorry for being what you are—a firefighter. A damn good one, too. This city needs an army of people like you."

Braden smiled and remembered why he respected this man so much.

"If anything," the Chief continued. "This was all my doing, Kid. I guess I spoiled Roger; he learned the wrong things from me. I thought I did a good job raising him alone but you just never know. It's a tough thing to raise a child, even with another parent. I just didn't see the signs...that, or I didn't want to see them. Can I give you a piece of advice, Braden?"

"Sure, Chief."

The old man took a hard swallow and hesitated, as if trying to find the right words. He looked away then back at Braden.

"Love your children," he said, choking back emotion. "But don't love them too much."

Braden was going to ask him how one knew when it was too much but seeing tears in the old man's eyes made him change his mind. Yet, in his heart he knew the answer; a parent never knows how much is too much until it's too late. You just do the best you can and hope it all works out.

The Chief wiped his eyes with the back of his good hand and changed the subject.

"Looks like the Mayor's going to give you another award, Kid."

Braden lowered his eyes. "I...I don't want it, Chief."

"Why not?"

"I didn't do anything to deserve it. Thom and Joni...they deserve it."

"Their families are taken care of and their legacies are assured. Someone has to put a live, brave face on what happened here. That's you, Kid."

"But I don't do this for the awards, Chief," Braden said. "I do it because it's in my marrow, it's in the blood that's running through my veins. It's who I am. Sure the money is good, the benefits are better...but the people I work with, the job itself...it's the best."

The Chief smiled. "I know, Kid. And I agree with you. But you'll accept that award and let me tell you why. What this station has gone through, the death, the destruction, the sorrow, has been felt by every other firefighter in this city. By accepting that award you're accepting it for them, too. It shows them that their job is worth the price they pay; that's more powerful than any paycheck or any benefit they'll ever receive. You have to accept it for them."

Braden understood and nodded.

The breeze picked up again and Braden saw that a brown leaf had somehow made its way up there and was swirling across the floor as if caught in an invisible dust devil. It scratched across the cement floor, spun up wildly, then rolled across the floor again until it was caught in the corner by the elevator where it lay there perfectly still.

"So what happens now, Chief?" he asked.

"Well, truth be told, Kid, I'm tired," the Chief answered. "I'm old, worn, and burned out. In the thirty years I've been here, I've done everything I can to keep this city safe and serve her well. I've been thinking that now it's time for me to ride off into the sunset and retire. I have a younger brother who lives in Arizona. Maybe I'll finish the year out here and then head down there in January. I've nominated Sam to the Mayor; he'll replace me."

"Sam will be happy about that."

"I don't know. The job entails a lot of paperwork and diplomacy. He may not be up to it, being the man of action he thinks he is."

Braden laughed.

"I just wish Jaclyn was alive and could go down there with

me. We always talked about it before she passed."

"I hear it's beautiful down there in the winter."

"Yeah, and I can catch the Cubs' spring training games. That tipped me off the fence. What about you, Kid?"

"I'm not going anywhere, Chief," Braden said, smiling proudly. "I'm a firefighter. I made a promise to this city and I intend on keeping it."

"Good for you," the Chief said. "Next year should be an interesting year for you and the city."

"Why's that?"

"It's an election year in Chicagoland, Kid, and nothing *ever* goes wrong in Chicago during an election year."

Braden didn't know why, but he picked up an element of sarcasm in the Chief's voice. He didn't pursue the subject any further. Some things were best learned from experience. What did the Chief say to him once? *Learn through pain, Kid.*

The Chief walked into what would be his office and stood in front of the window. It was still nothing more than a rectangular hole in the wall waiting for the frame and glass to be put in. But as they stood there, looking down over the city they both swore to protect, one at the beginning of his career, the other at the end, they were both thinking the same thing… *God, how I love this beautiful city.*

About Gregg

Gregg was born in Chicago, IL and currently resides in Lindenhurst, IL with his wife. He has a son who is a firefighter for Fox Lake and Round Lake, IL, and is the inspiration for the book. Gregg has studied writing and poetry at the College of Lake County, in Grayslake, IL and has six books previously published. His favorite authors are Hemingway, Bradbury, Asimov and Clarke. He is also an accomplished graphic artist.

Visit our website for our growing catalogue of quality books.
www.champagnebooks.com

www.ingramcontent.com/pod-product-compliance
Lightning Source LLC
Chambersburg PA
CBHW070826180626
46818CB00001B/406